Brynn huffed. "I don't know why I bother."

"Bother with what?"

"Talking to you!" she said, shaking her keys in his face. "Just when I think you're going to be nice, you get me all..."

Will took a small step closer. "Get you all what?"

Brynn swallowed dryly and resisted the urge to take a step backward. He was just inches away, and if she'd been slightly sweaty before she felt downright hot and bothered now.

"Please step away. Your man-stench is making my hair frizz."

He didn't move. "You didn't finish your sentence. I get you all what? Riled? Panting? Hot?"

"I was going to say nauseated," she snapped, starting to move around him.

He moved his body and blocked her way. "I don't think so, Brynny."

Brynn glanced at her watch and winced. Even with Will's help, she was probably going to be late. In the time she'd spent arguing with him, she might as well have waited for AAA. At least then she wouldn't be so...oh, damn, he was right. She *was* riled and hot. And possibly on the verge of panting.

Made for
YOU

LAUREN LAYNE

FOREVER

NEW YORK   BOSTON

Copyright © 2014 by Lauren Layne
Excerpt from *Only with You* copyright © 2014 by Lauren Layne

Forever
Hachette Book Group
1290 Avenue of the Americas
New York, NY 10104

www.HachetteBookGroup.com

Printed in the United States of America

First Edition: October 2014
10 9 8 7 6 5 4 3 2 1

OPM

Forever is an imprint of Grand Central Publishing.
The Forever name and logo are trademarks of Hachette Book Group, Inc.

The Hachette Speakers Bureau provides a wide range of authors for speaking events. To find out more, go to www.hachettespeakersbureau.com or call (866) 376-6591.

The publisher is not responsible for websites (or their content) that are not owned by the publisher.

To Melissa, Suman, and Jaimie: for the epic cubicle chats that inspired me to think beyond 9–5 and chase my dreams. I am indebted.

And to the women of Stratejoy (lookin' at you, Molly!) for giving me the tools to make it all happen.

ACKNOWLEDGMENTS

Even in my pre-published days, I'd always heard that the process of taking a manuscript from early draft to finished book required a team. And I thought, "Yeah, yeah, of course, the cover, the printing, etc., I get it." Well, I didn't get it. If being published has taught me anything (other than how to drink obscene amounts of coffee [and wine, definitely wine]), it's that there is literally a *team* behind every book that you see on the shelf or your e-reader.

In the past, I've defaulted to "and thank you, everyone who worked on this book!" and I've meant it from the bottom of my heart, but that's not quite sufficient for this book. *Made for You* went from being a messy jumble of words to the book you see today in a few short months. In publishing that is akin to a miracle, and definitely deserving of some shout-outs.

First, and foremost, I owe a big thank you to Lauren Plude (or, as she is known affectionately in my head, simply *Plude*, to account for that pesky same-first-name business). If I'm the book's mother, she's its kick-ass nanny who made sure it didn't grow up into a total weirdo. Thanks for helping shape the story, and for shepherding the book through the publication process.

Despite the old idiom "Don't judge a book by its cover," we readers and writers totally judge a book by its cover, and I, for one, am grateful, because this cover could not be more perfect for this story. Huge thank-you to cover designer Claire Brown for taking my directive of "Um, something pretty?" and getting this cover exactly right on the first try.

I used to think that writers were writers, and we could therefore put together our own copy just like we could a novel. Um, no. Different skill set. Thanks to Katie Panicali and Huy Duong for figuring out how to describe an 80,000-word book in a few fantastic sentences.

To senior managing editor Bob Castillo and senior production associate Jessica Krueger, for working all kinds of magic I'll never understand, thank you. You are heroes!

All authors know on some level that after writing the book, they'll have to sell the book, but that's something we can't do alone, and thank goodness for people like Marissa Sangiacomo who are there to hold our hands. Thank you!

To Amy Pierpont and Leah Hultenschmidt, I'm not going to lie...your names are the ones I whisper in soft, deferential tones. I don't know everything that you do, but I know it's a lot. *bows in gratitude*

To my copy editor Janet Robbins, I owe both gratitude and maybe an apology because honestly, I'm never going to know the difference between *lay* and *lie*, and sometimes I still stumble on *whom*, so thanks for kicking my butt.

And to production editor Jamie Snider, could you *be* any nicer? Knock it off. Seriously, though, thanks for being so great to work with and for being patient with me when I have "writer's brain." Which is always.

Lastly, to Nicole Resciniti, who's technically my agent, but mostly my advisor, therapist, plot guru, and friend: thanks for being my partner in this book and every book.

For anyone else who's touched this book whose name should be here and isn't, sincerest apologies, but know that I am *so* grateful!

Made for
YOU

*C*HAPTER ONE

*Accept the aging process with grace
and decorum.*

—Brynn Dalton's Rules for an
Exemplary Life, #32

*D*istributing toilet paper was not on Brynn Dalton's life list.

Neither was crying in a public bathroom at her own birthday party.

But if there was one thing Brynn was starting to suspect, it was that life's plans went to hell after thirty.

"Excuse me, um...ma'am? Would you mind passing some toilet paper? This roll is empty."

The slightly embarrassed question from the neighboring bathroom stall caught Brynn on the verge of a sob, and she blinked rapidly to keep the tears at bay.

"Oh. Sure." She kept her voice composed. Her voice was *always* composed.

Brynn carefully tore off six squares of toilet paper and folded them neatly. She was about to pass them under the stall when she paused. The tidiness of the bundle annoyed her. So instead of handing it over, she set the folded squares on her knee and slapped at the toilet paper roll again until she had an enormous wad of tissue. Brynn very slowly, very intentionally crumpled the toilet paper into a ball.

Much better.

Plus, now the poor lady on the other side wouldn't be in the awkward position of having to ask for some more toilet paper. And Brynn Dalton was *very* good about not putting people in awkward situations.

Brynn leaned down slightly and thrust the wad of tissue under the stall wall.

"Thanks," came the relieved voice. "You'd think a classy place like this would have enough TP stocked, huh?"

"You'd think," Brynn agreed politely. Not that she gave a hoot about the toilet paper stocking policies at SkyCity's private event venue.

"You here for the party?" the voice asked.

"Mm-hmm," Brynn said, becoming aware that she was on the verge of entering full-on conversation from a toilet seat.

What kind of crassness was this? Talking through bathroom stalls had always made Brynn uncomfortable. Weren't bathroom stalls supposed to be sacred places?

"Do you know the birthday girl?" the voice persisted.

"Oh yes."

"I've never met her," the other voice said. "I'm just tagging along as the date of one of her friends."

"Oh, nice," Brynn said, struggling to keep her voice polite.

Brynn heard Chatty Cathy's toilet flush. *Finally.* "Well, see ya," the voice said. "Good luck."

Good luck? What exactly did the stranger think Brynn was doing in here that required "luck"?

Then again, she had been in here for the better part of twenty minutes. And come to think of it...what *was* Brynn doing in here?

She knew only that she couldn't be out *there*. She'd rather be watching her dignity melt away while passing out toilet paper to strangers than face what awaited her:

Her thirty-first birthday, and a room full of people just itching to spot that first gray hair.

Brynn breathed a sigh of relief as she heard the sink faucet turn off, as the swish of the swinging door indicated that the talkative woman had returned to the party. *Finally* Brynn could commence what she'd come in to do in the first place.

Wallow. In private.

"Brynn! Brynn Dalton, are you in here?"

The door to the women's restroom banged against the wall and the click of a fast-paced high-heeled walk echoed through the marble bathroom.

Crap. Caught.

In an uncharacteristic burst of cowardice, Brynn contemplated lifting her feet above the ground so that her sister wouldn't be able to spot her shoes beneath the stall walls. She knew full well that Sophie Wyatt wouldn't think twice about crawling around on hands and knees until she spotted her prey.

Then again, knowing Sophie, she also wouldn't hesitate to look *over* the bathroom walls.

Resistance was futile.

The *tap-tap* of Sophie's heels paused outside the stall where Brynn sat hiding.

"I know you're in there, Brynn. I can see your boring brown shoes."

Brynn glanced down at her designer pumps. "They're not brown. They're nude."

"Seriously? *Nude* doesn't even count as a color."

Brynn's brow furrowed. What did Sophie mean, nude wasn't a color? The saleswoman at Nordstrom had told her that nude heels would make her legs look "impossibly long."

She tried to look at them through her more flamboyant sister's eyes. Okay, maybe the shoes were a *little* boring.

Just like you.

She pushed the disparaging thought out of her head. Self-pity wasn't Brynn's normal style, but it had been steadily fighting for room in her brain ever since she'd learned that the birthday she'd been hoping to sweep under the carpet was turning into a damn circus.

Brynn heard the neighboring stall door swing open and the clatter of Sophie's heels on the closed toilet seat. Warily, Brynn glanced up and saw her sister's accusing blue eyes staring down at her.

"I knew it!" Sophie said. "You're not even *going*. You're hiding in there."

"Well, if I *were* going, I certainly wouldn't appreciate the audience," Brynn mumbled.

Sophie waved away this objection. Younger sisters didn't put much stock in the value of privacy. Sophie folded her arms on top of the stall wall and rested her chin on her hands. "You okay?" she asked, her voice softening.

Brynn shifted uncomfortably, increasingly aware that the toilet seat cover was not meant for long stays. Exactly how long had she been in here? She'd only meant to hide out for a minute or two to catch her breath, but if Sophie had hunted her down, her absence must have been noted.

"I thought I specifically said no surprise parties," Brynn said, trying to keep her voice calm as she addressed her sister.

Sophie's brow furrowed. "When?"

Brynn's fingers went to her temples. "*When?* How about every birthday for the past decade?"

"I thought all that fussing was about your *thirtieth* birthday. I didn't know it applied to thirty-one as well."

The tick in her temple increased and Brynn fought to keep from screaming at her sister. But the thing was, she knew that the warped logic made sense in Sophie's bubbly, carefree head.

Just as she knew that Sophie would never have thrown this party if she'd suspected Brynn wouldn't like it. Despite her occasional bouts with obliviousness, Sophie was one of the kindest, sweetest people Brynn knew.

But it didn't change the fact that everyone in her acquaintance had seen the big fat "31" cake on the table, and now knew her precise age. And instead of looking at what she'd accomplished, they'd be looking at what she *hadn't* accomplished.

No husband. No fiancé. No baby on the way...

All of which would have been fine if those things hadn't been part of *The Plan*.

"I'm really sorry, Brynny," her sister was saying. "It's just that we haven't really done *anything* for your birthday since you turned twenty-one. I thought you'd be sick of quietly toasting with Mom and Dad like we do every year."

"Nope. The key word there is 'quietly,' Soph. If getting older must be observed, I like it to happen in a classy, understated way."

"But this *is* classy! It's the Space Needle. It's not like I dragged you to Cowgirls Inc."

Brynn stifled a shudder at the very thought of straddling a mechanical bull or doing body shots, or whatever they did at Cowgirls Inc.

"It is a lovely party," Brynn said, belatedly realizing that she might be hurting Sophie's feelings. The party must have taken months to plan, and here Brynn was acting like it was an execution.

Get it together.

Taking a deep breath, Brynn stood and opened the stall door and walked calmly to the bathroom mirror. She heard Sophie nosily clamber to the ground and follow her.

"You look pretty," Sophie said, looking at Brynn's reflection.

"Even with my brown shoes?"

"I guess they're not so bad," Sophie said kindly. "They're very *you*."

"Gee, thanks." But Brynn didn't take offense. They *were* her. And normally she took pride in being consistently subdued.

But today . . .

"I'm thirty-one, Soph," she blurted out.

"You always were good with numbers," Sophie said. "You know what else we could go count? The huge number of presents, and even bigger number of people here to see you."

"See me what, turn old and wrinkly right in front of their eyes?"

"Okay, stop," Sophie said, planting her fist on her hip. "Do you have any idea how obnoxious you sound? Thirty-one isn't even close to old, and you know perfectly well that you don't look a day over twenty-five."

Her sister's criticism chafed at Brynn's raw nerves. "Give me a break, Soph. Like *you've* never had a sense of panic over an impending birthday?" Brynn snapped. "I distinctly remember you going on a rampage about how your eggs were going to turn into raisins when you turned twenty-nine and Gray refused to turn his office into a nursery *just in case*."

"Yeah, but that's *me*. You know perfectly well that I am the whiner of the family. *You* always rise above pity parties. I thought it went against your moral code, or whatever you call that notebook of yours."

"It's my life list, not a moral code." She hated how snobbish her tone sounded.

Sophie's eyes narrowed. "Wait a minute. *That's* what this is about. Your stupid list."

Brynn began rummaging in her purse for her lipstick. Her *nude* lipstick. The same color she'd been using for almost a decade. "That's not it," she said primly.

Sophie snickered. "Oh, it *sooo* is. Isn't there a thirty-five-before-thirty-five clause or something in there? Or is that an entirely separate list, not unlike your Thirty Things to Do Before Thirty, and your Fifty Before Fifty list."

"If you're going to make fun of me, I'm not going to talk about this with you," Brynn said as she applied a careful swipe of the lipstick.

But Sophie had already latched on to the topic. "Your hyperorganized little mind is running through all of the things you were supposed to have done by now. That's why you want your birthdays to slink by unnoticed."

Something squeezed in Brynn's chest. "I just...I thought I'd be engaged by now."

There.

She'd said it.

And she knew how it sounded. She'd practically delivered a death blow to feminism. Modern women didn't need a husband. Brynn didn't need a husband.

Except...it was on her *plan*. And what was the point of having a plan if you didn't stick to it?

She didn't bother looking at her sister to gauge Sophie's reaction. She already knew her sister would be incredulous, and possibly a little outraged.

But Sophie wouldn't get it. How could she? Her younger sister had married the man of her dreams before the age of thirty, and was happier than she'd ever been in her life.

"But, Brynny, it's just not your time," Sophie said softly. "And I thought things with James were going great? He's looking for you, by the way."

James.

Right. She felt even more ridiculous for stressing about her marital status when she had a perfectly wonderful boyfriend. A boyfriend who was currently stuck making small talk with people he barely knew because she was lamenting the lack of a shiny ring on her fourth finger.

She was pathetic.

"Listen," Sophie said, helping herself to the sugar-free

gum from Brynn's purse. "I know you probably have some grand plan of where you're supposed to be by this exact date. But it doesn't always work like that. Or, you know, maybe marriage just isn't in the cards for you."

Again, that tightness in her chest. *Dammit.* "It is," Brynn said firmly. "I know it is."

"Okay," Sophie said with strained patience. "Then it will happen. Someday. But hiding out in the bathroom isn't going to get you there any faster. I hardly think James is going to get marriage-minded with a woman who spends inordinate time in the restroom."

True. So true.

Brynn gave her sister a spontaneous hug. "I love how you always say the right thing in the weirdest way."

Sophie hugged her back before tugging at the hem of her flouncy blue cocktail dress and dropping into a small curtsy. "I do my best."

"You know, you might have given me a *hint* about this party so I could have dressed accordingly." Brynn looked her sister up and down. "You're not supposed to outshine the birthday girl."

Sophie waved her hand. "Please. Outshine perfect Brynn Dalton? Impossible."

Brynn gave a forced smile. Because once upon a time it had been *very* possible to outshine Brynn Dalton. But now wasn't the time to take a trip down memory lane. Although, come to think of it, the whole hiding-in-the bathroom thing was an all-too-familiar blast from the past.

A past that involved crying in the bathroom through most of second grade. And third . . . and pretty much every horrible day up until she'd finally begged her parents for braces, contacts, acne medication, and a regimented weight-loss program.

At fifteen, she'd finally figured out how to do it right. It had been the start of her lists. Lists that kept her from ever being the one that stood out from the crowd to be pointed at and laughed at.

Her lists and plans had kept her from ever having to sit alone at lunch, or hook up with a guy who was out of her league.

Her lists were her life. And she wasn't about to fall off the wagon at age thirty-one.

Besides, coming in second place to Sophie was just fine with her. God knew she was used to it.

Her sister was especially sparkly tonight. Sophie's dress was the perfect color to offset her bright blue eyes. And unlike Brynn's own boring "brown" pumps, Sophie's were a shocking orange. The look should have been garish, but instead was completely charming.

"Charming" was something the younger Dalton sister had in large doses. If Brynn was the smooth and reliable one, Sophie was the fun, alluring sister. Even Sophie's *hair* was more fun. Despite the fact that their long blonde hair was almost identical in color and texture, Sophie's was always styled in a mess of wild yellow curls. Brynn's own long hair was kept perfectly straight. A style that suited Brynn perfectly even if it did feel a bit... boring.

"Not boring. Respectable," Brynn reminded herself under her breath. Although she'd learned early on that there were a lot worse things to be called than boring.

"Yeah, yeah," Sophie said as she dragged Brynn toward the bathroom door. "You're respectable, *and* you're beautiful, rich, and successful. Everyone adores you. Blah, blah. The only person who RSVP-ed 'no' to your party was Aunt Philly, and that's just as well because now we don't have to hear about her hemorrhoids. But—"

"There's a but?" Brynn interrupted.

Sophie paused at the door and spun back around. "You have to promise me to loosen up. Forget that damn list for once. Drink too much champagne and have drunk sex with James back at his place."

Brynn carefully kept her face blank. She and James hadn't been having much of *any* sex lately, but there were some things even one's sister didn't need to know.

"Fine," Brynn said reluctantly, "but if Mom starts on one of her rampages about how I'm not getting any younger..."

"I'll handle Mom," Sophie said as she shoved Brynn through the door. "You just get yourself some bubbly booze, and embrace another fabulous year in the life of Seattle's most gorgeous orthodontist."

"Yeah, because the competition is pretty stiff in that category," Brynn said as she plucked a glass of champagne from a passing tray.

"There you are," said a familiar male voice from behind Sophie and Brynn. "Everyone's been wondering what happened to you two."

"Ladies' room," Sophie said, sliding an arm around her new husband's waist.

Gray Wyatt raised an eyebrow. "The entire time?"

Sophie raised an eyebrow right back. "Do you really want details?"

Gray grunted and fell silent. Silence was something Grayson Wyatt did a lot of. Brynn should know. She'd dated the man for about five seconds of tepid boredom before he and Sophie had spontaneously combusted. Not that anyone ever remembered Brynn and Gray's romantic history. Probably because it hadn't been the least bit romantic.

"Thanks for the party, Gray," Brynn said. "I know you're friends with the owner of the restaurant."

Gray gave a polite nod. "The planning was all Sophie. If it was up to me, I would have planned something more…"

"Dull? Bland? Introverted?" Sophie supplied.

Gray's amused gray eyes met Brynn's over Sophie's head. "I was going to say 'mellow.'"

Sophie sniffed. "Yawn. People like you and Brynn have plenty of mellow in your life."

"Has anyone seen James?" Brynn asked, scanning the room for her boyfriend. He could hold his own in social situations, but she felt bad leaving him alone this long. Especially since he'd probably helped coordinate this whole disaster with Sophie. She should at least say "thank you."

"He was talking with your dad," Gray volunteered, taking a sip of his whiskey.

"The usual medical mumbo jumbo?"

"Yep. Didn't understand a word of it," Gray confirmed.

"Great," Brynn muttered. She was glad her father and boyfriend got along. She just wished they were able to connect on something other than ER policy and the latest heart-valve technology.

"Seriously, I don't know what you two talk about," Sophie said as she eyed a tray of passing spring rolls with a critical eye. "James is nice, but the man's like a machine.

He's practically been a part of the family for the past year, but I still can't get more than small talk and lengthy lectures out of him."

"You thought Gray was a machine when you first met him," Brynn countered.

Sophie cuddled up to her husband's side with a coy grin, and Brynn stifled the sting of jealousy at the easy connection between her sister and her husband. "Well, I may have made a mistake about that," Sophie said softly.

"A mistake? You?" Gray said blandly.

"Just the one. Unlike you and Brynn, who have so much red tape running every which way that you couldn't *possibly* make a mistake. You're both overdue. Mistakes build character..."

But Brynn couldn't hear her sister over the rushing in her ears.

He.

Was.

Back.

Look away. Look away now from The Enemy.

But she couldn't tear her eyes away from the tall man with dark blond hair who was ogling a redhead in a killer black dress. His dark jeans and white shirt should have been too casual for the occasion. But nobody would notice that he was underdressed. They'd be too busy basking in his wide smiles and hot gazes.

He was back.

Why was he back?

"Brynn, are you listening?" Sophie asked. "I was just explaining how maybe if you would slip up every now and then you wouldn't have to hide in the bathroom on your birthday."

Sophie couldn't have been more wrong about Brynn not making mistakes.

Because not so long ago, she'd made the most elementary of all mistakes.

And he was staring right at her.

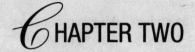

CHAPTER TWO

Be polite, even to those who
don't deserve it.

—Brynn Dalton's Rules for an
Exemplary Life, #19

Will knew exactly the moment she'd seen him. He felt it like a shock to the balls, and he wanted a shot of whiskey. Now.

It had taken a full fifty-seven minutes since he'd walked into the room until her ice-blue eyes had locked on him, and that was including the ridiculous amount of time she'd spent in the bathroom.

She made him wait another twenty minutes before seeking him out.

But what was seventy-seven minutes when you'd already waited a lifetime?

Will watched her approach, her expression schooled into one of polite indifference. She stopped several inches in front of him, and only the slight narrowing of her gray-blue eyes gave any indication that she wanted him dead. Which, of course, she did.

"William."

"Brynn," he said, matching her prim tone.

He felt a little jolt of disappointment at her vapid smile. It was the same courteous, reveal-nothing expression she'd given everyone else in the room. He'd been kind of hoping for that special brand of bitchy that she'd always reserved just for him.

"You're looking a little wider around the hips," he said with an insulting glance up and down. She wasn't, but the thought that she'd gained an ounce would keep her up at night.

Her smile slipped for a second, and for a moment he wondered if he'd struck a nerve. Normally he wouldn't dare touch the subject of a women's weight. He wasn't a *total* ass. But Brynn had had the same perfectly slim figure as long as he'd known her—she wouldn't tolerate anything else. Her physical appearance was flawless.

Her personality, however...

"And you're looking...man-whorish," she said with the usual venom.

Ah. *There* was the old Brynn. He nearly smiled. "So. Nice party," he said blandly.

"Yes, it was sweet of Sophie to put it together."

"Mm-hmm," he said, taking a sip of his red wine. "And exactly how intense was the urge to strangle her when you learned that she'd planned a surprise party instead of the usual dull birthday dinner with your family?"

This time the smile faded altogether. "Don't. Don't do that thing."

"What thing?"

"That thing where you make it a point of thinking you know me better than anyone else."

Don't I? He stifled the thought. For now.

She stepped closer and he caught the scent of her expensive perfume. The same one she'd been wearing for as long as he could remember. Change was not a concept Brynn Dalton embraced.

"What the hell are you doing here?" she hissed.

"Sophie invited me."

"To *my* birthday party? Sophie knows full well that we can't stand each other."

He ignored this. "Has anyone told you that your shoes are boring? They're the same color as your skin," he said.

"That's kind of the point. It's a look. A *classic* look."

Uh-huh. In Brynn's world, "classic" was simply a synonym for "risk-free."

Will pulled a champagne flute off a tray and handed it to her. "You need a drink."

"I've had plenty to drink," she snapped.

"Right, because you wouldn't want to get a little tipsy on your *birthday*. Are you really only thirty-one? Between the sagging and the wrinkles..."

She made a small rattling noise before snatching at the glass he held out. He watched as her eyes scanned the room, probably to ensure they hadn't caused a scene. She took a tiny sip of champagne and tucked a strand of honey-blonde hair behind her ears. Like the perfume, her hair hadn't changed in years. It was still in the same long, stick-straight style she'd worn in high school.

When he was seventeen, he used to fantasize about

how the ends of that perfect blonde hair would look against her bare exposed breasts.

When he was thirty, he'd had a chance to confirm it. *Beautiful.* His fingers itched at the memory, and he pushed the thought aside.

He was now thirty-three. And Brynn wouldn't be wanting him anywhere near her bra straps.

"You didn't answer my question about what you're doing here," she said, her thin body looking increasingly tense beneath her boring gray suit.

"That's because you didn't ask nicely."

Her nostrils fluttered briefly. "You've been gone for three years. You haven't so much as called my family on *Christmas.* You completely abandoned my parents without a good-bye and you never even come to visit Sophie, who's supposedly your best friend—"

"I've visited," he interrupted. "Not often, but I've been back to Seattle a couple times each year."

She blinked in surprise. "Do my parents know? God, Will, you were like a son to them."

Will leaned forward slightly. "Last time I was in town I stayed in your parents' guest room. The time before that, I slept on Sophie and Gray's couch. So you see, Princess...the only Dalton I was ignoring was you."

Will watched her reaction carefully.

But there was none.

Her expression hadn't changed a bit, and he felt a surge of frustration. The Brynn he'd known had been rigid but always willing to rise to the bait and show fire.

This version of Brynn wasn't just the illusion of ice— she *was* ice. He'd clearly made a mistake in staying away too long, and everyone else in her life had let her get too comfortable in her structured little routine, with all of her stupid rules and lists.

An older couple approached to wish her happy birthday, and Will watched as she smoothly thanked them for coming and asked about their children by name, which he was sure were filed away in some elaborate contact list somewhere.

She didn't introduce him to the couple, which suited him just fine. He was sure he wouldn't like whatever title he'd be given.

"How long until you slink back to Boston?" she asked him when they were alone again.

"A while."

"Could you be more specific?" she snapped.

"You know, Princess, whatever ailment had you in the bathroom for an hour has really messed with your mood."

"I wasn't in there for an *hour*," she snarled as she took another gulp of her champagne. Despite her claims of not wanting it, her glass was nearly empty. He was pushing her limits, exactly as planned.

It was time to get what he'd come for. "So who's the sallow-looking fellow you were dragging around like a whipped dog?"

Her eyes closed briefly. "Go away, Will."

He ignored this. "New boyfriend?"

"Not new. James and I have been dating for two years."

Will already knew that, of course. Sophie kept him updated. But he wanted to see if there was any change in Brynn when she talked about her guy. Not so much as a flicker.

Excellent news.

As if on cue, Brynn's mannequin of a boyfriend appeared at her side. "There you are, sweetheart. I figured you'd be making the rounds with the guests."

I'm not a guest, jackass. I know her better than you do.

Brynn set her hand on James's arm and Will was careful not to let his eyes linger on the touch. Careful not to punch the guy's bland features.

Brynn beamed up at her boyfriend. "James, this is Will Thatcher. He's an old friend of the family."

"Oh, sure," James said, with a nod of his boring, all-American head. "You're Sophie's friend, right? The one who moved to Boston?"

"Yup."

"So what brings you into town?" James asked. "Business? Pleasure?"

Pleasure. Definitely pleasure, Will thought, not letting himself glance at Brynn.

"Will doesn't do business," Brynn said casually. "He's unemployed."

Self-employed, he mentally corrected. But he didn't say it out loud. Didn't want to ruin the slacker playboy image she had of him just yet.

"Just reacquainting myself with my old stomping grounds," Will replied. "Wrapping up a few loose ends that I left hanging when I moved."

This time, he did glance at Brynn, but she didn't meet his eyes.

"That's right, you moved rather suddenly, right?" James asked politely.

Brynn let out a brittle laugh. "Slunk out in the middle of the night is more like it."

James frowned at her tone. No doubt he wasn't used to seeing his perfect girlfriend be anything less than pleasant. Will would have warned the guy what he was getting into, except Will had no intention of letting James maintain his status in Brynn's life for much longer. The very thought of it made his knuckles itch.

"Yeah, my departure was sort of a whim. Seattle just seemed so...*vapid* back then," Will said, taking a slow sip of wine and making it clear that it wasn't the city that was vapid, so much as the woman standing in front of him.

"Mmm, yes," Brynn mused. "It must have been disheartening to realize you'd slept with the entire female population in the area. Don't worry, there's a whole new set of girls who have come of age since you left."

"Gotta keep it legal," Will said with a grin.

"Disgusting," she muttered.

"Well, it was nice finally meeting you, Will," James said, breaking the awkward silence.

"Likewise," Will lied.

James slid an arm around Brynn's narrow waist. "Brynn, sweetheart, if you're done here, could you come with me for a second? There's something I've been waiting to do, and I want your full attention."

"Oh, I'm definitely done here," Brynn said. "William, it was *so* nice seeing you again. I'm sure our paths won't cross before you go back, so have a safe flight back to Boston."

Yeah, about that...

But it wasn't time to drop his little bomb just yet, so Will merely lifted a finger in response, and watched as James led Brynn away. Setting his wineglass on an empty table, he headed for the coat check. He'd done what he'd come to do. *Stage one complete.*

Excited murmuring caught his attention as he slipped on his leather jacket, and he turned back to see what the excitement was about. God knew it wouldn't be Brynn. "Excitement" wasn't in her vocabulary.

He was wrong.

Everybody's attention *was* on Brynn.

The crowd shifted slightly and Will froze as he took in the full picture.

In her hand was a tiny jewelry box.

A *ring-sized* jewelry box.

Will's gut twisted and it suddenly felt hard to breathe. *It's your damn fault. You stayed away too long licking your wounds.*

And now he was too late.

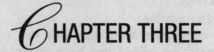

CHAPTER THREE

Marriage is about the man, not the bling.

—Brynn Dalton's Rules for an
Exemplary Life, #17

"You're quiet."

"Just tired," Brynn said, giving James a wan smile.

He gave her a boyish smile back, reaching across the car to tuck her hair behind her ear and admire her new earrings.

"Those really do look great on you," he said, sounding annoyingly self-satisfied.

They're two-carat-each diamond studs. They'd look great on a burro, Brynn thought.

Not that she wasn't appreciative. Diamond studs were right up her alley, even if the size of these were a bit ostentatious.

But for one heart-stopping moment, she'd thought she was receiving something very different.

Granted, he hadn't been on his knee or anything, but hadn't the guy ever seen a romantic comedy?

A small box presented to a serious girlfriend meant *engagement ring*.

Not big-ass earrings.

Being considerate wasn't perhaps one of James's strong points, but neither was he normally completely oblivious to social appropriateness. Hadn't he considered what everyone would think when he made a big show of presenting her with a tiny box?

Hadn't he considered what *she'd* think? She glanced down at her unadorned left hand before forcing herself to reach up and touch the new earrings.

She gave him the widest smile she could muster. "They're gorgeous. Thank you again."

"You're welcome," he said softly, before they settled into the companionable quiet of two people who had known each other for long enough to be comfortable with silence.

Sometimes Brynn thought they were *too* comfortable with the silence.

The steady click of his turn signal caught Brynn by surprise, and she sat up straighter when she realized where they were headed.

"You're not taking me home?" she asked.

James glanced across the dark car at her. "I thought we'd stay at my place tonight."

"You could have asked."

He blinked in surprise at her tone. "I can take you home if you want."

"No, it's fine," she said, slumping back slightly against the seat.

"It's just that you're so out of the way..."

Brynn closed her eyes and let James's lecture roll over her. He didn't like the fact that she lived thirty minutes away from the "action," and told her so at every opportunity.

The move had seemed a good idea at the time. She was sick of downtown living. Moving to the suburbs had meant more space, a garden, actual grass...and lots of family-minded neighbors. The move was supposed to be a *prompt* for James. A chance for him to see how happy the young families were pushing strollers on the side-walks and having impromptu BBQs.

But Brynn's plan backfired. James hated her house. Hated that she had to hire someone to mow the lawn and water plants when they went on vacation. And the guy never missed a chance to remind her that she was too young to be so far away from everything. Apparently he was so sick of the "wilderness" of suburbia that he'd re-sorted to kidnapping her.

After circling several blocks, James executed a perfect parallel-parking job. "You okay walking? We're a few blocks from my place."

"Now, see, if we were at *my* place, you could have just parked in the garage," she couldn't help griping.

James sighed as he pulled the keys from the ignition. "What's wrong, Brynn? You're irritable, and I'd like to understand why. So let's have it."

But she didn't even know where to start. How about with the fact that her thong was riding up her ass? Or that her boyfriend apparently had no intention of marrying her in this century?

Or the fact that nobody had told her Will Thatcher was back in town?

She made a low, growling noise in her throat. It wasn't fair to be mad at her family. They'd probably thought they were doing her a favor by not mentioning his arrival. It was no secret that Will and Brynn didn't get along.

But still, a little warning would have been nice. Sophie might have at least mentioned that she'd invited Brynn's mortal enemy to her birthday party.

Worst of all, the guy had looked...*good*. Brynn had always been so sure that the golden-boy good looks he'd flaunted in high school would give way to middle-age paunch and thinning hair. Instead, his blond, blue-eyed movie-star looks had improved with age.

His personality had not.

"I'm sorry," she said, giving James a weak smile. "I think I had too much champagne. I have a headache."

"No problem," he said, easily accepting her nonexplanation like she'd known he would. He opened his door. "I think you were entitled to a couple extra glasses. You're officially into your thirties now, after all."

"Oh, by all means, let's break out the confetti," she muttered under her breath.

James came around the car to open her door for her as he always did, but she beat him to it. Normally she liked his old-fashioned chivalry, but tonight she wanted to tell him to shove it. He set his hand lightly on her back and she resisted the urge to squirm away. It felt possessive for someone who didn't want to put a ring on it.

What was *wrong* with her tonight?

"It was nice seeing all of your friends in one place," he said, as they strolled along the quiet Seattle sidewalk. "And it was good to finally meet Will. Your parents and Sophie are always talking about him."

"Yeah, well, he's practically been a part of the family ever since he and Sophie became inseparable."

"Were they in the same class?"

"No, when Soph was a freshman, I was a sophomore and Will was a senior."

And can we please stop talking about him?

James frowned as they approached his apartment building. "So he was closer to your age, but better friends with Sophie?"

"Sure, they dated for a while," she snapped. "Why so interested in Will?"

James shot her a puzzled look as he let her into the building. "No reason. Just trying to put the pieces together."

"There's nothing to put together," she said, jabbing the elevator button. "He was a horny senior who asked out a pretty freshman. They didn't work out, but remained friends. Everyone thought they'd go all *When Henry Met Sally*, but then Sophie met Gray, and that's that. End of sappy story."

"Let's get you some aspirin, shall we?" James said with an amused smile.

Whatever. Anything to get rid of this edgy restlessness and self-doubt that wouldn't let go.

Ten minutes later, Brynn was changing into the lingerie she kept in one of his dresser drawers, when he came into the bedroom with tea and a bottle of pills.

"Thanks," she said gratefully. She really did have a headache. Brynn accepted the mug and glanced up at him through the steam. She sometimes forgot that James was handsome. Not in a showy way. His dark brown hair was kept short. Shorter actually than suited him, now that she thought about it. And his eyes were a nice, sexy gold color. He worked out daily, and it showed.

And yet, she couldn't remember the last time she'd felt genuinely attracted to him. The sex was infrequent and vanilla. And she didn't think it was all her. It wasn't like he was making accidental boob-brushes or reaching for her in the middle of the night.

But maybe that was okay. She was looking for a spouse, after all, not a sex toy. She'd never been one of those sappy, unrealistic types that expected the two should overlap.

"Shall we get you into bed?" he asked, turning the covers down.

Brynn felt both relieved and dismayed that this was apparently going to be another platonic night. "You're not coming?" she asked, crawling between the sheets.

"Nah, I recorded the Mariners game from earlier. You don't mind if I go kick back?"

"No, of course."

"Thanks, sweetheart." He brushed his lips against her forehead and ran a hand over her hair. "And Brynn?"

"Mm?"

"Happy birthday. I hope you don't think I was overlooking it. I was just playing it down, since I know you're not a fan of birthdays. I tried to tell your sister, but..."

"I know. Sophie is...persistent."

"But you're not upset about the party? Or are the earrings not what you wanted?"

Brynn set her hand on his. He was sweet. Oblivious at times, but sweet.

"Just the headache," she said, burrowing deeper into the blanket.

"Okay," he said, pulling the covers around her chin. "I'll make breakfast tomorrow?"

"That sounds nice. Just granola, though, since I won't have time to work out before my first appointment."

She heard the bedroom door close behind James and rolled onto her side to stare out at the cloudy night. A lump formed in her throat. Had her life really become a string of just-granola mornings?

Something was seriously wrong.

And it wasn't *just* that she was another year older.

It wasn't *just* that her boyfriend was proving to be a bit self-absorbed.

What *really* had Brynn terrified was that in the moment after she realized James wasn't going to propose she'd felt...

Relieved.

And she feared that the relief had everything to with the reappearance of one William Thatcher.

CHAPTER FOUR

Help your neighbors and they'll help you.

—Brynn Dalton's Rules for an
Exemplary Life, #98

Brynn hadn't even had a chance to get to her locker when her best friend pounced on her in the hallway, dragging her into an alcove.

"What the hell, Angela?"

But her annoyance faded into concern at the stricken expression on her friend's face.

"What's wrong?"

Her friend chewed her lip. "You haven't seen?"

Brynn glanced at the clock on the wall. She had seven minutes until first period. Not nearly enough time to deal with Angela's penchant for drama.

"Haven't seen what?" she asked impatiently.

Her friend wouldn't meet her eyes. "You know how

the other day after cheer practice you said someone had taken your bra out of your bag in the locker room?"

Brynn felt heat rising to her face as she looked around in embarrassment. *"Jeez, say it a little louder."*

"Well, I think I found it," Angela said, wrapping a hand around Brynn's wrist and dragging her toward the door.

Brynn's heart began to thud nervously.

Not again. *It couldn't be happening again. Not when she'd come so far.*

Moments like this were exactly why she'd refused to let her parents send her to St. Thomas Preparatory after eighth grade with the rest of her classmates. She needed a fresh start at the public school. Needed to find a place where she wasn't Dumpy Dalton.

Where people didn't stuff her book bag with candy bars, or make fun of her buckteeth whenever she had to give a presentation.

So far, freshman year at Truman High had been the best year of her life. She'd lost the weight... had even made the cheer squad. The acne medication had cleared up the worst of the pimples, and while the braces weren't exactly stylish, they'd already made a huge improvement on the huge front teeth she'd had her whole life.

But this? This felt a little bit like déjà vu.

Her pulse went into overdrive as Angela led her in the direction of the courtyard. Hardly a place where one's bra should be. Ever.

It took Brynn several seconds to register what she was seeing. A tiny scrap of white lace was very distinctly flapping in the breeze several inches below the American flag.

Through the roaring in her ears, she dimly became

aware of the crowds of students standing around and pointing. Laughing.

Eight years' worth of painful schoolyard memories came rushing back over her.

"Nobody knows it's yours," Angela said softly. "Just you and me."

Brynn's eyes remained locked on the small bra. Small to fit her small size. When she'd lost weight, her boobs had been the first to shrink. "No, Ang, we're not the only ones. It's you, me, and the jackass who did it."

Angela's eyes flew open. "Do you know who it was?"

Brynn's eyes scanned the courtyard until they found what she was looking for. Whom she was looking for.

His blue eyes locked with hers, much as they had a couple months earlier on the football field.

But this time, her stomach didn't flip in excitement. It turned in hatred. Three months ago, she'd thought Will Thatcher's interest in her had been, well...interest.

Turned out it was disdain. And disdain had turned into antagonism.

You started it, *she reminded herself. The first time he'd tried to talk to her, she'd been so nervous that she'd gone into what her little sister called Ice Princess mode.*

He'd been taking small hits at her ever since. Cat-calling her when she walked by, telling the boy who had asked her to the homecoming dance that she was a prude...

He'd even accidentally-on-purpose ran into her, knocking her notebooks all over the ground, only to taunt her as he'd helped her pick them up.

But this? This was a new level of mean.

Brynn's eyes narrowed at the smirk on his face.

She'd spent her entire life dealing with bullies. She could take on this one.

It was war.

And she was more than happy to engage.

* * *

Brynn took the last cookie out of the bakery bag and set it on her second-favorite white platter. She'd long ago stopped fretting about the lack of the homemade factor.

Did she wish that she'd mastered baking? Sure.

And she would. Someday.

But for now she worked sixty-hour weeks and barely had time to *buy* flour, much less use it.

And deep down, Brynn suspected that homemade was perhaps just a *touch* overrated. Why opt for homemade imperfection when you could just buy *actual* perfection?

Nobody had to know. Most of her friends thought she could rival Betty Crocker in a baking contest.

She hoped the new neighbors weren't gluten-free, or whatever, because they were about to have the best chocolate chip cookies that they'd ever had. Specialty's cookies were one of the few indulgences Brynn allowed herself once a month. Her butt wasn't going to fit into skinny jeans without a little self-control.

Brynn moved a couple cookies around so the plate looked symmetrical, and then headed upstairs to the bedroom to change her clothes. There was a fine line between casual-chic and casual-frump, and her favorite ratty athletic shorts were in the latter category.

Brynn had quickly learned that while yoga pants were *always* fair game in the suburbs (whether or not one actually did yoga), other athletic wear was not for public consumption. Probably because being spotted in well-worn gym shorts gave away the fact that one actually had to work out to look the way they did.

And Brynn definitely had to work at it. If she heard one more petty girlfriend complain about Brynn's slender figure being "unfair," Brynn was going to come unglued. She worked damn hard to keep her butt from wiggling and stomach from spilling over her jeans. She ran at least five times a week and did yoga on most weekdays. Maybe there were some women out there who were effortlessly thin. Brynn only aspired to make it *look* effortless.

She knew what it felt like when none of her clothes fit. Knew the despair of realizing she had to go up a size *again*.

And she was never going back down that path, no matter how much she hated the exercise or wanted the cookie.

Pulling on a casual white skirt and short-sleeved black turtleneck, she smoothed back her hair into a low ponytail and grabbed the plate of cookies and her keys. Showtime. The moving truck had been gone for a few hours now. Plenty of time for the new family to settle in, and plenty of time for her to have made *welcome to the neighborhood* cookies.

Brynn mentally kicked herself for not making it to last week's cul-de-sac party. She'd missed whatever scoop her neighbors had on the newcomer to the neighborhood. They probably had kids. Most people in Foxgrove Estates did. She only hoped they were the quiet, intellectual type of children, and not the throw-a-baseball-through-your-living-room-window types.

It didn't really matter either way, though. The sad

truth was, Brynn had little in common with *any* of her neighbors. They were all friendly and welcoming, but the group was made up almost entirely of families or couples. The only other single person was the elderly Mrs. Hoover, and she had her grandkids visit every weekend, which meant she was at least up-to-date on all the latest kid lingo. Meanwhile, Brynn had mistakenly thought Justin Bieber was a *Harry Potter* character, and the neighborhood's under-twelve population had yet to let her forget it.

The path to her new neighbor's front door was only a few feet from her own if she cut across the grass, but walking on the lawn didn't even cross her mind. What was she, an animal? Instead, she carefully marched down her driveway, across the sidewalk, and back up the new neighbor's driveway toward the front door.

As was typical in master-planned communities, this house wasn't all that different from her own. Lots of brick, unobtrusive cream-colored paneling, and a dark mahogany front door. James was forever rambling about how McMansion-style houses like hers lacked character, which was a bit hypocritical, coming from a guy who drove the same BMW as half the other doctors at the hospital where he worked.

But Brynn actually didn't mind the cookie-cutter nature of the neighborhood. Why did everyone think that character had to mean haphazard quirkiness? Her house did *too* have character. It was just uniform, organized character. Just as she liked it.

Nobody responded to her soft knock, so she tried the doorbell. She saw a shadow move through the slim glass partition in the door and straightened her shoulders and put on what Sophie referred to as her "orthodontist smile."

The door swung open and Brynn's vision went blurry as she felt her perfect smile crack.

She couldn't breathe.

It had never occurred to her that a single, good-looking guy would answer the door. And it certainly hadn't occurred to her that she would know him.

Intimately.

"Will, what the *hell* are you doing here? Tell me you're working for the moving company."

He leaned against the door and looked down at her. His faded jeans and tight white T-shirt were perfectly acceptable for moving-day attire and yet they annoyed her to no end. The jeans hugged body parts she'd rather forget, and the shirt displayed proof that he hadn't neglected the gym while he'd been whoring himself on the East Coast.

"Hey, neighbor," he said, shooting her a cocky grin.

Hope that he was just passing through town crumbled around her feet, and her fingers clenched her cookie platter.

"You don't live here," she ground out. "You can't."

He shrugged. "If you say so."

"You live in Boston," she said firmly.

"Sold my place last week," he said, reaching for the cookies.

Brynn slapped his hand away. "Well, you can't live here. I live *there*," she said, jabbing her finger at her house to the left.

"Do you now?"

Brynn narrowed her eyes at him. He didn't look the least bit surprised. He looked . . . smug.

Her jaw dropped open. "You knew? You hate me that much that you can't let me live in peace?"

"Now who said anything about hate?" he said in a low voice.

It might have been her imagination, but she could have sworn his eyes drifted down and lingered. Not on the cookies. Or rather, not *those* cookies.

Her mouth went dry.

"Are those for me?" he asked.

She jerked. "Are what for you?"

"The cookies you're about ready to drop all over my front porch."

My front porch. It had a terrible ring to it. Good Lord, the man was really planning to *live* here.

"Brynn?" he said, raising an eyebrow. "The cookies?"

"What? Oh. No. They're not for you," she said.

"What, are you selling them or something? A grown-up Girl Scout? Because your outfit needs some work."

"They're *my* cookies. And they're excellent. They're too good for you."

Will rolled his eyes and without warning hooked a hand around her upper arm and yanked her inside. "You're being ridiculous. Don't even try to convince me that you'd actually eat one of those cookies."

"Why wouldn't I eat a cookie?" she asked, weaving around moving boxes as she followed him into the kitchen.

"Please. You look like you haven't indulged in sugar since the tenth grade."

"Tenth grade," she mused. "Now which year was that, the year you ran my bra up the flagpole or the year you told the entire football team that I didn't wear underwear under my cheerleading skirt? Which was a total lie, by the way."

Actually, both of those things had happened in ninth grade. But she wasn't about to let on how well she remembered those moments.

Or how much they had hurt.

"Honey, I don't think anyone believed for a second that you went without underwear. I doubt you take your panties off to shower."

You've seen me without panties.

She pushed the thought aside. Immediately.

Since he didn't yet have any chairs, they squared off on either side of the kitchen island. Will's fingers toyed with the edge of the platter's plastic wrap and she jerked the cookies away, the juvenile action giving her a strange surge of satisfaction. Why did it feel so *good* to be impolite?

"Come on, Brynny. I haven't eaten all day and the cookies will just go to waste otherwise."

Her eyes locked purposefully on his sulky gaze and she edged the plate out of his reach, very carefully pulled one cookie from the plate. Keeping the eye contact she very slowly took a bite, making a big show of enjoying the way the bittersweet chocolate rolled over her tongue.

She'd just add an extra mile onto her run tomorrow. It was worth it to prove him wrong.

The cookie turned to sawdust as she saw the satisfied expression on his face.

He'd known she would eat the cookie. She'd played right into his hand.

Crap. Annoyed, she handed the cookie over to him.

Perhaps she'd get lucky and he'd have a recently developed chocolate allergy.

"So," she said, looking around the kitchen. "Care to explain what game you're playing?"

He helped himself to a second cookie. "Game?"

Brynn gave him her best withering glare. "Yes, game. There's no way you just *happened* to move next door to me. You're up to something."

"Maybe I just liked the neighborhood."

"You're a thirtysomething man-whore. The suburbs are the worst possible place for you."

Will rested his elbows on the counter and wiggled his eyebrows at her. "Maybe I'm here for the same reason you are."

Brynn leaned on her own arms to mimic his posture. "Which is...?"

"Convincing your boy-puppet that he should marry you and have little mannequin babies."

Brynn stood up straight, all traces of playfulness gone. The sting from James's nonproposal was still raw, and Will's jab hit a little too close to home.

"You know nothing about James," she snapped.

His eyes went serious for a moment. "I know you got those earrings the size of a small dog instead of a ring for your birthday."

Brynn carefully kept her expression blank. "I'm surprised you stayed that long. I'd have thought you'd be exploring the thong of some underage model."

He didn't rise to the bait. "Sophie filled me in on what I missed. I hope you ripped Jimmy a new one when you got home."

"His name is James. And I had no reason to be upset

with him," she said softly, fiddling with a cookie crumb.

To her surprise, Will dropped the subject entirely. "Want to help me furniture shop?"

Her mouth dropped open. "You're kidding, right? You honestly think I'd put myself willingly in your company?"

"Well, you are lingering here in my kitchen instead of setting my lawn on fire, so I thought it was worth a shot."

Brynn tapped manicured fingernails on the marble counter. What *was* she still doing here? "I'm leaving," she retorted. "Just tell me how long you plan to draw out this little joke."

"What joke?"

"This next-door-neighbor crap. You don't belong here."

"How do you know?"

"Well, for starters, your car only seats two people. That's about a quarter as many seats as you need to belong in this neighborhood."

"Maybe I'm on the hunt for a family."

"Everyone here already *has* a family. There's no possible reason you could want to live here other than to annoy me. Just come clean already."

Will stood up straight. "I hate to break it to you, Princess, but you're going to have to get used to me. I'm sorry I don't fit into the box you're trying to stuff me into, but I'm not going to apologize because I wanted a break from the swanky-high-rise-condo scene."

"Fine," she said, trying to keep her tone as cool as his. "You want your fill of minivans and Bed Bath & Beyond, have at it. But why *this* neighborhood? You can't tell me it was just a coincidence."

His face betrayed nothing as he lifted a shoulder. "Okay, fine, it wasn't a coincidence. As much as you'd like to think we don't have anything in common, there is one area where we're very much alike... we like the best. When Sophie said you'd moved to Foxgrove, I thought it was worth checking out. I knew you lived close, but I didn't know you lived right next door. That's the honest-to-God truth."

Brynn pursed her lips and studied him, looking for all possible signs of a lie. There were none.

"You really want to live next door to me?" she asked.

"Not particularly," he said, grabbing a third cookie. "But neither do I feel like reentering the real estate market just to get away from you."

She licked her lips nervously and asked the question that had been on her mind since he opened the door. "So this isn't about... you know..."

He leaned forward as though waiting for her to finish the sentence. "You'll have to forgive me, but it's pretty hard to read you beneath all that snooty pretension."

That snooty pretension is the only thing that keeps me safe from lechers like you, she thought.

"Well?" he prompted.

"You're being here has nothing to do with *that night*?"

"What night?" he asked, blue eyes all innocence.

"That night. The one, where we, you know..."

"Fucked like rabbits?"

Brynn winced. "God, Will."

"Yes, I do believe you called me 'God' a few times."

"You're appalling," she spat.

"Maybe. But you certainly didn't think so on *that*

night," he said, reaching out a hand to toy with the end of her hair.

She backed up into a pile of moving boxes. "Don't touch me."

His eyes went flat. "No problem. I don't need the frostbite."

"So funny," she snapped, as she grabbed her platter of cookies and headed toward the front door. "Just promise me you're not going to mention our little episode to anyone."

"They won't hear it from me," he said following her into the foyer. "But, Brynn, I've gotta tell you..."

"What?" she snapped, yanking open the door and turning to face him. "What do you need to tell me? That my ass looks big? That you can see my roots?"

"No," he said thoughtfully. "Although both are true."

"Nice," she muttered.

"But what I wanted to say, was that this is the second time you've arrived on my front porch. Once you offered sex. The second time offered cookies."

"And?"

"Well, I just wanted you to know..." His eyes went hot as they ran down the front of her body and she shivered at the memory of what they'd been like together.

"Yeah?" she asked, hating that her voice was husky.

Will leaned forward until his mouth was near her ear. "I think I like the cookies better."

With that, he grabbed the platter from her hand and slammed the door in her face.

Brynn stood there for several moments caught somewhere between anger and arousal.

And maybe something that felt like pain, which was

ridiculous. She and Will had been trading barbs since puberty.

But this one had felt...personal.

And she was pretty damn sure that where Will Thatcher was concerned, personal was tantamount to dangerous.

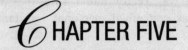HAPTER FIVE

*Friendships between men and women should be
avoided. They rarely end well.*

—Brynn Dalton's Rules for an
Exemplary Life, #48

*B*rynny, guess what?"

Brynn glanced up to where her sister danced happily
in the doorway, grateful for a relief from her honors biol-
ogy homework.

"What's up?"

Sophie bounced into her room, flouncing onto Brynn's
carefully made bed with gusto.

"Why are you still in your cheerleading outfit?" Brynn
asked, glancing at the clock. "I thought the freshman
practice was over a couple hours ago."

Sophie gave a mischievous grin. "It was."

Brynn's eyes narrowed, looking her younger sister up
and down for signs of trouble. "Did Mel bring you home?"

"Nope." Sophie twirled her hair and grinned.

"This guessing game is superfun, but just tell me whatever's got you so bouncy."

Actually, Sophie was always bouncy. And normally Brynn didn't mind in the least. She kind of liked having a sister who was queen of the freshman class. Brynn did her best to be friendly and outgoing, but it had never come naturally. Not like it did to her sister.

"I got asked to prom."

Brynn's eyes bugged. out. *"Prom? But you're a freshman!"*

"Yup. The only one going, that I know of." Sophie's voice wasn't quite gloating. But it was close.

"With whom? Sophie, Mom and Dad are going to totally flip. Not in the good way."

"Don't worry, he's totally the clean-cut kind of guy they want to see their baby girl with."

Brynn wrinkled her nose, trying to think of options. It would have to be a junior or senior. Freshmen and sophomores weren't allowed to prom unless asked by upperclassmen.

"Daniel Saunders?" Brynn asked.

"Nope."

"Nick McFain?"

"Uh-uh."

"Brian what's-his-name with the freckles?"

"Hasn't he had a girlfriend since like second grade?" Brynn shrugged. *"Who, then?"*

Sophie flopped onto Brynn's pillow and gave a little squeal. *"Will Thatcher."*

Something sharp seized at Brynn's chest.

She just didn't know if it was panic . . . or pain.

* * *

"How many copies of *The Shining* does one person need?"

Will glanced over to where Sophie was pulling his DVD collection out of a box. "There are multiple releases with different special features. And you're not putting them in the right order."

Sophie paused in lining them up messily on the shelf. "There's an order? For the exact same movie?"

"If you want to help me unpack, they go in order by release date," he said, returning to his own unpacking duties.

"Nobody *wants* to help somebody else unpack," Sophie muttered as she began turning the DVD cases over and checking dates. "It's just what friends do."

"Speaking of which, you were supposed to bring Gray with you. I need his help in moving my pool table to where I want it."

"First of all . . . there's no way you two can move the pool table on your own. It's probably time to extend your male social circle beyond one. And second, I didn't bring Gray because then you and I couldn't have our girl talk."

Will grunted.

Sophie cleared her throat. "Ahem. That was a hint to go fetch wine?"

He rolled his eyes, but headed into the kitchen to comply. Most of the time, having a woman as a best friend was useful. Hell, most of the time he barely even noticed that Sophie *was* a woman.

But there were times when a man would have been preferable. Times when he didn't want to *talk*.

Times like now.

But he hadn't been able to turn her away. He harbored a fair amount of guilt for ditching Sophie when he'd moved to Boston. Not that she'd ever guilt-tripped him about it...Soph always had his back. But he'd known she'd been hurt that he hadn't given her any warning about moving across the country.

The thing was, he couldn't have given her warning even if he'd wanted to. Because Will himself hadn't even *contemplated* the move until exactly three days before he'd actually gotten on that plane.

Weighing even heavier on his conscience was the one and only secret he'd ever kept from Sophie. The one that had him moving to Boston in the first place.

"White or red?" he called.

"Surprise me," she hollered back. He heard a crashing noise and winced. Sophie wasn't exactly the most careful of souls. Thank God he'd put all of the boxes marked FRAGILE out of her reach.

He poured them both liberal glasses of one of his favorite Cabernet Sauvignons and headed back to his living room. Sophie's expression was all innocence, and Will pretended he didn't see that his *Aliens* anniversary edition case had a new crack in it. He'd always found the movie overrated anyway.

Will smiled as Sophie took a massive gulp of wine. There was no swirling, no sniffing, no savoring on the palate. Just unpretentious good old-fashioned drinking. It was one of the reasons he loved her. There was nothing complicated about Sophie. At least, she'd never been complicated to him. She said what she wanted, did what she wanted, and before you could figure out whether she was brilliant or pure fluff, she'd already moved on, re-cruiting yet another person to her fan club.

"When are you going to get some furniture?" Sophie grumbled as she stood and stretched.

"Monday," Will said absently, taking in the unfamiliar setting that was his new backyard. He'd never really thought much about where he lived. Hell, he'd spent the better part of his twenties living in hotel rooms while he tried to secure investors. But he was surprised to find that he sort of liked having the extra space. He would have moved into a shoe box if that's what the plan required, but this was better. Much better.

"So," Sophie said, coming up beside him and gazing out at the newly stained deck. "When are you going to fill me in?"

Will didn't pretend to play dumb. But neither was he ready to come clean.

"I already told you," he said, keeping his voice light. "I was ready for a change."

That part, at least, was true. The constant moving, the sterile furniture, the high-rise city views had begun to feel a bit stale.

"Uh-uh," Sophie said, taking another gulp of wine. "If you'd wanted a change, you would have tried a new city. You wouldn't have come back to Seattle. There's nothing new here."

I don't want new.

"Does this have anything to do with my sister?" Sophie asked, turning to face him. "Is this like some new level of psychotic in the little war you two kids won't let go of?"

Will didn't answer. Didn't have to.

Sophie groaned. "Oh God, it *is* about Brynn. I should have known when you started asking so many questions about where she lived. And here I thought it was just a little good old-fashioned one-upmanship, but it's something more, isn't it?"

"You act like I'm out to ruin her life," Will grumbled. Sophie's tone didn't bode well for him. Sophie and Brynn were close. If Soph thought Brynn didn't want him around, this was going to be one painful uphill battle.

"I know you guys get some sort of perverse enjoyment out of the whole fighting-like-cats-and-dogs thing," Sophie said. "But isn't it getting a little...old?"

For a second Will wanted to tell Sophie everything. About that night. About his agenda. About how seeing Brynn again made him feel like a pathetic boy trying to get the attention of the girl he liked by pulling her hair.

But he couldn't risk that Sophie would tell all to her sister and scare Brynn off before he even had a chance.

"She's happy, you know," Sophie said softly.

Of all the things that Sophie could have said, that, quite possibly, was the worst.

What if he was wrong? What if his presence here did nothing but make her miserable? He wanted to shake her up and challenge her, not ruin her life.

"Tell me about this James guy," Will said, trying to keep his tone indifferent.

Sophie looked at him closely. "I thought I already did. In fact, I *distinctly* remember giving you the full scoop on the phone the other day."

"You gave me the résumé version," Will said, turning and leaning against the window. "I want the paparazzi version. This guy could be my neighbor one day soon."

"I doubt that," Sophie muttered, settling onto one of the larger moving boxes.

"Oh?" Will asked. Casually. Too casually. "You don't think he's 'the one' or whatever you women call it?"

Sophie shrugged. "On paper, they make sense. And God knows my mother's done enough interrogating of the guy to determine that he definitely wants a family someday. So he and Brynn are pretty much perfectly aligned right down to their hourly to-do lists."

"But...?" Will prompted.

"There's something missing," Sophie mused.

"You always think that about Brynn's boyfriends," Will said. Not that he ever disagreed with Sophie.

"That's because she keeps choosing the wrong ones," Sophie said, waving her wineglass around wildly. "She picks these perfect guys that are mirror images of herself. And she wonders why she gets bored."

"She said that? That she's bored?" Will asked.

"Well, no," Sophie admitted. "Admitting boredom would be akin to admitting *mistake*, and that would send her over the edge. But it's obvious that there's no spark."

"Maybe Brynn doesn't want spark."

"That's just the problem. She *needs* it."

He wanted to ask more questions.

How many guys had Brynn seen since he'd left?

How many had she slept with?

Did she ever mention him?

But Sophie was already looking at him suspiciously.

"Want pizza?" he asked, wanting to distract her.

"I had a salad for dinner."

"So?" he asked, pulling his cell phone out of his pocket.

"So *of course* I want pizza," Sophie said, heading into the kitchen, presumably for more wine. "Hey, you want me to start on this pile of boxes here?"

Naturally, she'd spotted the breakable items. "Nope, I want to finish up in here first," he called. "Bring that bottle with you."

"What's with the cookies?" Sophie asked, returning to the room just as he finished ordering the pizza.

"What?"

"The cookies on the counter," she said, gesturing with the bottle. "They're awesome."

"Brynn brought them over. She made a big show about them being homemade, but I call bullshit."

"Yeah, those are definitely from Speciality's," Sophie said with a dreamy look. Then her eyes narrowed on him. "So Brynn knows you're here, huh? I bet she shat a brick when she saw you."

Will gave a wry smile. "Let's just say she needed a tranquilizer. She thinks I'm here to make her life miserable."

"Well, aren't you?" Sophie asked.

Will was taken aback by the seriousness in his best friend's tone. He guessed he'd always known on some level that Brynn came first in Sophie's life. Sibling relationships were like that...not that he had any personal experience.

But it still chafed that she was so sure that he had nothing to offer other than annoyance. Not that he'd given either woman reason to think otherwise. For as long as he could remember, it had been him vs. Brynn, with Sophie doing her best to play mediator without taking sides.

The sad part was, he couldn't even really remember

when the war had started. He knew from Brynn's perspective it had started when he, as a hotshot, cocky high school junior, had snagged her bra from her cheerleading bag and put it up on the flagpole on a dare.

She had responded like a cat in a bath. And then, just because she'd become a pro at ignoring his very existence, he'd gone for the one thing that had gotten a rise out of her: her baby sister.

But Sophie had turned out to be, well...*Sophie*, which had turned into perhaps the one lasting platonic friendship in all of history between a freshman girl and senior boy. But despite his lasting friendship with Sophie over the years, and his eventual welcome into the Dalton family, Brynn and Will had never grown out of their roles as childhood adversaries.

He supposed he couldn't really blame Sophie for assuming he was here to cause trouble. But if his best friend didn't believe he might have good intentions, how the hell was he supposed to convince his worst enemy?

More disgruntled than he cared to let on, Will grumpily set Sophie back to work on unpacking his DVD collection. He'd have to rearrange everything later, but at least the monotonous task of lining them up by name and by year would keep her from rattling on about Brynn.

An hour later they were chewing on messy, cheesy pepperoni pizza, and Will became increasingly aware that Sophie's attention was on him, and not the pizza.

Hardly typical behavior for his best friend.

He tried not to look at her. Not only because he knew the woman could read him like a book, but when she was serious like this, it spooked him how much she looked like Brynn. Same long blonde hair, same wide-set eyes, same mouth...although Sophie's mouth was invariably a lot more smiley than Brynn's.

"You know that I know, right?" she said, breaking the strained silence.

He irritably set his empty plate aside and walked over to one of the half-unpacked boxes. "Know what?" he asked, setting a picture of his parents on the shelf.

"About you. And Brynn."

His fingers faltered for a moment on the frame, and he felt a burst of hope. Brynn had sworn him to secrecy on their one night together, but if she'd confided in Sophie about it, maybe she wasn't as ashamed of the encounter as she let on.

"What do you mean?" he asked casually.

"You're in love with her."

His hand jerked, and the picture shattered on the floor, but neither of them moved to pick up the broken glass.

He hadn't expected her to know *that*.

A million denials ran through his head, but he couldn't bring himself to utter them. Lying to his best friend by omission was one thing. Lying straight to her face felt wrong.

"Does Brynn know?" he asked finally, hating that his voice sounded like a nervous kid before asking someone to prom.

"No," Sophie said softly. "I think she's still as convinced as everyone else that you hate her guts."

He didn't hate her guts. Not even close. Although sometimes he thought he should. The woman could be downright witchy, and was so rigid, she was one good tantrum away from exploding into a million pissy pieces.

But she could also be sweet. Not to him, of

course...*never* to him. But he'd spent enough time watching her over the years to know that she helped old ladies take grocery bags out to their cars, and went on a fishing trip with her dad every summer even though she *hated* fishing. He'd also rummaged through her mail under the guise of pissing her off, and knew that she contributed to about nine hundred different charities.

She was also funny as hell, assuming one liked the prickly, caustic type of humor. He did.

None of that explained why he was completely, irrevocably wrapped up in her, but he was. Had always been.

He'd been sixteen, and he'd simply *known*. Known that she was the one. Even when she was busy tearing his heart out.

Will sighed and resigned himself to coming clean with Sophie. "How did you find out?"

He'd been so fucking careful. Then again, moving next door to the woman perhaps wasn't the height of stealth.

Sophie fiddled with the case of *Psycho*. "I wish I could say that as your closest friend, I've known all along. But the truth is, I didn't really have a clue until her birthday party the other night. When James handed Brynn that jewelry box, and we all thought...Well, I saw your face."

Will winced. "Was it that obvious?"

She shrugged. "To others you probably just looked disgusted. But as someone who knows you best, you looked...devastated."

"I wasn't *devastated*," he said. "Quit making a frigging soap opera out of this."

"Use whatever man-phrase makes you comfortable," Sophie said with a dismissive wave of her hand. "The point is, I *saw* you. It's why I called you immediately after you headed out. To let you know it wasn't what you thought."

"Thanks for that," he said quietly.

Those moments after he'd walked out of the party thinking he'd lost Brynn for good had been some of the worst of his life. He'd seen Brynn in a white dress walking toward someone who was not him, and it had clawed at his chest like a heart attack.

Sophie's phone call had come just in time to stop him from getting good and thoroughly drunk.

"Although, to be honest," Sophie was rambling, "I feel like an idiot for not seeing it before. True love hiding behind the squabbling couple is like the oldest romantic-comedy trope there is."

"Except in the chick flicks, it's generally mutual," he said, leaning down to pick up the shattered picture frame.

"True," she said, coming over to help grab the bigger pieces of shattered glass. "But you have a plan, right? That's why you moved back? That's why you moved *here*?"

Will grunted. It was bad enough to know his secret was no longer a secret. He really wasn't in the mood to have a pow-wow about it, even with Sophie. *Especially* with Sophie. She was Brynn's sister, and as much as he trusted her...

"Soph, you won't say anything, right? To Brynn? Or even to Gray?"

She hedged slightly. Secrets had never really been her forte.

"Please, Sophie. Just give me a little time."

"But I could help! I could play matchmaker, but be supersmooth about it."

Will gave her a look. She was about as subtle as a battering ram, which she knew full well. Smooth was absolutely not in her repertoire.

"Fine," she muttered. "I'll keep out of it. For now. But Will..." She stood, gingerly holding shards of glass with the tips of her finger. "You know that I'm rooting for you, but if she doesn't feel the same way..."

"She's a big girl, Soph," Will said, trying to lighten the mood.

"I know," she said, with a lift of her shoulder. "But she's fragile under all those matching outfits, ya know?"

Actually, he didn't know. Brynn had always been so damn *flawless*. But he'd always suspected that there was some piece of her that he was missing. All her die-hard dedication to perfection had to come from somewhere, he'd just never been able to figure out where.

Probably because they hadn't had a civil conversation in...ever.

"Fragile how?" He knew he was prying, but the cat was already out of the bag. Might as well get a little information out of it.

Sophie was silent for several minutes. "Maybe 'fragile' wasn't the right word. Brynn would kill me just for saying the word. But sometimes I think she's made it her life's mission to erase an imperfect childhood by being a perfect adult."

Will took a sip of wine. "By 'imperfect,' I'm assuming you mean she once placed second in a spelling bee and never forgave herself?"

Sophie gave him a look. "You *have* seen some of our old photo albums, right?"

"Yeah, because that's what every heterosexual guy

longs for. To rummage through his friend's family albums."

"Well, if you *had* seen them, you'd know that Brynn hasn't always been quite so..."

"Prim? Humorless? Slightly dead behind the eyes?"

"Well, I can tell you two are going to have sweet pillow talk," she said. "Let's just say she didn't exactly hit the beauty-queen jackpot."

Will's eyebrows crept up. He hadn't met Brynn until she was a little freshman hottie. He'd never done much thinking of what she'd been like before that.

"So? We all had awkward years," he said with a shrug.

Sophie licked her lips and looked pained. "Brynn's was more like an awkward *decade*. Actually, 'awkward' doesn't even cover it. She was my big sister, and I idolized her because she was funny and sweet, even if she was a little—okay, *a lot*—overweight, and she was shy, and she had this gap the size of Africa between her teeth, and..."

Will held up his hand with a half laugh. "Tell me you have a picture of this. I can't *believe* all this blackmail material was right at my fingertips and I didn't even know it."

Sophie was in his face in a flash. "Don't you dare, Will. I know you two like your games, but don't touch those years. Seriously."

His smile faded.

Whoa. What is going on here?

"We've all got a few rough memories," Sophie said more softly, "but kids can be cruel, and Brynn got more than her fair share of it."

The pieces began fitting together and Will felt something tighten in his chest at the thought of a chubby, awkward Brynn who would have wanted so badly to fit in.

"How am I just now finding this out?" he asked softly.

"Well, gosh, I can't imagine why Brynn wouldn't have shared all this with you while you were torturing her," Sophie muttered.

"Okay, in my defense, by the time I met the girl, she was queen of her freshman class."

Sophie shrugged. "On the outside, sure. Inside she was still Dumpy Dalton. That's what they used to call her."

Will rocked back on his heels. *Christ.*

He swallowed dryly. "Soph, you ever wish you could go back and do things all over again? I mean, like all the way?"

She gave him a look. "Will, my husband once assumed I was a Las Vegas hooker. So no, *of course* I wouldn't want a do-over."

He smiled slightly at her sarcasm, but his mind was already back on Brynn. For the first time, he was finally starting to see things the way they really were.

And a part of him—a big part of him—wanted nothing more than to cradle her to him and tell her that she was not that little girl anymore. That she didn't have to try so hard.

But the smarter part of him knew that Brynn Dalton would take anything looking even remotely like pity and shove it up his ass.

He'd have to stay the course. At least for now.

Sophie's eyes narrowed on him. "Oh God. I know that look. You're *planning*."

"Maybe," he said, giving her a boyish grin. "Would that be so bad?"

"Well…" she said in a thoughtful voice, flouncing toward the kitchen. "Let's see. There was that time that Brynn told Vicki Morales that you had crabs, and you got so pissed that you let the air out of the tires of the car my parents bought her for her sixteenth birthday. She'd had the car for exactly four days before you put it out of commission, and I honest to God thought she was going to kill you…"

Will had started to follow Sophie into the kitchen, but he stopped abruptly at the long-forgotten memory of Brynn and that car. He felt a small smile slide over his face.

Little did Sophie know that she'd just provided the next step in his plan.

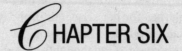

CHAPTER SIX

A tasteful watch is always in style,
as a lady is never late.

—Brynn Dalton's Rules for an
Exemplary Life, #21

*B*rynn was going to be late.

She *never* ran late. The inability to keep track of the hour and plan for potential mishaps was just so *crass.*

"And of course it would be today," she muttered as she pulled her cell phone out of her purse.

Normally Brynn's work schedule could withstand the occasional delay. She trusted her partner completely, and Dr. Wee would be more than happy to cover one of Brynn's patients.

But today, Brynn *really* wanted to be there in person. Seattle's mayor was bringing her daughter in for an initial consultation. And while it was hardly the president, the mayor was still something of a local celebrity. It was just the sort of reference that Brynn could put on her website that would set her apart from the other orthodontist practices that were popping up with increasing regularity.

Only one tiny problem...

Her tire was flat. Beyond flat.

She flipped through the list of contacts on her phone until she found AAA. She'd been a member ever since buying her first car. She'd never needed assistance before, but she'd found it prudent to plan for emergencies. She just wished it hadn't happened today.

Brynn patiently pushed all the requisite numbers to get through their automated call-intake system and calmly explained her situation to the woman on the other line.

"What do you mean it'll be ninety minutes?" Brynn exploded.

Suddenly her silk blouse started sticking to her back. She hissed in frustration. She hated perspiration. It was so...pedestrian.

"I'm sorry, ma'am," the polite voice was saying. "We'll get there as soon as we can, but we only have so many available agents."

She glanced at the Chanel watch she'd bought herself for her thirtieth birthday. The mayor's daughter would be in her office in a little over an hour and ten minutes. There was no way she'd make it in time. Dr. Wee would just have to take the appointment with Liz Blanton.

Unless...

Brynn's eyes fell on the house next door.

Will's house.

The thought still made her vaguely queasy.

"You know, I think I'll see if an, um...friend can take

care of the tire for me," Brynn heard herself saying to AAA. "Thank you anyway, though."

She dropped her phone back into her purse and delicately pulled at her shirt with her nails to keep it from sticking to her body. Of course this *would* happen on what would probably be Seattle's one hot day of the year.

Although, truthfully, she wasn't sure what was making her sweatier: the weather, or the thought of asking Will Thatcher for help.

But Brynn was nothing if not practical. AAA wasn't nearby, and she knew firsthand that Will was just a few hideous steps away. She'd seen him preening in front of his kitchen window that looked directly into hers.

She avoided looking in the direction of his house as often as possible, but the occasional glance had been inevitable. Best as she could tell, Will Thatcher did not seem to own a shirt. He probably enjoyed the reflection of his own pecs too much.

Brynn started marching toward his front door. If he wanted to torture her by living next door, she'd just let him see exactly what it meant to be *neighborly*.

She should have been prepared for it when she opened the door, but she still gaped. "For God's sake, Will, put some clothes on. You're going to scare the neighbor kids."

Will stretched and leaned against the door. "Yeah, but their moms will be happy."

"Gross," she muttered, scooting past him into the air-conditioned home, being careful not to brush against his impeccably carved chest.

He made a valid point, though. The soccer moms would be drooling if they could see him. The man was wearing only black boxers, and the rest of him was nothing but golden skin and defined muscles.

"Why are you all shiny?" she asked with a sneer as she gingerly scraped a nail down his bicep. "You look like you just got done with a wrestling playdate with Hercules and Achilles."

"Is that your way of saying I look like a Greek god?" he asked as his fingers locked on her finger. She jerked her hand back. She hadn't meant to touch him.

"That's my way of saying you need a shower," she snapped. "And would you quit with the flexing? You look like you're having seizures."

"Can I help you with something or did you interrupt my workout just to come ogle me?"

Right. Keep your eye on the prize. And not that *prize. Do it for the mayor's daughter.*

Brynn tried to let her eyes go soft while maintaining her smile. It wasn't easy when she had the irrepressible urge to strike at him. Or maybe pull him closer. Or maybe...

"Brynn?"

"I need help," she blurted out.

His cocky grin abolished all traces of the sexual awareness she'd been feeling a second earlier. Or mostly abolished them, anyway. If only he'd put a shirt on...

"I have a flat tire," she said, trying to keep her voice helpless and innocent. "And I called for help, but it'll be a while, and I have an important appointment at work, and I know you hate me, but if you could just be a decent human for like thirty seconds out of your entire year—"

"Sure," he said, interrupting her plea-slash-demand. "I can help."

"Oh," she said, surprised by the lack of a fight. "Thanks... You know about cars, right?"

"Seems to me all women assume that men being born with a cock somehow correlates to auto-mechanic expertise, but in my case, you'd be correct."

She gave him a bland look. "Were you just looking for a reason to say 'cock' just now?"

He grinned. "Maybe. Probably. Let me put pants on and I'll come take a look."

"Don't forget a shirt!" she called after him. "I wouldn't want you to be embarrassed when all of the neighborhood dads see your beer belly!"

She let herself out the front door and headed back to her own driveway, where she called her partner to let her know she'd be late, but that she wouldn't miss the Blanton appointment.

At least she hoped she wouldn't. If Will could use his hands on her car like he had on her body...

Firm palms bracketing her waist, pinning her to the mattress as his head dipped lower, licking and loving...

"Ah!" Brynn rapped her knuckles against her head in a futile effort to erase the mental images from her mind. It had only taken her an entire year to forget how good it had been between them. Taken her two more years to remember all of the reasons why they should never ever do it again.

She was not a savage.

She was a lady.

And ladies did not fantasize about soulless men who made a career out of making themselves disposable.

"So what happened?" Will asked from behind her. She turned, expecting him to still be half-naked just to annoy her. Thankfully, he'd thrown on jeans and an old college T-shirt. Unfortunately, neither did much to hide the body beneath it.

Think of James. James is fit. James is sexy. James is—

"Oh, you know, I just went off-roading on a bunch of spikes," she snapped to distract herself. Fighting with Will was vastly preferable to thinking about his really delicious-looking shoulders.

"Probably just a nail or something," Will said, ignoring her bitchiness as he knelt to look at the front left wheel. "You got a spare?"

"Of course I have a spare."

Actually, Brynn had no idea if she had a spare. But her car was only a year old and was pricey as hell. Surely that meant they threw in one of the extra wheel things, right?

Will gave her a look that said he knew exactly what she was thinking as he popped the trunk and began rummaging around.

"You golf?" he said, pushing aside her teal golf bag.

"Taking lessons," she muttered. "I belong to a group."

"Of course you do," he said, finding a hidden compartment and pulling out the spare tire.

"What's that supposed to mean?"

"It means," he said, as he swung the tire out and rolled it to the front of the car, "that everyone I met at your birthday party belonged to some club of some sort."

"You say that like it's a bad thing. There's nothing wrong with cultivating my interests."

He paused in the process of setting up some sort of tools. "Do you ever listen to yourself? *Cultivating your interests?* Is that really what you want your life to be about?"

Brynn felt her temper rising. "You're seriously lecturing me on how to live my life? You, who hasn't been in the same place longer than a couple years? You, who has no idea what it's like to maintain a steady job? You, whose longest relationship was determined by how long it took you to figure out the color of her sheets..." She broke off, running out of breath.

Will was looking up at her with a cocked eyebrow. "Oh, I'm sorry, Ms. Dalton. Here I thought you wanted me to help you out."

Think of the mayor's daughter. Think of your career. Think of the big picture...

"Right," she grumbled. "Sorry. Please commence with the man-moves."

He snorted at her grudging apology, but returned to swapping out her tires. She told herself to watch what he was doing so she could learn how to do it herself. Not that she had any interest in being Ms. Do-It-All-Herself, but she sure as hell wouldn't be asking *him* for a favor in the future.

But she couldn't concentrate on what he was doing. Her mind kept going back to his barb about her clubs and hobbies. *Is that really what you want your life to be about?...*

There was nothing wrong with her life. And she didn't understand why he'd said "clubs" with such disdain. Lots of women were in a book club. And a knitting club. And a yoga club...and...okay, maybe most women weren't in *all* of those clubs like Brynn was, but how was she to remain balanced if she didn't dabble?

Plus this way, if she had a falling-out with one group, she'd have the other ones to fall back on.

See? It was just good sense.

"So what's so important?" he asked, maneuvering the spare tire into place with ease.

"What?" she asked, distracted by her internal moping.

"What's the big hurry that you couldn't wait for Triple A? Must be important if you resorted to knocking on my door."

Seconds ago, Brynn had thought her reasoning completely sound. But for some reason now, when faced with Will sitting on the hot, hard pavement wrestling with her dirty tire, it felt a bit...shallow.

"Just an important client," she said, striving for confident nonchalance. He was sweating, and it made his dark blond hair curl just the slightest bit and his shirt stick to his torso. It should have looked messy and unkempt. It *did* look messy and unkempt. It also looked...good. Really good.

"I didn't know there was a such thing as an important client in orthodontics."

"Why do you always do that?" she asked, tilting her head at him.

"Do what?"

"Belittle my career. You always make it sound like I sold my soul to the devil or something."

Will stood and absently rubbed some tire grime off his hands as he examined his handiwork. "Just seems boring to me. Not to mention superficial. You get paid God knows how much money to tell kids they need to have you fiddle with their mouths in order to be attractive."

"Now hold on," she snapped. "First of all, you're the last person to lecture me about noble careers. You're not exactly curing cancer yourself. And second of all, several of my patients' oral situations cause real pain and medical issues for them. I'm a doctor. Of teeth. And do you know how many little girls have sat in my chair, crying because someone made fun of their overbites? *I fix that.*"

"Well. Let's just get you a Wonder Woman cape, shall we?"

Brynn huffed and began digging in her purse for her keys. "I don't know why I bother."

"Bother with what?"

"Talking to you!" she said, shaking her keys in his face. "Just when I think you're going to be nice, you get me all..."

Will took a small step closer. "Get you all what?"

Brynn swallowed dryly and resisted the urge to take a step backward. He was just inches away, and if she'd been slightly sweaty before, she felt downright hot and bothered now.

"Please step away. Your man-stench is making my hair frizz."

He didn't move. "You didn't finish your sentence. I get you all what? Riled? Panting? Hot?"

"I was going to say 'nauseated,'" she snapped, starting to move around him.

He moved his body and blocked her way. "I don't think so, Brynny."

She sighed and tried to look unperturbed by his presence. "What do you want, Will? Money? You want me to pay you for playing Mr. Handyman?"

Just to piss him off, she started to pull her wallet out of her purse. His expression went stormy, just as she'd known it would.

"Keep your money," he growled.

"And have you lording this over me? I don't think so. How much do you want?"

Brynn glanced at her watch and winced. Even with Will's help, she was probably going to be late. In the time she'd spent arguing with him, she might as well have waited for AAA.

At least then she wouldn't be so...oh, damn, he was right. She *was* riled and hot. And possibly on the verge of panting.

"I've gotta go," she mumbled, tearing her eyes away from his. "Think about whatever ridiculous price you want to put on your little hero-task and let me know."

Will moved so quickly Brynn didn't have a chance to react before he'd pressed her against the side of the car, his hands bracketing her waist.

Then his lips were on hers, and his mouth was every bit as firm and hot and wrong as she remembered. There was nothing soft about the kiss, and she stiffened as his tongue pushed between her lips and moved in silky possession against hers. She knew what he was doing...he was punishing her, torturing her, teasing her with the knowledge that she wanted him even as she hated him.

And she loathed knowing that he was right. She did want him. Hated that he could *make* her want him against her will. Still, she refused to let her hands slide around his neck to pull him closer, even as they itched to grab his head and give in to the onslaught of desire that rushed from her neck to her toes.

Instead she clenched her fist around her keys and refused to give in to her soaring hormones, even if it was the best kiss she'd received in *looong* while.

Her mind flitted to James much too late, and her eyes widened in realization.

And guilt. Bone-searing guilt.

James.

She pushed at Will's chest frantically. He pulled back and searched her eyes, and she gave him her most condescending expression. The one that said *That's right, you just kissed me senseless and I didn't kiss you back.*

But oh God, how she'd wanted to.

Think of James, she reminded herself.

But James didn't kiss like that. No *nice* man kissed like that.

"Well…I'd say your price was a bit high, but I'll consider us even," she said haughtily as she pushed him aside and climbed into the driver's seat.

Will didn't move as she closed the door and turned on the ignition. She'd been expecting a gloat, but instead he seemed…thoughtful.

Nah. Thoughtful wasn't in Will's wheelhouse.

"You've got a little issue there," she said as she put on her oversized sunglasses.

He didn't respond, so she waved in the direction of his crotch. "You, um, seem a little…aroused." She didn't bother to hide the gloat in her voice.

"What can I say? Bitchy, ungrateful women apparently do it for me," he muttered.

She put the car in reverse. "Thanks for helping with the tire," she called. "And thanks for making me feel like a prostitute to pay for it."

Brynn gave one last jaunty wave before she began driving down the street. She hated that he'd probably leave the flat tire sitting messily in her driveway, but it was worth it to make the dramatic exit.

And she'd needed to get out of there, fast. Another second with Will pressed against her and she wouldn't have been thinking about braces, or the mayor's daughter, or James. Heck, she probably wouldn't have even made it into the office.

Thank God she hadn't kissed him back. She wouldn't do that to James.

Or to herself.

She heard her phone vibrating in her purse, and reached for it as she pulled to a stop at a red light.

It was a message from Will. *You kiss like a houseplant. And you still owe me a favor.*

All the smugness she'd felt a moment ago began to fade. Every instinct told her that being in Will Thatcher's debt was very, *very* bad news.

CHAPTER SEVEN

*A solid career will never let you
down the way a man can.*

—Brynn Dalton's Rules for an
Exemplary Life, #39

She needn't have worried about not making it to work on time.

The mayor and her daughter were fifteen minutes late, and neither an apology nor an acknowledgment of the tardiness was forthcoming.

Basically, she was indebted to the devil's son over a flat tire for nothing. Awesome.

"But I don't *want* braces," Lizzie Blanton said, folding her arms over her thin preteen waist, and sounding more like a spoiled five-year-old than an eighth grader.

"I can understand that," Brynn said with a reassuring smile. "Few kids that come in here *want* braces, but I can pretty much guarantee you'll be grateful you had them when you're grown-up."

Lizzie gave a huff. "That's ages away."

Brynn and the mayor exchanged a commiserating glance over Lizzie's head. *Not as far as you think, honey.* After her near breakdown in the bathroom on her birthday, Brynn knew all too well how fast time went. No matter how carefully you planned, no matter how diligent you were, time kept chugging along and soon you were thirty-one and falling rapidly behind on all the things you'd thought you'd have checked off by now.

She wished someone would have told her when she was twelve not to let any of your life goals depend on someone else. Because even the most perfect guy could drag his feet to the altar and then you were *screwed*.

"Dr. Dalton?"

"I'm sorry, what?" Brynn said, forcing her attention back to her sulky patient.

"I can wait for a couple months? At least until after yearbook pictures?"

"I don't see why not," Brynn said with a careful glance at the mayor, making sure she wasn't contradicting parental preference. "My braces recommendation for you is primarily for cosmetic reasons at this point. You won't be doing any harm to your teeth or jaws if you hold off."

Actually, Lizzie Blanton's mouth would be just fine without braces for a *lifetime*, but Brynn wasn't about to volunteer that.

Still, the cosmetically fueled recommendation brought to mind Will's accusations that her career choice was superficial and shallow.

He was wrong.

She knew firsthand that having straight teeth wasn't always about vanity.

Sometimes it was about confidence.

Twenty minutes later, the mayor and her daughter were off to buy some frilly "fro-yo" milkshake the mayor had promised, and Brynn was in her office reading a mind-numbing article about some newfangled retainer.

But she couldn't concentrate.

It seemed she couldn't go two minutes without some flare of self-doubt creeping into her brain, and the latest offender was wondering why she'd busted her ass to get to work for such a mundane appointment.

Not that there was anything wrong with the daughter or the mother, but they'd been pretty standard patients. She waited for the zip of excitement that she'd just met the *mayor*. But...nothing.

Knock it off. You love your job. You're just irritated because you let Will Thatcher kiss you.

And the kiss had been fierce and unwanted. And if she'd felt a little bit of a tingle, it'd definitely been irritation. Not lust.

Brynn jumped at a knock on the door, seeing her partner and friend standing in the doorway.

"So how'd it go with the pseudo-celeb's daughter? Was she a total prima donna?" Susan Wee asked.

Brynn smiled in welcome, gesturing her partner into her office. As far as work relationships went, Brynn and Susan were perfectly suited.

They were both calm, and friendly without being bubbly. Most importantly, they were damn good orthodontists.

When Brynn had decided to start her own practice,

she'd known a partner would be inevitable, but finding someone she could trust and who wouldn't drive her nuts had taken longer than expected. Susan was younger than Brynn had wanted—only a couple years out of school—but her work was flawless and her chair-side manner was perfect.

The fact that the women had become friends was icing on the cake.

"I wouldn't say Lizzie Blanton is a prima donna," Brynn said, idly tapping her pen against her desk. "She is, however, a major brat."

Susan shrugged as she dropped into the chair across from Brynn. "She's twelve. Of course she's a brat."

"I don't think I was," Brynn mused, pursing her lips.

"Me neither," Susan said cheekily. "I was a perfect child. And pretty perfect now, if I do say so myself."

Brynn forced herself to smile back. It was a long-running joke between the two of them. Perfect jobs, perfect boyfriends, perfect lives...

It was supposed to be a point of pride, having crafted her dream life through sheer organization and hard work.

But today it felt...stale.

Damn Will Thatcher.

Her wave of self-doubt should have been limited to one day of birthday blues, but instead her discontent had been hovering above her head like a cartoon storm cloud. His unexpected presence brought back too many memories of her less-than-stellar moments.

Like the time she'd keyed his car. Or the time she'd told his junior-year girlfriend that he was gay.

Or the time she'd woken up in his bed. Naked.

Don't go there. The man had no bearing on her future.

Maybe that was her problem. Brynn was a big believer in always keeping one eye on the future, but perhaps she was trying to focus on too much at once. Her life list had become overwhelming instead of being the beacon of focus it was supposed to be. Perhaps it was time to focus on just one item.

The most important one.

Marriage.

And James *would* propose this year. She was sure of it. And then her *next* birthday would be perfect.

Except...while focusing on the future *usually* centered Brynn, today it wasn't working. Did she really want to spend her life merely ticking off days until her next big Life Event?

Wasn't there supposed to be...more?

"You okay?" Susan asked, tilting her head to study Brynn. "You seem kind of off."

"A little PMS," Brynn lied. "And the Blanton meeting gave me a headache. The mayor seems so levelheaded on TV, but up close she's a little...intense."

"Aren't they all when it comes to their darlings' teeth? Slight overbites are the quintessential first-world problems."

"Does it ever get to you?" Brynn asked. "The fact that the majority of our clients come in for cosmetic reasons?"

Susan lifted a shoulder. "I guess I sort of knew it coming into it, ya know? I mean, I know it's not saving lives, but it's good money, good hours..."

"But is it fulfilling?"

Susan blinked in surprise. "Of course. I love my job."

Brynn loved her job too. At least, she was pretty sure she did. Sometimes it felt a little less like love, and a lot more like...*contentment*.

But that was good enough, right?

"I'll grab our lunches," Susan said, standing. "You bring a salad?"

"Yeah," Brynn said distractedly. It was Wednesday; of *course* she'd brought a salad.

"Cool. I have some Midol in my purse. You'll feel better by the time your one o'clock gets here."

"Thanks, Sue," Brynn said distractedly as her tiny friend walked out of the office with perfect posture.

Her smile slipped as soon as her friend was out of sight. Somehow she didn't think Midol would fix whatever was bothering her.

CHAPTER EIGHT

Take one day a week for solitude and reflection.
Sundays are "me" days.

> —Brynn Dalton's Rules for an
> Exemplary Life, #76

*B*rynn had spent an inordinate amount of time wondering what "favor" Will would call in for helping with the flat tire.

She should have known better than to ask him for help. Heaven forbid he just do the decent thing and help a girl out.

But a week had passed and he hadn't done more than wave at her from his kitchen window or "accidentally" knock over her recycling bin with his lawn mower.

There certainly hadn't been any mention of her supposed debt.

So she'd forgotten about it. Mostly. Sure, there'd been a few nights where she'd fantasized about the clever ways she'd turn down his undoubtedly crude suggestions. But for the most part, she hadn't thought about Will.

Hadn't thought about how much he annoyed her.

Hadn't thought about how easily he'd agreed to help her out with the tire, even though she'd treated him like crap.

Hadn't thought about the fact that they could be in each other's bedrooms in under five minutes.

And she *certainly* hadn't thought about what his hands had felt like on her on that night three years ago.

So when his face had popped up in her kitchen window on a Sunday morning as she'd been sipping a cup of coffee and daydreaming about what to do with a day to herself, she hadn't expected it. And she screamed.

"Goddamn it, Will!" she yelled through the pane as she wiped coffee off her pale pink silk robe. Temper spiked at the sight of his smirking face and she slapped her palm against the glass. And that made her even madder. Now she'd have to clean up the coffee *and* the handprint.

He pointed in the direction of the back door that entered into her kitchen and disappeared.

Please. Like she would let him interrupt her productive Sunday routine. She had laundry to do. And then she was going to clean the fridge. And eventually she was going to alphabetize her bookshelf, which she'd really been putting off for way too long.

Brynn ignored the first knock at the back door as she cleaned the spilled coffee off the granite countertop.

She ignored the second knock as she got out her organic, nontoxic glass cleaner and returned her kitchen windowpane to its usual pristine state.

The third knock made her smile as she refilled her mug. Rejection would do Will Thatcher good.

But then she started losing track of the knocks because the fifth one turned into the eighth, and then the twelfth, and then there was no end.

Go upstairs and take a shower, she ordered herself. *Do not open that door. Not when this robe barely covers your ass.*

The knocking went from an insistent tapping to a strange rhythm.

Good God. The infantile moron was tapping out "Jingle Bells" on her door. Clearly he had a death wish.

"Go away, Will!" she called out.

"I love this song, don't you?"

"Love it!" she hollered back.

...oh, what fun, it is to ride...

"Say, sweetie...I'm out of coffee..."

She rolled her eyes. "Oh? No longer welcome at Starbucks after sleeping with their entire staff?" she asked, wandering to the other side of the door so she wouldn't have to yell as loud.

"Don't be snobbish. There are a couple male baristas that didn't interest me in the least."

"Lecher."

"Prude."

...a day or two ago, I thought I'd take a ride...

"Will, if you don't stop with that infernal Christmas carol, I'll tell my mom that you were the one who finished off her favorite Cognac during winter break freshman year."

"I already confessed. And now she buys me my own bottle every Thanksgiving."

"Of course she does," Brynn muttered.

...jingle bells, jingle bells...

"Come on, Brynny, you owe me a favor."

She paused at that. He wanted a cup of coffee as his favor? Hell, she'd been imagining something a little more...torrid. If coffee was all he wanted, she'd give him the whole pot.

"Okay, fine. I'll give you coffee. But then you're leaving."

The knocking slowed. Then stopped. The doorknob rattled impatiently.

Taking a deep breath, she opened the door. She swallowed dryly. His hair was slightly damp and he smelled like soap, having obviously just showered. *Yum.*

"Wearing a shirt today, I see," she said, closing the door behind him as he immediately headed toward the coffeepot. He found the cupboard with the mugs on the first try, and damn if that didn't annoy her. He'd been gone for three years. He had no right to know how she organized her kitchen shelves.

He poured himself a cup before leaning back against her counter, eyeing her over the steaming mug. The scene was unexpectedly domestic and she resisted the urge to squirm under his gaze. His worn jeans and casual green button-down fit him entirely too well.

"You know, this is the first time I've been in your house since we became best friends and neighbors?" he asked.

"And the last time. Is the one cup enough, or do you need another to go?"

He ignored this. "I'm ready to call in my favor."

She nodded in the direction of his coffee mug. "You just did."

He held up the plain white porcelain cup in disbelief. "This? You think I rolled around on the hot pavement and wrestled a dirty tire for a cup of coffee? Please. I've got my own coffee back home."

Brynn all but felt steam come out her ears as she realized she'd been played. "You said you were out of coffee."

"Lied. I just needed a way to get in the door so we can talk about my due."

"The only thing you're due is my foot up your ass on the way out," she snapped, opening the back door and making a sweeping outward gesture.

He sighed. "You and Sophie. Both cranky in the morning. Your poor parents."

Will pushed away from the counter, idly shutting the door as he wandered into the living area.

"All-white décor. Shocker."

Brynn closed her eyes in resignation. Short of forcibly pushing him out the door, he wouldn't leave until he got what he wanted. And no way was she touching him.

"All right, let's hear it. What do I have to do to even the scorecard? What sort of humiliating adventure do you have cooked up? Lap dance? Striptease? Orthodontist appointment?"

It wouldn't be the last one. Will's teeth were perfectly straight, perfectly white. Sharklike.

"Interesting suggestions, Brynny," he said, idling toward her until there were just inches separating them, her back against the door.

Stupid, stupid, Brynn. She knew by now not to let herself get backed into a corner with this guy. He *always* took advantage.

"So the lap dance is an intriguing suggestion, but I find I'm…" His eyes skimmed over her, on the coffee stain splattered all over her breast.

Brynn sucked in a breath, every *physical* instinct telling her to arch her back to push herself into him, even as every *mental* instinct told her to knee him in the balls.

"You find you're what?" she asked. *Crap.* Her voice was way huskier than the situation warranted.

His eyes flicked back up to hers, his head inclining just slightly toward hers. "Not interested," he finished in an equally husky voice.

She let out a hissing noise, and this time her mental and physical instincts were completely in sync. But he saw it coming, and grabbed her knee and pushed it easily away before she could make contact with his special bits.

He'd moved away before she could register the feeling of his fingers on her knee, giving her that classic Will Thatcher grin. The one that said *I've got your number.*

She straightened, primly tugging the hem of her robe into place, ignoring the brand his thumb had left on the inside of her leg.

"So, back to the debt," he said, taking a sip of coffee as though nothing had happened. "Go get showered. The Marilyn Monroe getup won't do."

Her nostrils fluttered. "You're calling it in *today*? I have plans."

"What plans? Vacuuming your car? Ironing your sheets? Reading some boring biography?"

It was a little too close to her actual plans, and she kept her mouth shut as she moved to top off her coffee, instinctively topping his off as well just because he was there.

"Thanks," he said gruffly. For some reason this quiet

and unexpected bit of manners unnerved her even more than the flirty Will and she felt herself blushing.

"Spit it out already," she said, refusing to meet his eyes.

"Well, actually, I already told you the other day, but you seem to have forgotten. We're going furniture shopping."

Brynn's mug clanked noisily on the counter. "Furniture shopping?"

"Good hearing, Brynny. And yes, furniture shopping. I plan to have *lots* of female company, and hence I need a female's opinion. You qualify. Barely. None of this white stuff, though," he said, gesturing at her clean color scheme.

"Make Sophie do it."

"She's busy."

"So am I," Brynn ground out.

"Not with anything interesting. And you owe me, remember? Wouldn't you rather get it over with?"

"I'd rather you'd have just changed my tire as a favor, not as something to lord over me until you could decorate your bachelor pad."

Will drained his coffee before rinsing his cup and placing it in the dishwasher, in the exact right spot on the top shelf. Upper right corner, handle facing in. *How'd he know?*

"I'm not shopping with you."

He shrugged and then moved so quickly she barely had time to swallow her mouthful of coffee. He was on her in a second, his hips pressing into hers.

Don't move. Do. Not. Move. Why could she never breathe around this guy?

It wouldn't have mattered if she moved. She could already feel him, hard and hot even through the denim of his jeans, his erection pressing into the flatness of her stomach.

"I can think of another way to return the favor," he said, his eyes never leaving her. "One you might like better?"

His hips moved ever so slightly and Brynn bit her lip against a moan. *It's just memories of before. That's all.*

"I'll go shopping with you," she whispered softly, keeping her gaze locked on a spot over his shoulder.

He moved away as quickly as he moved in, his grin triumphant.

Brynn didn't know what bothered her more, that he'd won the battle, or that he was apparently more enthused about the idea of furniture shopping than sex with her.

"My driveway in thirty minutes?" he asked.

"An hour," she said, setting her mug aside in resignation. So much for her quiet, productive Sunday.

He gave her a none-too-soft slap on the ass, like a coach swatting his second-string running back.

"Good girl," he said, grabbing her elbow and ushering her in the direction of the stairs. "Go shower now, you look like hell."

She probably did. God knows she was *in* hell.

CHAPTER NINE

The home is an oasis—it should be treated as such.

—Brynn Dalton's Rules for an
Exemplary Life, #12

Does this little toy car of yours have heated seats?"
Brynn asked as she peered at the fancy buttons of his
sports car.

Wordlessly, Will punched a button and turned his attention back to the road. Brynn studied him out of the corner
of her eye. They might not get along, but she'd known him
long enough to know that silence and Will were never a
good combination. Her body went on high alert.

"You shouldn't have offered me a ride if you were going to sulk the entire time," she said.

"Had I known you were going to chatter the whole
way, I probably wouldn't have offered."

Brynn straightened her shoulders and gazed out of the passenger window and tried not to let his words sting. He'd never made a secret that he didn't like her, but she couldn't quite understand why her company was so repellant to him. And she really couldn't understand why someone as open, loving, and sweet as her younger sister had befriended such a selfish oaf. His entire existence revolved around casual sex and business ventures. He had zero substance.

"I don't understand why Sophie loves that bar so much," Brynn mused as she stared out at the line of red brake lights on either side of them. "It's so out of the way."

Will made a sharp turn to take a side-street detour, and Brynn braced her hand against the dash, surprised by the sudden movement. She was about to nag him for driving like a freaking NASCAR driver when his outburst obliterated the sullen silence.

"Don't you ever get tired of being selfish?" he exploded.

She snapped her head around to look at his clenched profile. "Excuse me?"

"I'd just think you'd get sick of yourself after a while. I know I do." His knuckles tightened on the steering wheel.

"What—"

But he wasn't done. His voice took on a whining, high-pitched mimicking tone. "Sophieeee, you need to sit through a hellish double date to make my life more convenient. Why doesn't everyone pick a bar that's closer to me? Mommy, Daddy, it's been ten minutes since you've praised all of my superpredictable accomplishments. Gray, why aren't you adoring me the way I deserve to be adored? Gosh, Will, you're so mean to me."

The unprovoked attack sent a river of emotions rolling

*through her, the anger hitting her hardest. How dare he
of all people accuse her of being selfish?*

*The sharpness of her anger was followed quickly by an
automatic denial. Will didn't even know her, not really.
She was a good person. Sure, maybe she'd asked Sophie
for an unfair favor, but Sophie was resilient. Nothing
bothered her.*

*But as hard as Brynn tried to hang on to her anger,
doubt crept down her spine. Was he right? Was she selfish? Brynn didn't mean to be. She loved her sister, and
would never want to sabotage her happiness. But did
Brynn even know what Sophie's version of happy looked
like? Had she really stopped to assess what was going on
with her sister, or had she just assumed that her own pri-
orities were more important?*

God, she was selfish.

The last emotion was perhaps the worst of all.

Hurt.

*Hurt that it had to be Will of all people who'd held up
the mirror and forced her to see her own narcissism.*

*Oh no. Not tears. Not now. She could not let Will
Thatcher see her cry.*

"Are you crying?"

"No," she said, the word soggy.

"Shit," he said softly.

Exactly.

*He pulled over to the side of the road, and Brynn was
surprised to see through the haze of her tears that they
were outside of her condo building. Grabbing her purse,
she fumbled at the door, desperate to escape Will and the
flood of emotions he'd thrown at her.*

"Thanks for the ride," she muttered tersely.

Again with the damn manners! She should have told him to go screw himself, but even at her most vulnerable, she couldn't get the words out.

"Brynn," he said softly, putting a hand on her arm.

"Don't you dare," she hissed, turning to face him, suddenly not caring that he was seeing her with puffy eyes and black rivers of eye makeup running down her cheeks. "Don't you dare insult me, outline every single flaw I have and then turn around and try to make it better. You wanted to hurt me and you succeeded. At least have the balls to own your victory."

"I never meant to hurt you," he said, not breaking eye contact. "I just can't stand the way you were trying to push Sophie down so you could pull yourself up."

"Of course, we wouldn't want your poor precious Sophie to suffer," she said scathingly, hating the words she heard coming out of her mouth.

"This isn't about Sophie!" he said more sharply. "This has never been about Sophie!"

"Oh really?" She scoffed. "So it's just coincidence that you're taking her side on everything. You just don't want to see me happy, so you're doing your best to ensure my relationship with Gray never has a chance."

"You don't even like the guy!" Will yelled. "This isn't about Gray or Sophie, it's about you trying to control absolutely every little detail in your life because you don't know what you really want."

"I do know what I want! I want Gray. He's perfect for me. Smart, successful, genteel..."

"The man's a Goddamn mannequin, which is exactly what you think you want because you can ensure he fits into your plastic life."

"Why are you acting like this?" she whispered, staring into his blazing blue eyes. "I know we're always bickering, but you've never been cruel before."

"God, Brynn." He turned away and stared out the front of the car, running his fingers through his blond hair and muttering a string of curses.

"I don't expect an apology," she said quietly. "I know better. I just want to know why."

"Why? Why?!" His voice had taken on an agitated tone, and he sounded completely unlike the controlled and manipulative Will she knew so well.

"This *is* why, Brynn."

A rough hand slid behind the nape of her neck and jerked her over to the driver's-side seat. Firm lips slammed down on hers as he held her head still and took control of her mouth.

She parted her lips on a surprised gasp and his tongue flicked teasingly across her bottom lip. Brynn moaned. She didn't know if this was supposed to be her punishment, her embarrassment, or simply more ammunition that he could use against her, and she didn't care.

She didn't care that they hated each other, didn't care that she was lying awkwardly across the middle console of his car like one of his groupies.

She didn't care that he probably had some sort of agenda or that she was most certainly going to regret this in the morning.

Because at this moment, all she cared about was kissing Will.

His tongue slid against hers in a silky stroke and she moaned again. Winding her arms around his neck, Brynn pressed closer, letting her tongue tangle with his in a kiss *that wasn't civilized or rehearsed or practiced. Kissing Will was a lot like dirty dancing. It was heady, instinctual, and it gave her the urge to move her hips.*

They kissed like they argued. Savagely, taking as much as they gave. His hands tilted her head to the side so he could press deeper, and this time it was Will that let out a low groan. His mouth broke away from hers, and his lips softly pressed against the side of her mouth, skimming along her jaw before gently brushing her cheeks, her eyelids.

Reality crashed down as Brynn realized what he was doing. He was kissing away her tears. He cupped her face gently, as though using his lips to try and erase the pain he'd caused.

And suddenly it just felt too... tender. Animal passion had been safe. She could blame that on the champagne and their anger.

But kindness and tenderness from Will... she couldn't... she wouldn't...

She pulled away sharply.

"Brynn," he said quietly, reaching out to her again.

"Don't," she said. "Just don't."

Clutching her purse, she scratched at the door again, shoving it open in clumsy haste. She set one foot out into the stormy night before hesitantly looking back at him.

"You won't... you won't tell anyone about this, right? We'll just chalk it up to a moment of absurd insanity?"

Any softness that might have been in his eyes vanished. "Don't worry," he snapped. "Your secret is safe with me. You think I want anyone knowing that I failed to get a hot reaction from Ice Princess Brynn? You're just as cold as everyone thinks you are."

She didn't let his words sting. She was already numb.

"*Good night, Will,*" *she said stonily as she climbed out of the car.* "*If you've given me some sort of disease, you'll be hearing from me.*"

She'd barely slammed the door before he peeled away from the curb with a squeal of tires. Typical, *she thought. Slowly her snarl faded as she stood hunched in the rain, staring after his long-gone taillights.*

That was a mistake. *The realization came as a shock. Because Brynn Dalton did not make mistakes.*

* * *

"No. Absolutely not ever. The dining room table was fine. The living room furniture was tolerable. Your home office collection was pushing it, but I absolutely draw the line at *shopping for your bed.*"

Will gave her a patronizing pat on the shoulder. "I understand. Too many memories?"

Brynn's eyes narrowed as he'd known they would. "Seems to me there's not much to remember."

"Oh? Is that why you were panting at me in the kitchen this morning?"

"Oh baby, *yeah*, because conniving men in ratty jeans who steal my coffee really turn me on." She brushed past him, shoulders back as she headed in the direction of the mattress store.

He gave a little smile of victory. He'd been gently manipulating her all day long, turning her "two hours" max into a full day of shopping.

So far the day had gone exactly as he'd planned. He hadn't counted on her holding out *quite* so long before letting him into her house, and the chorus of "Jingle

Bells" was still banging through his brain. But it had been worth it just to see her in that sweet little pink robe. Even the messy coffee stains hadn't been able to distract from the long toned legs.

Legs he remembered wrapped around his waist all too well. And his head. And his...

"Thatcher, you coming, or what?" Brynn snapped from up ahead.

Oh, I wish.

"You know, manipulating my whole day is really pushing it, considering that putting on my spare tire took you all of twenty minutes."

"Twenty difficult minutes," he corrected, holding open the door for her. "So far all you've had to do is wander around in the air-conditioning and test couch cushions for comfort."

"I still think you should have gone with the café au lait–colored one," she said, as she frowned around at the enormous collection of mattresses.

Will had dragged her to the Bellevue Collection, a mass of multiple upscale shopping centers that had a variety of furniture stores within walking distance.

"Was the café au lait one the boring beige one?"

"No. Beige and café au lait are *not* the same thing. Although both can be nice, and neither is boring."

"Says the woman with all-white future."

Will threw himself back on the first mattress in the row, knowing immediately that it was too soft for his preferences. But he had every intention of drawing *this* part of the shopping adventure out as long as possible. Every intention of reminding her of him on a mattress. Of her on a mattress *with him.*

"What do you think of this one?" he asked casually. Apparently *too* casually, because she immediately narrowed her eyes at him.

"Oh no," she said, crossing her arms. "I'll endure you bouncing on a mattress that hundreds of other people have writhed around on, but I'm not playing."

"C'mon," he said, turning the corner of his mouth up in the half smile that always got women all riled up. "What if I take you to an early dinner at Purple after this?"

Brynn rolled her eyes. "Save that smarmy smile for one of your groupies. And how'd you know I like Purple?"

I know everything you like. Everything.

Instead he rolled his eyes right back at her. "Well, let's see, it's an upscale, totally pretentious wine bar that pretends *not* to be pretentious. How could you help yourself from liking it?"

He saw her hesitate. Brynn was always a sucker for New Zealand Sauvignon Blancs, and Purple's menu had a handful of them.

"No thanks," she said, pressing her lips together. "I should get home. I should call James."

Will noticed that there was a pause before the last sentence and carefully hid his grin. She'd barely mentioned that marble boyfriend of hers all day, and he knew she was only doing it now to tell him to back off.

No can do, Brynny.

"Suit yourself, Princess. This mattress is no good anyway."

"Too small to accommodate your depraved tendencies?" she asked sweetly as he rolled off.

"No. Too small for yours," he said with an eyebrow wiggle.

She stiffened slightly. "I have no intention of sharing a mattress with you today or ever."

"Just as well. I think you wore out the one I had last time."

"I hope you get bedbugs up your ass," she muttered as he threw himself onto the next mattress.

Will took his time with the mattresses. He already knew which one he wanted. He'd been getting the same brand for years. It was just always easier to get a new one rather than deal with the hassle of shipping it every time he moved. But Brynn didn't have to know that.

"Hmm, I think this one has just a little too much give," he muttered, pretending to test the current mattress. "Say, Princess, could you straddle me for a minute so I can get a sense of how much leverage a woman's knees could get on this thing?"

She ignored his request, and instead tapped a long finger against her lips and pretended to study the mattress. "You know, that's a valid point. I seem to remember you just sort of *lying* there, so considering the woman will have to do all the work, it's good that you're paying attention to the female needs. Especially if you want her to come back for more. Oh, wait, you don't *do* repeats."

He gave an exaggerated sigh and moved on to the next mattress in one fluid movement. He watched carefully as she checked her watch, although he didn't think she was really in a hurry. In fact, for most of the day, she hadn't seemed to mind being with him. Much. He'd intentionally let her pick all of the furniture. Well, except for that awful beige couch.

He'd known all along that the thrill of being able to

decorate a house from scratch would be too much for her to resist, and she'd thrown herself wholeheartedly into the task, asking the sales people millions of questions, trying dozens of different options before informing him firmly, *this one*.

He knew he was pushing it with mattress shopping, but it was a necessary step in his plan.

A salesperson approached them warily as Will rolled around on each mattress, and Brynn patiently explained that no, they didn't need any help, that her acquaintance merely wanted to try them out. All of them.

The salesguy gave a tentative smile and wandered away as Brynn pulled out her buzzing cell phone, her eyes scanning the incoming message.

It was the moment he needed. Taking advantage of her distraction, Will rolled to his knees, hooked his arm around Brynn's waist, and tugged, flopping both of them back onto the mattress with just enough of a jolt to make her purse whack him in the chest before he rolled her beneath him.

Or almost beneath him.

Mostly she was just wiggling and muttering obscenities at him.

He rolled onto his side, locking his arm around her waist and pulling her into the little-spoon position.

"So now what do you think about this one?" he said against her ear. "It's hard, but I'm kind of thinking it's just right."

"Oh, wow, a blatantly obvious double entendre. How unexpected of you."

But she was smart enough to know that every one of her wiggles rubbed her ridiculously tight ass against his erection. Other than her heaving breath, she lay perfectly still.

"We're making a scene," she said under her breath. Will almost smiled. She was curled up on a mattress with her worst enemy and she was worried about making a scene.

He rolled onto his back, but not before he'd clamped his hand around her wrist so she couldn't wiggle away. "Now tell me honestly, what do you think about this mattress?"

She was still for several seconds before she rolled onto her back next to him. "I want a whole bottle of wine, Will."

Victory.

"Fine."

"And their baked brie plate."

He smiled. "You got it."

"And there's this salad . . ."

"No, no salads," he said, unable to stop himself from rubbing his fingertips against the sensitive skin of her inner wrist.

She hissed in a breath. "Well, if I get the rich cheese dish, I have to get the salad."

"Says who?"

"My thighs," she said primly.

"Honey, I've seen your thighs. They don't care whether you have the salad or the cheese or the Goddamn crème brûlée."

Brynn loved crème brûlée. Not that she would ever admit it.

"I guess I could do an extra session of yoga tomorrow."

He snorted. "Yoga? You?"

She rolled her head to the side to scowl at him. "What's that supposed to mean?"

"I dunno, it just doesn't really seem like you. Doesn't that require patience?"

He felt her eyes studying his profile, and it took everything in him to not turn toward her and meet her eyes. And then to roll on top of her and kiss every cheese-loving, yoga-hating bit of her.

"I don't really like yoga," she admitted finally. She sounded surprised, although he didn't know if it was surprise at the realization or surprise that he'd been the one to note it. She'd never exactly been one to know herself.

"So it's decided. Cheese, no salad?"

This time he did turn his face toward hers, putting their lips just inches apart.

Will waited for her to whip her head away from his in panic, but she surprised him, remaining perfectly still except for the wary eyes that searched his face.

"Why are you doing this?" she asked quietly.

"Making you skip the boring salad?"

"Everything. The next-door-neighbor thing. The out-of-coffee ploy. The furniture shopping. And now dinner?"

He locked his eyes on hers, telling her the truth for the first time in a long time. "Don't you ever get tired of fighting, Brynny?"

He kept his tone light, but she must have read the intensity in his gaze because her blue eyes went slightly wide. "Do you?"

I don't mind the squabbling. I just want more.

But it was too soon. She still looked like a wary cat ready to call her stupid boyfriend at the first sign of her being turned on. And he knew he could turn her on. Easily. Her eyes kept moving to his lips and her pupils were dilated.

She wanted him. She'd wanted him when she he'd kissed her in the driveway last week, and when he'd rubbed against her in the kitchen this morning, and she wanted him now.

But she wouldn't take him. Not until she'd gotten rid of Jimmy what's-his-name. If he kissed her now, she'd hate him. Hate herself for liking it when she was supposed to be loyal to an absent boyfriend.

He allowed himself one more lingering touch of his fingers on her palm. Just enough to remind her of what it had been like with them. Enough to have her sucking in her breath and springing away from him.

Clearing his throat and hoping his erection wasn't *that* obvious, Will glanced around until he spotted the salesguy he'd shooed away a few minutes ago.

He rattled off his desired size and model to the short, eager-to-please employee, who took rapid notes, and couldn't resist sneaking a look at Brynn.

She looked properly furious.

"You didn't even *try* that mattress," she hissed after he'd given his payment and shipping information. "That brand of mattresses is over on *that* side of the store, and we haven't gotten there yet."

"Yeah, I don't really want something new. I like the one I had before."

He didn't know if the double meaning was unintentional or if his subconscious had made him say it, but he found himself meeting her eyes all the same, watching for any sign of understanding.

But she lowered her eyelids as soon as he tried to meet her gaze.

Too soon, he thought, sucking back a sigh.

"Come on," he said, patting at her butt. "Let's go get you that baked brie."

The wine bar was just around the corner from the mattress store, exactly as Will had planned.

"What is it with women and wine bars?" he asked, as Brynn led them to a spot at the bar. He would have preferred sitting at a table so he could see her—read her—but he knew that was too date-like for her.

"They're our response to sports bars," she said, gracefully sliding onto the high stool and arranging her skirt around her knees like the perfect lady she so wanted to be. "Except there's no peanuts on the ground, no obnoxious TVs, and very few leering men."

"Except for me."

She smiled at him, and then looked surprised for smiling. "Yeah. Except for you."

Two cheese appetizers, a crème brûlée, and a bottle of wine later, Will was guiding a very tipsy Brynn toward his car. He'd deliberately let her drink more than her share of the bottle, not only because he was driving, but because she'd clearly needed it to forget that she was with the enemy. Maybe even *enjoying* herself with the enemy.

For the first time in their history, they'd shared a meal, just the two of them, and there hadn't been a single argument or jab. She'd even laughed.

God he loved her laugh.

"I'm *drunk*," Brynn said with emphasis, swinging her purse into the backseat of his car and dropping messily into the passenger seat.

She didn't object when he scooped her legs up, tucking them into the car. Didn't object when his fingers lingered on her smooth calves.

"You're not drunk. Just...happy," he said, closing the door carefully behind her.

The ride home was mostly silent, other than the radio, which she changed every two seconds.

It started to rain as he exited the freeway, and though it was raining more often than not in Seattle, he wondered if she remembered the only other time they'd been alone in his car together.

It had been raining then too, but she hadn't been tipsy. Just good and pissed about something he'd said and his own temper had spiked until he'd almost told her everything. And then he'd lost his mind and kissed her. Their first kiss.

He wondered if she ever thought about it.

Will pulled into her driveway, and she gave him a puzzled look. "You could have parked in your own garage. I could have walked."

"It's raining," he said, not looking at her. *And if I let you anywhere near my house right now, I won't let you go.*

"Don't tell me there's a gentleman hiding in there," she said with a giggle, stabbing at the buckle on her seat belt and getting it on the third try.

"If there is, I'll never tell," he said, reaching into the backseat for her purse.

"Well, thanks," she said, clutching her purse to her chest. "I um...I had a good time."

"You sound surprised."

She snorted. "Well, yeah. It's probably the first time I didn't want to kill you."

"Unlike the last time we were in a car in the rain."
Whoops. He hadn't meant to go there.

Her eyes clouded over. So she did remember.

"You were mad at me," she added softly.

Dammit. Her voice sounded tiny and hurt.

"Honey, we're always mad at each other," he said, trying to lighten the mood.

But she wasn't having it. "No, I mean you were *really* mad at me. You told me I was vapid and selfish because I was trying to boss Sophie around, and Sophie's all you ever cared about."

He refused to let his expression change. "I don't remember that."

"Well…I do. And then because yelling at me wasn't bad enough, you had to punish me by *kissing me.*"

He swallowed, desperate for the flippant sarcasm that normally came so easily to him. But it was nowhere to be found. Her eyes were open and wounded and a little raw. As though that evening had hurt her. *As though his opinion had mattered.*

"I didn't kiss you to punish you," he said finally. It was more than he wanted to say, but he had to do something to vanquish the lost look in her eyes.

"Then why?"

Her eyes were locked on his lips and his hand was cupping her cheek before he was even aware that he'd moved.

"You don't know?" he asked, his voice a little gruff.

She gave a sad smile. "I do know. I've always known."

His heart lurched and he forced himself to swallow and keep his gaze on hers. "Yeah?"

She nodded. "You wanted what you couldn't have. So

you took it. Just like when we slept together. I was the lone holdout on your endless line of bedpost notches, and once you checked me off the list, the challenge was over. And then you left."

His heart felt like it tumbled into his stomach, and he didn't know if it was in dismay or relief. His hand dropped away from her face.

She didn't have a freaking clue.

He didn't know if he was disappointed or relieved.

He let himself shrug. "Yeah, well...if it's any consolation, you were worth the wait."

He expected her to get pissed, but the wine had made her soft. "You're not getting in my pants again with the sweet talk, Thatcher."

She patted him playfully on the cheek climbing out of the car and going into the house without a glance backward.

Will waited until the door closed behind her before dropping his forehead onto the steering wheel and letting out a string of oaths.

He'd known that the game he was playing would be difficult.

But he hadn't anticipated it being painful as well.

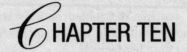

CHAPTER TEN

*There's no indignity in ending a
relationship—as long as you're
doing the ending.*

—Brynn Dalton's Rules for an
Exemplary Life, #44

*B*rynn had barely had time to take off her shoes after
a particularly hellish day of removing braces when there
was a knock at the front door.

She took a deep breath, rolling her shoulders in an at-
tempt to prepare herself for the confrontation. She wasn't
entirely sure she was ready to see Will again. It had been
three days since their surprisingly amiable day of shopping together.

Three days since that...*moment* in the car. Three days
since she'd thought he was going to kiss her.

Three days since she'd *wanted* him to.

Three days to feel guilty about wanting it.

And as though her guilt had some sort of beckoning power, it wasn't Will on the other side of the door.

"James!"

"You sound surprised," he said with a small smile. He looked every bit as exhausted as she felt; she was oddly reassured by the tension around his eyes and the strained smile. It reminded her that they were the same. Serious adults with grown-up jobs. Not playboy entrepreneurs who spent all day working on their six-packs and flirting with the recently divorced Tammy Henderson across the street.

Not that she'd been spying or anything.

"Well, I am a *little* surprised," she admitted, standing aside to let him in. "You haven't exactly been returning my calls."

Calls she'd made out of guilt. Out of need for a reminder that she should not be even close to thinking about kissing Will Thatcher.

"Sorry," he said, rubbing a hand across the back of his neck. "Terry has the flu, so I've been on call for five days straight."

Brynn made the appropriate sympathetic noises as she pulled a bottle of Pinot Noir off the wine rack and poured them both a glass before joining him on the couch.

"You want to order in?" she asked. "Or I could make some carbonara? I have some of that good pancetta."

He shook his head slightly, taking a healthy swallow of wine. And then another. "I can't stay long."

Brynn frowned in confusion. "You drove all the way over in rush hour, and you're not sticking around for dinner? You're the one who's always informing me how out of the way I live."

He didn't respond, just took another of those big swallows before topping off his glass. Brynn's frown deepened. James was a total wine snob. He was a big fan of what he liked to call the three *S*s. Swirling, sniffing, and sipping. There was no *gulping* of wine in James's world.

And he *loved* her carbonara.

Something was wrong.

Brynn took a small sip of wine and ordered herself not to panic. He'd said he was tired. And he was always in a bad mood after a long streak of being on call with little sleep and hurried meals. He was still in his scrubs, for God's sake. She was worried for nothing.

She casually swung her leg over his, letting out a small sigh of relief when he didn't shift away or push her off.

"Do you have tomorrow off?" she asked, watching his face closely. "I think I have a slow day. I could pass off a few appointments to Susan."

"Brynn, we need to talk."

There it was.

She had the slight urge to throw up. Surely she wasn't being...dumped.

Brynn had a near-perfect record. Other than the time in tenth grade when Patrick Mulligan had reneged on his homecoming date offer in order to take the better-endowed Carrie Lowry, Brynn had always been a dumper, never a dumpee.

But looking at the resigned, detached expression on James's face, she had a feeling that was about to change.

"Sure, what do you want to talk about?" she asked, hating the false bright note in her tone. One octave higher and she'd be squeaking.

He set his hand on her knee. Squeezed. "I think we need to take a break."

Brynn didn't let her smile slip. Couldn't even if she wanted to. It was frozen on her face.

"A break, James? I'm not sure anyone beyond junior high really knows what that means."

He let out a small exasperated sigh. As though *she* were being the difficult one. "It means I'm not sure I want to do this anymore."

"You're not sure," she repeated in a flat voice.

He rubbed a hand through his hair. Hair that suddenly seemed unbearably *boring*. "I care about you, Brynn. I really do. And we're perfect together, it's just…"

Brynn set her wineglass on the coffee table with a clink. "We *are* perfect together, James. We want all the same things, we like all the same people…"

"I know," he said, giving her a sad smile.

"Then *why*?" Her voice was a whisper now.

His lips tightened and something like guilt flashed across his face, and Brynn felt it like a knife to the gut.

Still, she made herself ask it. "Is there someone else?"

His fingers flexed on her knee again, but she could no longer stand his touch, and pulled her leg back so that she was sitting upright. It was better posture anyway.

"I didn't cheat, Brynn. I would never do that."

She relaxed slightly. And she believed him. James was one of those guys with an iron-rod moral code. He wouldn't run around on her. And yet…

"But you have feelings for someone," she prompted. She kept her eyes locked on the tulip arrangement on her coffee table, but she felt him shift beside her.

"More like the *potential* for feelings," he said awkwardly.

Oh, please. Now she did turn to face him. "Come on. At least give it to me straight. Who is she? Someone you work with?"

Please don't let it be that cliché.

He cleared his throat. Took another sip of wine. For a second, Brynn almost felt sorry for him. She knew firsthand how hard it was to break up with someone.

But her sympathy began to fade as she realized she'd never dumped someone because she had feelings for someone else.

She intentionally pushed aside her recent attraction to Will. That was a result of too much wine and too few shirts on his part.

James cleared his throat. "Well, you know Maggie?"

Brynn's mind went blank for a moment before her eyes bugged out. Oh, surely not. "Maggie, as in your neighbor?"

He colored slightly. *Bingo.*

The world that had been starting to tilt around Brynn now felt completely upside down. She'd only met Maggie a couple times, usually when they'd just returned from vacation and she'd come over to drop off the mail that she'd been collecting.

Maggie was...well, frankly, she was a total mess. Brynn had a dim recollection of a tiny, fake redhead whose clothes were always just a little too big and careless, whose fingernails were always chipped and who laughed too much.

Maggie was James's opposite. Maggie was *Brynn's* opposite.

It was ironic, really. Brynn had been trying so hard to be structured and normal and *acceptable* so that James would propose.

Apparently he hadn't wanted perfection at all.

"I didn't realize you two were close," she said stiffly.

He started to put a hand on Brynn's back, but stopped when she tensed and instead took another sip of wine. His sips were calmer now. As though he could relax now that he'd dropped the bomb and would be done with her.

"It's not like anything's happened," he said again. "But she's come by a couple times recently to drop off UPS packages that she'd signed for, to let me know that maintenance came by to fix the air-conditioner...that kind of thing."

"And what, you're drawn to...what? Her split ends? The gap between her teeth? Jeez, James, isn't she an artist?"

"She paints. Does some freelance graphic design stuff," he said quietly. Almost guiltily.

"Of course she does," Brynn muttered.

She felt like a bitch, but she couldn't help it. She was pissed. And baffled. She ignored the fact that hurt hadn't yet registered. That would probably come later.

"It's just...she's different from me. Different from us," James said.

"Ya think?" she snapped.

"I like the difference. She's unpredictable, quirky. She doesn't care what people think of her, doesn't care that she's saying the right thing, doing the right thing, *being* the right thing. Maggie...she makes me feel...alive."

But being different sucks. How could this Maggie woman stand it?

How could James stand it?

"And I made you feel...dead?" Brynn asked, keeping her voice calm.

He put his hand firmly on her knee. "No. *No*. But, Brynn, don't you ever get sick of us? Sick of our plans and our checklists and the way that we know every little step that's going to be in front of us?"

She stared at him. "Obviously, *I* don't know every little step in front of me. I certainly didn't see *this* coming."

"You didn't? I thought for sure you'd been feeling me pulling away. I thought you'd been pulling away too."

She wasn't in the mood to deal with the truth behind that statement. Sure, things hadn't been perfect the past couple months, but that didn't mean she'd been expecting to be discarded so he could dally with a Bohemian.

"I thought you were getting ready to *propose*," she blurted out.

He went still. Brynn felt both foolish and relieved for having said it out loud.

"I thought we were headed in that direction too," he said quietly.

She relaxed slightly. At least she hadn't been *that* far off base.

"What changed?"

And why don't I care more?

He linked his fingers with hers, giving her a squeeze meant to comfort. She found herself squeezing back.

"It's nothing you did, Brynn. It's us together that isn't working. I realized I want more than a lifetime of white furniture."

Something sharp and nagging snuck beneath her baf-flement. She distantly recalled Will's disdain for her white furniture, and his refusal to get the leather café au lait sectional she'd suggested. The café au lait couch that was nearly identical to the one she'd helped James pick out.

God, had Will known what she hadn't? That nobody, not even James, wanted a woman with white furniture and piles of notebooks full of plans?

And suddenly Brynn realized that what was *really* eating at her wasn't that James was breaking up with her.

It was that James was *right*.

She *was* sick of herself. Sick of her life.

Sick of the fact that her life plan was blowing up in her freaking face.

Brynn needed a vacation.

From herself.

CHAPTER ELEVEN

*Cosmetics should be used to enhance
one's natural self—never to change.*

—Brynn Dalton's Rules for an
Exemplary Life, #8

Are you sure you wanna do this, honey? You're a hot blonde."

Brynn met the eyes of the hairdresser in the mirror. Her usual guy was out, and her regularly scheduled appointment wasn't for another week and a half, but Brynn hadn't wanted to wait. She was done waiting.

The old Brynn would have been freaked out by the orange-haired hipster holding a pair of scissors behind her head. The new Brynn wanted to bring it on.

Well, the new Brynn who'd had a glass and a half of Chardonnay for courage at lunch prior to entering the salon.

"I'm sure," Brynn said with a reassuring smile. "It's just time for a change, ya know?"

The girl gave a bored shrug. "Your hair, your life."

Damn straight. It's my life. It's time to start living it.

Brynn had been giving herself these types of pep talks all day, every day in the week since James had walked out the door. One day to wallow. One day to be mad. One day to flip through her life list in an effort to get back on track...

One day to stash her precious life–road map on the top shelf in her closet for retirement. *Temporary* retirement. She wasn't giving up on her plan altogether. She still knew what she wanted long-term. But maybe in order to get there, she needed to let go. For the short term.

"All right, then, if you're sure..."

"I am."

The hairdresser shrugged and went to work.

Brynn had come prepared. After the shampoo process, she dug into a pile of trashy magazines and didn't look up once. Not to see the hair fall away. Not to see it darken in color. If her peripheral vision caught big chunks falling to the floor, she refused to let her brain absorb it.

"All right, hon, take a look."

Brynn took a deep breath, letting her eyes finish reading an article that she wasn't really absorbing.

Then she looked up.

She looked...different.

"So what do you think?" Orange Hair asked. "I think the dark really brings out your eyes."

Brynn nodded, turning her head from side to side. The girl was right. Brynn had never thought much about her eyes before. They were a light, ordinary blue. But with the dark brown hair, they looked piercing and sort of dangerous.

Or maybe she just *wanted* them to look dangerous.

Either way, the look was precisely what she'd wanted. She felt a surge of satisfaction. *Meow.*

"I like it," Brynn said reverently, running a hand over the shortness. She'd expected to miss the comforting length that had been there her entire life. Instead, the choppy, shoulder-length cut felt light and freeing.

"The grow-out's going to be a pain," the woman said, taking a long sip of her water. "You'll need to come in every few weeks unless you're okay with blonde roots."

But Brynn was barely listening, too busy staring at her own reflection. She had to give the girl credit, the look was exactly what she'd envisioned and hadn't known how to convey.

Brynn hadn't asked for it, but the girl had added some lighter brown streaks in the otherwise chocolate-colored look, and added several layers around the face. She'd also resisted the urge to go too short, so the longest layers brushed against Brynn's collarbone. It was edgy without being sloppy. Dark without being gothic. Modern without being trendy.

"I wish I had a longer name so I could go with a nickname for a little while," Brynn said to no one in particular. "You know, like go with a secret identify for a few days."

"How about Bee?"

Brynn winced. So okay, maybe no on the name change.

But there were plenty of other things she could tweak. And she planned to start...

Now.

After paying for her new look and leaving a hefty tip,

she hit up the next stop on her vacation-from-life plan. No not a plan. No more plans.

The receptionist at Brynn's office looked up in surprise as she strode in the door. "Hey, Dr. Dalton. I thought you were out this week?"

"Oh, I am," Brynn said with a bright smile. *And I'm about to be out a lot longer than that.* "When Dr. Wee is free, could you tell her I'm in?"

"I like the hair!" Erika called after her as Brynn headed to her office.

Brynn dropped her purse onto the chair and stood for a moment with her hands on her hips, taking in the perfectly tidy desk, the alphabetized journals on the shelves, the neat row of fake plants she'd set along the window because they looked more uniform than real plants.

"It looks like a robot lives here," Brynn announced to the emptiness.

She reached out and moved her stapler a few inches so it wasn't neatly in line with the pen holder and the paper clip dispenser. She promptly moved it back. Maybe she wasn't quite ready for that. Brynn reached out again. Moved it a half inch forward.

There. That was okay. Baby steps.

"Rearranging?"

Brynn glanced up toward the voice and saw a very curious-looking Susan standing in the doorway.

"Sue, we need to talk."

Susan entered and, closing the door, looked as unruffled and unperturbed as ever. It was how Brynn had always thought of herself. At least until her thirty-first birthday had brought it all crashing down around her, turning her into a high-strung, self-doubting train wreck.

"What's with the hair?" Susan asked, settling into one of the chairs. "Midlife crisis?"

"God, I hope this isn't the midpoint," Brynn said vehemently, tucking her hair behind her ear and liking that it didn't stay there the way it used to.

She dropped into the other guest chair next to Susan rather than across from her on the other side. "Things have been okay here, right? Since I've been out."

Susan arched an eyebrow and folded her hands in her lap. "You mean in the all of four days that you've been gone? Yeah, we've been just fine."

"Dr. Anders is doing okay?"

"Yeah, Blake is great. He's a little green, but conscientious...asks questions when he has them. And the patients love him. Especially the thirteen-year-old girls."

"I bet," Brynn said absently. Blake Anders had been doing a residency with them, but when Brynn had called in "sick" for the week, he'd been asked to take on more hours.

She only hoped that he'd be open to taking a *lot* more patients for the next few weeks.

"What's going on, Brynn?"

Brynn took a deep breath, forcing herself to meet Susan's eyes. "I think I need some time off."

Susan didn't flinch. "Longer than this week, you mean?"

"Yeah. I'm thinking more like...through the end of the month."

"Okay, no problem. As long as you need."

Brynn stared at her partner in exasperation. "You're supposed to freak out. At least a little bit."

Susan gave a small smile. "Oh, believe me, if I didn't

have Blake, I probably would. But honestly, we'll handle it. You'll be missed, but you've gotta do what you've gotta do."

Brynn sucked in a breath. Just like that. It was so *easy*. She'd been half expecting—hoping—that Susan would protest. Maybe try to talk her out of it.

No going back now.

"Well, okay, then," Brynn said. "I'll make sure all of my patient notes are updated, of course. And I'll contact them all personally to let them know I'll be on leave. And you can call me anytime. And I'll check in..."

Susan put a hand on her arm. "Brynn. We've got this. You take care of you."

Brynn nodded. "Yeah. Okay. I will."

"Look, I don't mean to pry, and I understand you want privacy, but..."

"I'm okay, Susan," Brynn said with a reassuring smile. *On the outside, anyway.* "There are no scary health issues or suicidal impulses, I just need some time, you know?"

"Totally. My sister had this total epiphany last year, and went on this three-month-long backpacking trip through Asia. When she came back, she gave up law and opened up her own organic bakery."

Brynn blinked. "Well, I'm not planning on *quitting*. And I can't bake worth a damn. And backpacking? When did she shower?"

Susan gave a slight laugh. "Okay, I can see that you need this break more than I thought. Seriously, though, don't give yourself any expectations for the next few weeks, okay? Not even good-intentioned ones."

"Sometimes the good-intentioned ones seem to do the most damage," Brynn muttered.

"Too much of a good thing, and all that," Susan agreed.

"Yeah, I guess."

Susan glanced discreetly at her thin designer watch. "I've got a patient in five. You'll let me know if you need anything?"

"For sure. And I'll get all my notes together and have them to you and Blake by the end of the week."

"I know you will," Susan said breezily, heading toward the door. "And Brynn? Have fun, okay? Whatever that looks like...mimosas for breakfast, skydiving, Vegas, monkey sex...just go for it."

Brynn tilted her head and narrowed her eyes at Susan. "You say that so easily. Have you ever gone for it?"

Susan gave her a cheeky smile. "No. But I'm only twenty-seven."

Touché.

CHAPTER TWELVE

*When you feel the urge to do something
irrational, sleep on it.*

—Brynn Dalton's Rules for an
Exemplary Life, #9

*Brynn Dalton maintained a very a strict list of Do
Nots.*

*Perms. Trans fats. Cubic zirconia. Tequila. Glitter nail
polish. Airplane bathrooms. Casual sex. William
Thatcher.*

*The last two items of her list were completely unre-
lated, of course. At least, they were supposed to be.*

*But then that kiss in the car had happened, and Brynn
couldn't seem to separate "Will" from "sex." And after
an uncharacteristic three glasses of Pinot Grigio, it was
getting a lot harder to remember why exactly "William
Thatcher" and "casual sex" were on her Do Not list at
all.*

Combining the two wouldn't be so horrible, would it?

Yes. Yes, it would be very horrible, *said her brain.*

But fun. Really hot, sexy fun, *said her loins.*

Clearly, it was her loins that had done the majority of absorbing the three glasses of wine she'd just consumed at her monthly sorority reunion.

She wasn't drunk. Just tipsy. And tipsy was not something Brynn did often because it left her feeling reckless.

Brynn Dalton did not do *reckless. Come to think of it, she should probably add it to her Do Not list. Nothing good ever came from being impetuous. That was where STDs, unwanted pregnancies, and broken hearts came from.*

And yet here she was, standing outside Will Thatcher's home and debating the unthinkable.

It bothered her that he lived in a homey town house. Hotshot bachelors like William Thatcher were supposed to live in monolithic high-rises. Brynn had been here before, of course. He'd hosted an anniversary for her parents two years earlier, and she'd also been by a couple times to pick up an inebriated Sophie.

But she'd never really picked up the details before. Like a friendly blue welcome mat. Why would a man who could barely be civil have a welcome mat?

The dark green of his front door was also all wrong. Hunter-green accents were for her *future home. They did not belong at the enemy's abode. And the dented brass knocker looked like it had been well used. Probably by a constant stream of female visitors.*

The flower pots bothered her more than anything. They were empty now thanks to Seattle's chillier-than-usual winter, but she couldn't help but wonder what he planted in the summer months. Flowers? Herbs? Or maybe something more stark and manly, like palms. Not that she could see him out here watering the damn things. Or maybe she just didn't want to picture it.

Brynn squeezed her eyes shut and told herself to walk away. Contemplating a one-night stand with public enemy number one was dangerous enough. Humanizing the bastard would be a disaster.

Damn Carrie for pushing that last glass of wine. *Although it wasn't really fair to blame her friend. It wasn't like Brynn didn't know her own limits. The monthly sorority reunions were notoriously boozy. Granted the sugary Jell-O shots of college had given way to overpriced wine bars, but her group of girlfriends still knew their way around their drinks. Brynn usually limited herself to one or two glasses, but she had the day off tomorrow, and she'd really hoped that third glass would help rid her of the itchy feeling.*

Instead it had led her here. Enemy territory.

"This is insane," she muttered. "I'm *not* that *drunk.*"

There were plenty of less dangerous men with whom she could scratch her itch. That accountant she'd gone on a date with last week would probably be willing. Or an ex? She thought briefly of Gray but quickly discarded the thought. They hadn't slept together when they were dating, why would they sleep together after they'd broken up?

Besides, something clearly was happening between him and her sister. Not that Brynn could actually see something developing there. They wouldn't make it past the first date when Sophie insisted on rowdy karaoke and Gray wanted to go to the opera. Something she'd told him straight-out when he'd driven her home after the emer-

gency room the other night. Sophie would kill Brynn if she knew she'd interfered, but Brynn hadn't been able to resist the opportunity to talk with Gray.

The soft looks that Sophie had been shooting Gray were not harmless employee-to-employee glances. Brynn hadn't seen her sister look at anyone that way in years. Sophie choosing to care about something was a rare gift, one that Brynn had made damn sure Gray knew to either accept or return with care.

"Will?"

"Brynn." *His voice was low and gravelly. She felt the smart part of her slipping away, and her reckless feeling increased tenfold.*

"Hi, um...why are you calling me?" *she asked in a too-casual high-pitched voice.*

He was silent for several moments. "What are you doing on my front porch?"

Oh God. *She squeezed her eyes shut.* "You know?"

"I saw the cab and watched you teeter up my walkway in death heels. Pretty sexy shoes for an orthodontist."

Brynn scowled at that. She hated how he always undermined her career, as though being an orthodontist meant you had to be frumpy and wear clogs.

"Yeah, well, I was just leaving," *she grumbled.*

The door opened so suddenly that she nearly fell forward. Their eyes locked for several heated moments, and moving on unspoken agreement, they silently hung up their cell phones without saying another word.

Will had braced his arm on the doorjamb as though barring her entrance.

Not exactly a welcoming start, *Brynn thought with a pang.*

Then his hand slid up several inches as he lifted his eyebrows in invitation, leaving just enough room for her to slide under his arm if she wanted to.

She wanted to.

Swallowing dryly, she ducked under his arm so she was standing in his foyer. He closed the door with a quiet click, and they still said nothing.

She studied Will closely, waiting for smugness or mockery, but his face was carefully blank.

"I, um... I just thought I'd stop by. You know, to say hi, and stuff," she said, her voice husky.

His eyebrow quirked at the mention of "stuff," but instead of giving her a hard time, he just nodded and gestured toward the kitchen. "Let me get you a glass of wine."

"Oh gosh, no. I've had plenty," she said, following him into the kitchen.

He paused in opening the fridge. "You're drunk?" Something like disappointment flashed across his face.

"No, just a little buzzy. And getting less so by the minute."

"Coming from a not-so-great date?" he asked, pouring her a glass of ice water.

"No, just a girls' night." She lowered herself onto the leather bar stool and fixed her eyes on her glass as he poured himself some sort of amber-looking liquid.

"And you came by to say hi," he said, taking a long swallow of his drink.

"Mm-hmm," she said, tracing a drip of condensation down the side of her glass.

The wine buzz was fading, but the recklessness wasn't. Her mind kept returning to The Kiss from the car. It had been running over and over through her brain like a track on repeat. And the more she thought about it, the more she wanted to do it again. Take it further.

But not like this. He was supposed to be his usual crude self. She wanted hot, meaningless anger sex. Something she could walk away from without so much as a bruise on her emotions.

This quiet, contemplative Will set her on edge. She didn't know how to speak with him in any language other than "feud."

Why didn't he call her bony or snobby or vapid and set her temper off so that she could storm out? Storming out was immature, but smart. Practical. Necessary. Storming out was very Brynn.

And that was the problem. She was sick of herself. She wanted a break from being the organized, uptight, no-sex-before-the-fifth-date goody-goody.

Who better to give her a night's vacation from perfect *than a man who spent more on condoms in a year than he did on food?*

Brynn shook her head to try and clear it. She was making herself dizzy with all of this waffling. Either she wanted to jump his crass bones, or she didn't. Make up your mind.

And then the most disturbing thought of all hit her. What if he didn't want her?

She'd taken for granted that he was a womanizer, but for all her complaining about him going through women faster than a toddler went through Cheerios, he'd never made a move on her. Not in high school, when they'd run in the same social circles. Not in college, when he'd practically lived at her house over Christmas break. And certainly not in their adult life, when their once-harmless bickering had turned into very real dislike.

Not until that rainy night in his car, and she still wasn't sure that the kiss hadn't been more about punishing her than passion.

The thought of being rejected by Will was almost enough to bring back the practical, self-preserving Brynn. And yet still she didn't move.

Just do it. You have the rest of your life to be boring.

Brynn set aside her untouched water glass and stood.

Keeping her eyes locked on his moody blue gaze, she slowly made her way around his kitchen island. She continued her slow approach until there were only inches between them. Still he didn't move or speak.

Brynn let her eyes move over him the way she'd seen him check out women a thousand times before. He was wearing a tight black T-shirt, jeans, and a scowl. He looked like every woman's bad-boy fantasy. Perfect.

Licking her lips nervously, she pulled the glass from his hand and set it on the counter. She felt a little thrill of gratification when something dark and dangerous flashed through his normally bored eyes.

She hesitantly ran her manicured fingernails lightly over his rib cage, closing her eyes in ecstatic panic when she heard him suck in a sharp breath.

Rough fingers clamped around her wrist. "Brynn, wait—"

No! *Desperate to stop him from thinking this through, she rose to her toes and kissed him. It was a soft kiss, just the merest brush of her lips against his. But still, she shuddered. He tasted warm and smoky and strangely addicting.*

She kissed him again, lingering this time. His lips moved just slightly beneath hers. Not quite returning the kiss, but not pulling back either.

He's letting me decide, *she realized. Whatever she was feeling was nothing like the manic passion of the car, and that alarmed her. This kiss was softer. Nicer.*

And every instinct was screaming that "soft" with William Thatcher was dangerous. "Soft" wasn't what she was here for. She wanted hot, animalistic sex on the floor of his bachelor pad, not soft, heady kisses in his homey kitchen.

Determined to banish all traces of tenderness, Brynn wound her arms around his neck and pulled his head down to her. Her lips were firmer this time, and she nipped at his bottom lip. He stiffened, and for a fraction of a second she had the horrible sensation that he was going to pull pack. Push her away.

He doesn't want me, *she realized in horror.*

Then Will moved so quickly that she nearly lost her balance. Sliding one arm around her back, he hoisted her onto the kitchen counter, even as his other hand slid around the back of her head.

She closed her eyes and waited for the crush of his lips, but his fingers clenched in her hair and held her still. His eyes had gone so dark they were almost black, and he stared into hers with an unreadable expression.

"You'll hate me if we do this," he said gruffly.

"I already hate you."

"Then why are you here?"

She almost laughed at that. She had her legs around his waist and he had to ask? "Isn't that kind of obvious?"

"Just sex?"

"Yes. And just this one time. And, Will...if you tell anyone about this, I will kill you."

His head tilted back slightly, and something unidentifiable flashed across his face before he resumed his usual bored expression.

"Well, if it's one-time sex you want, you've come to the right place," he said with an evil little grin.

Then his mouth closed over hers, and she resigned herself to the inevitable.

She was going to become one of William Thatcher's women.

* * *

Will knew Brynn would be back around. Knew it was only a matter of time before she ended up on his front door looking to scratch an itch she couldn't even identify.

But he sure as hell didn't expect *this* Brynn.

"Sweetie, what the hell happened to you?"

Although he was pretty sure he already knew, and he wanted to kill that sallow-faced James for doing it to her. Not that Will hadn't seen it coming.

Not that he hadn't wanted it.

But it hurt all the same to see it.

The long yellow hair he'd so often dreamed about sinking his fingers into had been replaced by a dark brown hack job, and instead of her usual minimal makeup, her blue eyes were dark and smoky and...

Oh, who was he kidding. This version of Brynn was *hot*. A hot mess, perhaps, but still hot.

But this wasn't *his* Brynn. This was the wounded, messed-up, lost version.

He'd wanted her to come to him, just not like this. But he'd take what he could get.

"Bad day?" he asked easily, leaning an arm against the doorjamb and locking his eyes with hers. He didn't give her an extended once-over. It was what she wanted, but not what she needed.

Instead he kept his face blank. This was her game now. He just needed to know the rules.

"Can I come in?"

Her shoulders were thrown back in a show of confidence and she had that subtly defiant look on her face that he knew all too well, but her eyes told another story.

Her eyes were terrified. Vulnerable.

He let her in.

"What's with the outfit?" he asked, stepping aside so she could enter. "Was it bordello-chic day at the office?"

"I didn't go into the office," she said, heading to the kitchen like she owned the place. "Well, I mean, I did. But not to work."

He raised his eyebrows behind her back. Brynn not working on a random Thursday. That was new.

"I didn't go to work all week, actually," she added.

Shit.

"Oh yeah?" he asked, going to the fridge and pulling out a bottle of wine. It was one of her favorites, but he didn't let her see the label. He was worried this version of Brynn would start asking questions that the real Brynn wasn't ready to hear the answers to. Like why he kept her favorite wine stocked. Always. Just in case.

She nodded in thanks as he slid a glass across the counter, then picked up it up and wandered toward the living area.

"The furniture looks good."

"Even with the 'gaudy' couch?" he asked, pouring a glass for himself.

She shrugged and flung herself on the black leather couch as though she hadn't launched a one-woman crusade against the "pinnacle of trashiness" just a week earlier.

He wanted to sit next to her. To have her swing her legs over his knees, kick off the scary shoes she was wearing, and talk about whatever had her dressing up like a harlot wannabe.

Wanted to tell her that she didn't have to try so hard. She didn't have to try to be perfect, or in this case, try to be *imperfect*. That with him, she could just *be*.

Still, Will had to admit, while the clothing was completely out of character, she pulled it off well. He was used to seeing her in cardigans and silk and perfectly tailored slacks, so this new look was a shock to the system. The dark jeans fit her like a second skin, cutting off at trim ankles to reveal high-heeled black patent leather stilettos that could kill a man. And the shirt, if you could even call it that, was fitted, red, and tiny. It wasn't low-cut…he didn't think Brynn Dalton was ready for *that*, but it was one of those strapless numbers that stayed up only because it was tight as hell.

One tiny tug downward, and…

"So what's with the midlife crisis?" he asked, taking a sip of wine and sitting in the chair across from the couch. Distance felt really important right about now.

"Why does everyone keep calling it that?" she asked with a frown. "Do you all think I'm going to die at sixty-two?"

"With all the organic shit that you eat, and nine thousand fitness classes? I doubt it."

"I quit my job today," she announced, taking a too-big sip of wine.

Will was careful to keep his face bland even as he felt a little flare of panic. "Oh?"

She took another sip of wine. "Well, not *quit* quit. Just . . . a sabbatical."

He relaxed slightly. Not because he cared about whether or not she ever went back to orthodontics again, but because he didn't want her making any decisions when she was all torn up over a guy. At least he was pretty sure that's what it was, but damn if he'd ask. She'd come this far. She'd have to come a little bit further.

"And what do you plan to do during this sabbatical?"

She narrowed her eyes at him slightly. "You're being nice. Why are you being nice?"

Because you're broken. "Just checking out your new look."

"Oh." She glanced down at herself before running a nervous hand through her short hair. "You like it?"

"It's different."

Brynn held out her glass for a refill. "That's what people say when they think something's awful and they're trying to be polite."

"When have I ever been polite?" he asked.

"True. Can I have more wine? What kind is it? It's good."

He stood to head toward the kitchen and ignored her question. "Why is it that you seem to need to be drunk in order to be in my presence?"

"Not drunk. Although I *have* been having a lot of wine

lately. Just...I dunno. Look, I live like twenty steps away. And if I have a little headache tomorrow, it's not your problem."

Will obediently went to the fridge for the bottle. Two glasses wouldn't kill her, but no way was he going to let her get drunk. That was the easy way out.

"So when did he dump you?" he asked bluntly as he refilled her glass.

To his surprise, she didn't even flinch. "Last Wednesday."

He eyed her closely as he topped off his own glass. "You seem...okay with it."

Brynn flopped back on the couch, and to his relief, she didn't immediately dive into the wine. "Of course I'm not okay with it. I thought I was going to marry the guy."

Something clenched in Will's chest but he forced himself not to move. "I take it he had other plans?"

"Your way of asking if there was someone else?"

Yes. "No."

"He didn't cheat," she said, looking down at her black-painted nails as though surprised they belonged to her. "But he 'met someone.' This crazy, dumpy woman who's not at all his type."

Will gave a slight nod. "Those are always the ones that get you."

Her eyes locked on his. "Have you ever had one of those? A woman that's not your type, I mean?"

You have no idea.

"I don't know that I have a type," he replied.

"That's true. You've always been of the *if it has boobs I'm on it* mentality."

Will hid his wince. Her tone was so matter-of-fact, and she wasn't entirely wrong. Based on what she'd seen of his behavior over the years, he *did* seem to pant over anything with the right reproductive parts.

"For what it's worth, you're better off without him," he said, trying to redirect the conversation back to her.

Brynn narrowed her eyes. "What's the catch? That almost sounds like a compliment."

"Just because I don't like you, doesn't meant I can't like Jimmy less."

She gave a little laugh at that. A soft, self-depreciating, *tiny* laugh, but she wasn't busting his balls or getting huffy or throwing her wineglass at him just for being alive.

Could this be ... *progress*?

"So what's next in this little crisis?" he asked, gesturing at her with his wineglass. "Piercings? Motorcycle? Tattoo?"

To his surprise, her face lit up at the last one. "A tattoo! Do you think I should get one?"

Oh no. She was worse off than he'd thought.

"Well, you know ... those are kind of ... permanent." Will shifted uncomfortably at being put in the role of the responsible one. "Do you think this, um ... phase is permanent?"

"Oh gosh, no," she said, running a hand over her newly dark hair and taking a little sip of wine. "This is just a month-long hiatus to clear my head and get back on track. A vacation. But it would be good to have a little reminder, don't you think?"

"How about a little less *forever* kind of reminder? Like ... spiky earrings or a charm bracelet or something? Hell, you could just put those trampy clothes under your bed when you're done with them, and use those as your memento."

But Brynn wasn't paying attention. She had that thoughtful-Brynn expression, which usually meant she was cataloging her dry cleaning, but apparently this time meant tattoo deliberation.

"Maybe just a little quote on my ankle, like *seize the day*, or something," she said excitedly.

"Or, hell, why not just go for a huge tarantula tramp stamp? Or a python crawling up your torso." He snapped his finger as though enlightened. "Wait, no. How about that ridiculous life list scrawled across your butt?"

Brynn sniffed. "For the record, that list is retired for a few weeks. But even if it weren't it would never fit on my butt. It's much too extensive and detailed..."

He shook his head. "This isn't happening, right? We're not actually having this conversation?"

"Oh, come on. Of all people, I thought you'd get behind my little rebellion."

Will's hand paused briefly as he brought the wineglass to his mouth. "Is that why you're here? Because I'm the only person in your life that won't freak out because you've gone off the deep end?"

"Sophie would be pissed if she heard you talking right now," Brynn replied, sitting up straight and setting her wineglass on the end table that she'd picked out. "She'd totally kill to see me through this little transformation. She's only been pushing for me to let loose for about a decade now."

"So why aren't you at Soph's, then?" he asked, standing and grabbing both their glasses before heading to the kitchen. She'd barely touched her second glass, but he needed to do something with his hands to keep them off her.

Brynn trotted after him. "Well, let's see...It's a Tuesday, so she must be having copious amounts of sex with Gray."

"How did you know *I* wasn't having copious amounts of sex before you barged in here?"

Brynn leaned her forearms on the counter and studied him. "Lucky guess. You haven't had any women over since moving in."

He arched a brow at her. "Spying?"

"Observant. So what gives? You haven't been this celibate since the womb. Waiting for some STD medication to kick in?"

Why do you care?

"Why are you really here, Brynn?" he asked. It felt strange to cut through the bullshit with her. They were all about the bullshit. But he didn't know his way around this new Brynn. And losing his footing now would completely derail his plan.

"I wanted to talk. And you live next door." She didn't meet his eyes.

Will crossed his arms over his chest and leaned back against the kitchen counter before making a rude buzzing noise. "That's not it. Try again."

Brynn licked her lips slightly. Lips that were just a shade brighter than her usual look, and more kissable than ever. "I don't know what you want me to say."

Yes, you do.

He itched to go to her, but he had to know what she was after first. Jogging her memory seemed a good place to start. He let his eyes go slightly sleepy as they raked over her, lingering on her mouth once more. "Really? So you don't remember the last time we were alone together in a kitchen?"

She picked at a fingernail—a sure sign she wasn't herself, because the Brynn Dalton he knew would never settle for a less-than-perfect manicure. "Sure, the day you moved in. I brought homemade cookies."

"They weren't homemade, and you know it. You *also* know that's not the kitchen encounter I was talking about." He pushed away from the counter and began moving carefully toward her. Decisively enough to let her know he wasn't fooling around, but not so quickly as to scare her off.

"Well, you said the *last* one," she said primly.

He resisted the urge to grind his teeth as he oh-so-slowly backed her against the counter. "Sorry. I should have said *the last one that mattered*. You know, three years ago...a different kitchen...a certain surprise drop by..."

Will slowly moved his arms until his hands were on either side of her hips on the counter. Watching her closely, he was ready for anything. Ready for her to scamper away. Ready for a scathing cut-down. He was even ready for the potential slap, because maybe this new Brynn wouldn't tolerate being backed into a counter. God knows the old Brynn hadn't.

But of all the things Will was prepared for, it wasn't for her to stand on her toes and kiss him. Hard.

Before he could register her soft body against his, she was *on* him, her fingers sliding around his neck at the exact moment her tongue slid against his.

And if maybe there was a tiny voice warning *not like*

this, he didn't pay it the least bit of attention. Instead he took what she was offering, because God*dammit*, it had been too long.

Will slid one hand up along her side, letting his palm brush the outside of her breast before clamping a hand around the back of her head and jerking her mouth closer so he could take control of the kiss. He heard her little gasp of surprise as his tongue pushed into her mouth and slid hotly along hers before he drew back and raked his teeth along her bottom lip. His other hand remained planted on her hips, his fingers digging into her tight little butt as he let himself rub against her once, twice. Three times. Refusing to kiss her again until she moaned in acquiescence. And when she let out a low frustrated moan, he gave her what she was looking for, taking her mouth again and again in hot, drugging kisses.

Distantly he became aware of her doing a little claiming of her own. The woman who was tugging at his hair and writhing against him was not the refined, cautious Brynn he knew.

He'd seen only glimpses of this Brynn once before on a night all too similar to this one. A night that had ended with her treating him like a tawdry one-night stand to be ashamed of.

The memory had him pulling back. Hell, it was the *only* thing that could have him pulling back.

It took her a second to realize that his mouth was no longer on hers, although he couldn't bring himself to take his hands off her. Not yet. His fingers slid around the back of her neck, tipping her head up and forcing her to meet his eyes.

"Brynn."

She touched the tip of her tongue to her swollen upper lip, and her eyes held a beguiling combination of confusion and want, and he almost dove in again.

But first he had to know. "What are you doing here?"

He waited for her to tell him that they'd made a mistake. Another one. Waited for her to tell him that she wanted another one-night stand with no strings attached. Waited for her to break his heart. Again.

But Brynn wasn't done with the surprises tonight.

Her blue eyes lifted to his, made slightly edgy with a dark smudge of makeup. "I was kind of thinking you might be part of my midlife crisis. You know, as a fling."

Will forced himself not to respond. It wasn't as much as he hoped and yet was more than he feared.

He didn't want to be her rebound. Or at least not *just* her rebound.

And yet, God help him...

He was going to say yes.

$\mathscr{C}$HAPTER THIRTEEN

A woman's body is a temple.
It should be treated as such.

—Brynn Dalton's Rules for an
Exemplary Life, #55

$\mathscr{Y}$ou can't be serious about this."

"I'm always serious," Brynn said, shooting Will a death glare. Honestly, for a guy who'd sworn to be her personal tour guide through the land of rebellion, he was turning out to be a total stiff.

Starting with the night he'd verbally agreed to her frenemy-with-benefits suggestion before dumping her on his front porch and telling her he was *tired*. She'd assumed he'd come around the next day to collect. He hadn't. Nor the day after that.

Then he'd dropped by with pizza, and then left without so much as a kiss.

Hell, she half expected him to show up with flowers,

and that scared the *crap* out of her, because it would mean he was *up to something*.

So Brynn had done what she needed in order to regain control of the situation.

She'd taken him to a tattoo parlor.

"What do you think about this one?" she asked, pointing toward a tiny purple butterfly. "Maybe on my butt or something?" *Where nobody will ever see it.*

Will glanced over her shoulder at the binder. "Don't embarrass yourself."

Brynn turned the page and planted her finger on a skull with pink roses for eyes. "Okay, then, how about this one?"

"Not unless you're a cross-dressing trucker."

"If you're not going to help, you might as well go home."

"Really? Because if that's an option..."

Brynn clamped her fingers around his wrist, enjoying the way the dark blue of her new manicure looked against his forearm. "You said you'd have a fling with me."

Will let out a long-suffering sigh. "Which I thought meant no-strings-attached sex, not hanging out in a dirty tattoo parlor on a random Friday morning."

"It's not dirty! I did a lot of research for one that was clean and respectable." *And you turned down the sex.*

"There!" he said, jabbing a finger at her. "That right there is proof that you shouldn't get a tattoo. You researched first? Tattoos are supposed to be spontaneous. Or at the very least, about the ink itself, not how often the place dusts."

"I don't care how often they dust so long as the needles are clean," she said with a lot more confidence than she felt. Actually, she *did* care about how often they dusted, but there weren't exactly a whole lot of high-class tattoo parlors out there.

"We are not having this conversation," Will muttered. But he reluctantly lowered himself into the seat next to her. She'd been sitting in the small waiting area for nearly twenty minutes under the guise of deciding on her "ink." But she was pretty sure both Will and the kid behind the desk knew what she was up to.

Stalling.

As if on cue, an irritable-looking woman came out of the back room where the pain happened, and Brynn did her best not to gape. Save for her face, the woman was literally *covered* in tattoos, most of them resembling animals you'd find on a safari.

Brynn mentally crossed predatory animals off her list of choices. Too many teeth.

"Where's, um, the guy that was here earlier?" Brynn asked, gesturing helplessly in the vicinity of the grungy welcome desk. He'd been clean-cut and sweet-looking. Nothing like this woman.

Safari Woman snorted. "Christian? He's on his lunch break. He doesn't do much other than phones and cleanup anyway."

Cleanup? Clean up what?

"I'm Jody. I'll be doing the art."

Brynn worked up a smile. "Almost ready, just debating a few options."

Jody raised a skeptical pierced brow. "Uh-huh. You sure about this? Because don't take this the wrong way, but you don't look like my normal clientele."

She didn't? Because she'd tried, she really had. Brynn

resisted the urge to glance down at her outfit. She'd wanted to go with the new black leather pants that made her ass look surprisingly fantastic, but it was too hot, so she'd gone for the shortest skirt in her wardrobe. One that seemed to have matriculated from her college closet, paired with a red tank top that was just a little too low to be respectable.

And red shoes. The shoes were key to this whole thing.

But apparently she didn't look tat-ready. *Should have gone with the leather.*

"No, I'm doing this," Brynn said firmly. She turned back to the binder in desperation. "I just need..."

Warm fingers caught her chin, and she found herself looking up into Will's familiar gaze. "You don't have to do this, Brynn. Nothing to prove. Nobody else even knows you're here, and I won't tell a soul."

"Not even Sophie?"

She didn't know why she'd asked. She didn't care if Sophie found out, but it was important somehow, that she and Will could have a secret.

Especially if she was going to sleep with him. Again.

"Not even Sophie."

Her heart swelled. *Stupid heart.* She took a deep breath. "I am sure about this," she said, giving him a small smile. "I need to branch out, ya know? For me?"

Will studied her closely, his eyes never leaving hers. "Okay, then. Do you trust me?"

Brynn sucked in a small breath. *Did* she trust him? Will Thatcher, her long-term tormentor? The one guy who never failed to make her behave badly?

The very same guy whom she was now begging to *help* her behave badly?

He was unreliable, unpredictable, and incorrigible. But he was here, and that was something. And the way he was looking at her...

"Yeah, Will. I trust you."

* * *

"What do you mean I have to keep this bandage on for a couple hours? I want to *see* it."

"And you will. In a couple hours."

Brynn pursed her lips and let Will lead her toward his car as they left the tattoo parlor. "Okay, fine. But I need to use the restroom before we go. Look, there's a Starbucks—"

Will's finger snaked around the tiny strap of her tank top as she strode toward the coffee shop. Brynn froze, knowing one good tug would send the twins spilling out for all of Aurora Avenue to see.

"You'll have to hold it," he said simply, his hand cupping her elbow and leading her more firmly toward the car.

"But I need to pee," she protested.

"No, you don't. You want to hide out in the stall and take a look at your new shiny tattoo."

She shot him a glare and dropped into the passenger seat. "Something I wouldn't have to do if you'd let me get it someplace *respectable*."

"Trust me, the hip was your best bet. If you hate it, nobody will have to see it. And it hurt less than other spots because the hip is more fatty."

Her mouth dropped open slightly. "How in *God's* name do you have as many notches on your belt as you do when you go throwing around words like 'fatty' to women?"

"Oh, I don't say them to actual women," Will said, as he carefully pulled out into traffic. "Just to you."

She made a face and turned to stare out the window, even as her fingers itched to explore the faint throbbing of her hip. It didn't hurt as much as she'd expected. Probably because it was so *fatty*. But she was dying of curiosity.

"You're really not going to tell me what it is?" she asked, turning to study his profile.

"That was the deal. You want me to stick with you, hold your hand, and not tell your mom, you had to let me pick, and you have to see it for yourself."

"This is quite possibly the most nuts thing I've ever done. I let a guy who's dedicated his life to torturing me mark me for life." She whipped her head around again to study him more closely. "Oh God, it's not like a picture of your face, is it? Or your name?"

His mouth turned up in the tiniest of smiles. "Now, would that be so bad?"

"Yes! Yes it would be so bad! To spend the rest of my days forever reminded of my biggest mistakes?"

Will glanced at her briefly before returning his eyes to the road, and she felt a little jolt of surprise at the unreadable expression on his face. She'd expected a retort. Maybe a put-down. But instead he'd looked...wounded?

Naaaahhhh.

He knew full well what they had. Ridiculous sexual chemistry and the long-term compatibility of a Bengal tiger and a canary.

"It's not a canary, is it?" Brynn blurted out. "The tattoo?"

Will rolled his eyes. "You are so weird."

"At least give me a hint—"

Will held up a hand as he stopped at a red light before the freeway on ramp. "No more tattoo talk for the next two hours."

"But—"

"No. Just because you're in this weird wild-child mode is no reason you need to have the patience of a four-year-old at church. Trust me, that tattoo will be there in two hours."

"It'll be there a hell of a lot longer than that," Brynn muttered darkly.

"Regrets already?"

"Hard to say since I don't know what it is. I mean if you've slapped a pair of hairy testicles on my hip bone, I'm sure as hell going to have some regrets. But the experience itself? The decision? It feels...liberating, ya know?"

"Sure, I know. But I'm surprised *you* do. You went from country-club prude to inked-up hooker so fast I'm getting whiplash."

"Yeah, well, getting dumped will do that to you. Hey, you're going the wrong way. You're headed into the city."

"Am I?" he asked, looking totally unperturbed.

She narrowed her eyes at his too-casual tone. "Where are we going?"

"Just thought it might be nice to get your mind off your tattoo for the next couple hours."

Or until I can get to a bathroom and see what we're dealing with, she mentally amended.

"Fine. So what's your plan? I don't want something I've done before, I want something—"

"I know. You want to rob a bank or learn how to throw knives, but how about we start small? You already let me brand you, how about you take the rest of the day in baby steps and just relish playing hooky on a weekday?"

Brynn frowned. "But I've already been playing hooky for a week."

Will snorted. "Yeah, I've seen the way you play hooky. You apply all that black stuff on your eyelids like you're going daytime clubbing, and then go garden. You wiggle into leather pants to get the mail. You get a tattoo and then want to get a freaking *butterfly*. Oh, and let's not forget... you ask a guy to be a fling, and then don't so much as move to kiss him."

Whaaaaaaa... Talk about crossed wires.

Brynn's mouth dropped open. "I kissed you first that night! And for the record, it was you who threw me out."

"Sure, so you could have a chance to think about your harebrained idea. I wanted you to sleep on it."

"So that's what you've been doing? Waiting for me to make move number two? I mean I asked you to go get a tattoo with me, for God's sake."

"Holding a woman's hand in a tattoo parlor isn't exactly a fling, Brynn."

She swallowed, remembering his moment of kindness in the tattoo parlor. "Well... thanks for doing it anyway."

The second she'd lain back and Jody had told her to take a deep breath, she found herself reaching for Will's hand. He'd taken it without question and held it the entire time, firm and sure. For some reason she had a feeling she'd be remembering that moment long after they were done with each other.

Still, she was more than a little annoyed at him. He was

making her work for what she'd already asked for. It had been hard enough to put herself out there the first time, and now he wanted her to do it again?

Brynn folded her arms across her chest. "I told you I wanted a fling. I don't know what more you want."

"It's easy after two glasses of wine, the thrill from a new look, and a fucking hot kiss."

"It's not easy when it's you! We're like Harry Potter and Voldemort. We're nemeses."

Will shook his head as he got off the freeway. "I'm talking sex and she's talking *Harry Potter*."

"I thought you'd appreciate it. You like black-magic movies and stuff."

"I like horror movies, Brynn. *Harry Potter* does not qualify."

Several moments lapsed as Brynn tried to figure out her next move while simultaneously trying to ascertain where they were going.

"So what do you want from me?" she asked quietly, as Will pulled into a parking spot in the middle of tourist central.

He turned off the ignition and faced her, one arm draped over the wheel in a way that was so intensely male that she wanted to take the tiniest nibble out of his bicep.

"I want you to ask me again."

She didn't pretend to play dumb. "But you already said yes the other night."

"Only because I was hard and could see your nipples through that slutty top you were wearing. Ask me again. And I'll say yes again. But you have to ask while sober. Maybe even begging a little."

She held his gaze. "You're playing games with me."

Will gave her a faint smile. "Sweetie, isn't that the entire point? To make a big game out of your 'vacation' before you go back to real life?"

There it was again. That raw, honest look on his face that was completely unlike the Will Thatcher she'd come to know and hate over the years. He was intentionally messing with her head. He had to be.

And yet...

"William Gregory Thatcher. Will you have a fling with me?"

His tiny smile turned into a full grin and her entire stomach flipped over. *Oh dear.*

And then he was out of the car before she had a chance to register why something so simple as a smile made her swoon.

"Hey!" she called, scrambling to unbuckle her seat belt. "You said you'd say yes!"

"And I probably will," he said, putting on his sunglasses and taking in the crowded scene as though he didn't have a care in the world. "But first you must be tested."

Brynn resisted the urge to slam her forehead on the hood of the car. "Tested how? We're in the middle of Seattle Center. What do you want me to do, run through the fountain naked?"

Will gave a mock shudder. "Ain't nobody wanna see that. And besides, your tattoo can't get wet yet. No, I'm thinking more... science center."

It took several seconds to register. "You want to take me to the science center? As in the Pacific Science Center? As in school field trip, nerdy grade school nirvana?"

"Yup." He was already heading that way.

"But Will," she said, scampering after him in her high heels. "I'm supposed to be living on the edge. This is even more mundane than my *regular* life."

He stopped so suddenly she would have skidded past him had he not grabbed her hand. Brynn assumed he was steadying her, but he kept pulling her closer. Then closer still. Until they were standing chest to chest, hip to hip in the middle of a crowded courtyard.

"Does *this* feel mundane?" he asked, tilting his hips forward slightly.

"Will!" she hissed at the contact with his erection. "You're..."

He shifted his hips again to confirm it. "Yup."

"There are children around."

"Somehow I don't think two adults dry-humping is going to outrank cotton candy with the six-year-old set."

"We are *not* dry-humping," Brynn said, her hands going to his chest to push him away. Except she didn't. Okay, maybe they were *kind of* dry humping.

He carefully scanned the crowd for gawkers before slowly lowering his head as though to kiss her cheek and then missing, and landing behind her ear, where there were about a thousand nerve endings.

"Is that a yes to the fling?" she asked, hoping he didn't notice her slightly breathless voice as his tongue flicked across her earlobe.

Will pulled back almost as quickly as he'd moved in. "Mmmm, too soon to tell. I'll have to see how you perform in the bubble race."

Brynn stared in exasperation at his back as he strolled toward the admissions gate of the center as though they hadn't just necked in public.

She chewed her lip.

She hadn't been lying about it being field trip heaven in there. Every school in the area made an annual trek there. Including hers. And every damn year, her class had been instructed to pick a partner to stick with for the day. But there was always an odd number. And Brynn had *always* ended up with one of the chaperones.

Which had been fine, really. Because at least the chaperones hadn't called her names and hidden her lunch box.

"Come on, Princess!"

She took a deep breath. *You can do this. You're an adult.*

You're not that little girl anymore.

"God, I hate you," she muttered as she set off to follow Will.

It was a sentiment she'd been thinking and saying for years. But for the first time, she wasn't even remotely sure it was true.

CHAPTER FOURTEEN

No sex without love. We're not savages.

—Brynn Dalton's Rules for an
Exemplary Life, #24

"Admit it, you had fun," Will said they crossed from his driveway to hers. Over the grass this time. Because rebels did that sort of thing. Still, Brynn might have been just a *little* careful not to let her heels pierce the lawn.

"The Science Center was fun," she conceded as she dug her keys out of her purse. "But the Ride the Ducks adventure was a monstrosity."

"Come on, that's tourist gold!"

"Perhaps. But it's local trash."

Will followed her into her dark foyer without asking permission to come in, and Brynn was surprised that she didn't have the slightest inclination to ask him to leave, even after an entire day spent in his company. When had spending time with Will gone from miserable to...fun?

It's just this weird phase you're in. In a couple weeks you'll wake up and realize that he's a schmuck and that you have a tattoo.

Brynn's eyes went wide at the thought. "My tattoo! I entirely forgot!"

Will gave her a slow, smug smile. "Which was exactly the plan."

She threw her purse onto the entry table and immediately reached for the waistband of her skirt to finally inspect the new marking on her hip.

But Will moved faster than she did, capturing both her hands in his and bringing them purposefully against his chest. "I'll do that," he said in a strained, gruff voice.

She froze. Any girl past puberty knew that tone. It was the one that said, *I want you naked. I want you to scream.*

Brynn swallowed and forced her eyes up to his. They were dark and smoky, exactly as she'd known they would be.

"Will, I..."

He lifted one hand to her face, unfolding her fingers and planting a hot kiss on her palm, the tip of his tongue just barely making contact with her skin.

And just that one touch was enough to have her moan. This was why she'd picked Will for her fling. The guy knew his way around sex.

Or maybe he just knows his way around you. She pushed the thought out of her mind. No way would she get through this night by *thinking*.

"I still want to see my tattoo," she whispered.

Will backed her up slowly until she was against the wall. "Later."

And then his lips found hers, and he kissed her long and slow and hard.

Brynn forgot all about her tattoo as she let her arms wind around his neck, pulling him closer, not caring that she seemed needy, not caring that they were using each other for sex, or maybe companionship or some other weird, possibly unhealthy connection she didn't know how to name.

The kiss wasn't gentle, but it was different from the other kisses they'd stolen from each other. It was purposeful, each giving as much as they took.

Will's hands were roaming over her back as he deepened the kiss, and Brynn raked her nails lightly over the back of his neck, relishing his guttural low moan.

Brynn had never understood the big deal with kissing. It had only ever been the obligatory first step toward the main event, but kissing Will was an event all its own.

He pressed hotter, deeper, his arms locked so tightly around her that she couldn't breathe. Didn't *want* to breathe. Dimly she became aware that there was a certain desperation to his kiss. As though there was something darker at play than standard male horniness.

When he finally released her mouth, they were both gasping for air as their gazes locked and held for several seconds. Without warning Will dipped his head and ran his tongue along her exposed collarbone before moving his mouth to her neck and sucking.

"You're going to give me a hickey," she said, her voice crackly.

He pulled back slightly letting just the tip of his tongue

soothe the spot he'd just ravished. "You want me to stop?"

No.

"Upstairs," she said, digging her fingers into his shirt collar and pulling him downward so her lips could reach his neck. Will let her nibble and suck for several seconds, but when her hands started to travel toward the button of his shorts, he pinned both her wrists together in one hand and, before she could register surprise, slung her over his shoulder.

It took Brynn several seconds to realize that she was upside down, staring at Will's back. Not a position she thought she'd be in. Ever. Good view, though.

She reached down to pat his very nice butt when she realized they weren't heading in the direction of her bedroom.

"The stairs are the other way, cowboy."

This time it was her butt that was getting patted. "*Nice* girls do it in bed, Brynn. Wild women like you? They do it on the couch."

Brynn squealed he tossed her unceremoniously on her couch. Her white couch. She gaped at him. "We can't do it here, it's *white*."

Will was already unbuttoning his shirt. "Exactly."

Brynn struggled to get into a sitting position, not letting her shoes touch the pristine upholstery. Just because she was letting loose didn't mean she didn't have some standards.

She froze when she felt Will's warm palm on her inner thigh. Her eyes fluttered shut as his hand slowly slid upward until his pinky finger brushed her *there*. And then he was cupping her new black satin panties and she was lost.

"Fuck the couch," she said, slumping backward and pulling him on top of her.

"It's not the couch I'm after." He slipped a finger under the elastic of her panties, his finger barely touching her as he stroked and teased.

"Will."

He plunged a finger inside her, roughly and uncompromisingly, and Brynn arched her back in surprise.

Will shifted until he was lying over her, his lips finding hers as he added another finger and began touching her in firm, sure strokes.

Brynn's fingers played over the sharp lines of his abs as she returned his kiss hungrily, even as she writhed beneath his hand. It wasn't enough, and she was on the verge of begging for more when he shifted the angle of his hand slightly until his thumb found her sweet spot. He pressed and circled, once, twice, and then she was lost, her body shuddering in a helpless orgasm.

When she finally stopped shaking long enough to open her eyes, she was horrified to find him studying her face with a small smile.

"Were you watching me?" she accused, squirming in embarrassment.

"What's the point of doing all that work if I don't get to watch?" he asked, giving her a swift peck on the lips before rolling off her.

She whimpered at his absence. "You're leaving?"

Will gave her a smoky look as he deftly unbuttoned his shorts and stripped down to a pair of tight black briefs. "Not even if you paid me."

The sight of a mostly naked Will was so arousing and achingly familiar that before she'd realized she'd moved,

Brynn pulled herself into a sitting position, resting her hands lightly on his hips. Keeping her eyes on his, she pulled him toward her until his waist was at her eye level and he was standing over her. Other than using a single finger to tuck her hair behind her ear, Will didn't move. Brynn was in control and vulnerable at the same time, and the combination was intoxicating.

The old Brynn had never been much of an initiator in sex, but this was the new Brynn. Moving ever-so-slowly, she dipped her head forward, planting a lingering kiss on his erection through his briefs. His hips bucked forward and he let out a sharp hiss before closing his hands around her head.

"Brynn..."

She kissed him again, parting her lips slightly to let his warm breath rush over him before carefully curling her fingers into the waistband of his briefs and pulling down, exposing him to her gaze. To her mouth.

Will let out a string of curse words that belonged in a trucker pit stop as her lips found his bare skin. She teased him slowly, and he let her, her lips brushing and tongue flicking lightly until finally she wrapped her lips around him and sucked, just once, but enough to have him uttering a hoarse "fuck" before tugging her head back roughly.

"Not like that," he whispered, his fingers brushing his cheek.

Brynn felt her cheeks heat in mortification. She'd forgotten that Will had turned sex into a pro sport over the years. He'd probably had a thousand women do that a hell of a lot better than her awkward attempts.

"No" he said sharply, his fingers tightening. "Stop

whatever you're thinking. I just don't want to do it that way. Not the first time."

"But it's not our first time," she said, trying to joke her way out of her embarrassment.

Will's grip loosened slightly and he ran a hand over her cheek. "It's the first one that counts."

Brynn didn't have time to ponder what that meant because then he pushed her back onto the couch, following her down and planting gentle kisses along the tops of her breasts before tugging her top down and slipping a tongue under the low cut of her black bra. She whimpered when his tongue flicked her nipple and together they awkwardly shed her shirt and bra until she was wearing nothing but a tiny skirt and damp panties underneath him.

"Pretty," he said softly, before wrapping his mouth around her nipple.

She'd never been well endowed, but Will made her forget about that as he loved her, giving gentle attention to each breast until the new Brynn took over, pulling his head firmly against her as he sucked hard.

"I feel like we're doing things all out of order," she said, her back arching.

Will chuckled, blowing warm air over her cold nipple. "Baby, if you think there's an order to sex, you've been doing it all wrong."

She wanted to protest, but then he tugged her panties to her knees and was inside her with a firm hard stroke, and somewhere amid the searing pleasure she wondered if he was right, that she had been doing it wrong, because it had never felt so right as right now.

Brynn let her hands roam wherever they wanted, nails

raking his flat nipples before clutching greedily at his firm hard butt, pulling him tighter, harder against her.

Will began to move faster, his hand moving between their bodies and finding her sweet spot as they both watched down where their bodies were joined. His fingers ceased their playing long enough to grab Brynn's right hand and guide it down until she was touching herself.

With a groan, Brynn began to touch herself in the small circular motions she liked, as his greedy eyes took it all in.

It was dirty and elemental and so fucking *good*, that Brynn barely had a chance to register that she was going over the edge again until lights exploded in front of her eyes. She hadn't yet caught her breath when he grabbed both of her hands, this time pinning them above her head as he rode her harder, his eyes burning into hers as he let out a sharp yell, thrusting into her one last time before he let his own shudders take over.

Neither of them moved for God knew how long, until Brynn finally wiggled her fingers, which were starting to fall asleep.

"I've gotta pee," she whispered.

Will grunted and rolled over just enough for her to scoot out from under him, as she half walked, half waddled to the bathroom wearing only her tiny skirt.

She didn't bother to look in the mirror, knowing she wouldn't like what she saw, but as she was righting her skirt after peeing, she felt an unfamiliar bandage.

The tattoo.

Her fingers shook in nervous anticipation. Allowing another person—especially Will—to select a tattoo was one of the riskier things she'd ever done. And so wildly out of character, she didn't feel even remotely like herself.

And she kind of loved it.

Brynn shimmied her skirt down to her ankles and very carefully removed the bandage from her upper hip. She was surprised that it didn't hurt, especially after the grinding gymnastics she and Will had just done on her couch.

She braced for the worst as she stood on her toes so she could see the tattoo in the mirror. She'd been expecting something funny, or clever, or downright embarrassing, but she frowned when she realized it wasn't a picture at all. It was a saying.

There it was in tiny black letters.

One step closer…

Her mind went blank, and she waited for understanding to register. She didn't hate it. It felt…intriguing.

But why?

She was obviously missing something. One step closer to *what*?

It was unlike Will to be cryptic.

And that bothered her more than anything.

CHAPTER FIFTEEN

Hollywood can never compare
to a good book.

—Brynn Dalton's Rules for an
Exemplary Life, #61

I'm telling you right now, up front, I don't like gore."

Will grimaced as he set a bowl of popcorn in her lap. "And I'm telling you up front, if you call my classic horror collection 'gore' one more time, you'll never get laid again. At least not by me."

Brynn gave him a smug look. "What makes you think I need you?"

"You may not, but *she* does," he replied, gesturing crudely between her legs.

"That's disgusting," she said, stuffing a handful of popcorn in her mouth. *And so true.*

They were lounging on Will's nonwhite couch, and she was wearing ancient booty shorts from college, and one of Will's undershirts. Her hair was a mess, and she didn't have any makeup on beyond the remnants of yesterday's mascara.

And she felt the most fabulous she had in months. Years. Maybe forever.

"I could get used to this whole life-vacation thing, ya know?"

Will gave her a bland look over her shoulder. "Perhaps that's a sign that this shouldn't just be a vacation."

She took a small sip of wine and considered. "Nah. If I live like this forever I'll get huge." *Again.*

"Great, maybe your boobs will grow."

Instead of getting offended, she found herself grinning confidently. "You *like* my boobs."

"Sure, when I can find 'em."

Her smile only widened as she licked buttery salt off her fingers. This was just right. Her and Will bickering like old times with the added benefit of sex. And wine.

And apparently horror movies.

"So how many of your lady friends have you subjected to this?" she asked as he finally pulled a DVD case from the shelf.

"What do you mean 'subjected'? Chicks love this."

"You haven't put any of them through this, have you?"

His hands paused for a second. "No. None."

Brynn's smile faltered slightly. This wasn't supposed to be special—it was supposed to be like any other of his short-lived fling.

She certainly wasn't looking to be different in Will's life.

Although perhaps it was inevitable that their situation be unique. Lifelong enemies didn't become temporary lovers every day. Though Brynn was no longer sure that sex was all they were doing anymore. There'd been plenty of it over the past few days, and yet here they were getting ready to watch his scary-movie collection together.

Not at all typical fling behavior.

When she'd hatched her ridiculous, spontaneous seduce-Will-Thatcher plan, she'd had it in her head that they'd alternate between tearing at each other's clothes and going back to having nothing to do with each other.

But it had been a week since they'd screwed on her couch, and the days that had followed hadn't been anything like she'd been picturing. She hadn't counted on moral support, or lazy Sunday breakfasts, or *friendship*.

But here they were.

"Okay, so what is this?" she asked skeptically as he plopped down beside her on the couch and dug his hand into the popcorn bowl. "*Psycho*? *Scream*? That *Nightmare on Elm Street* business?"

He shook his head, eyes already locked on the screen with a dreamy expression. "*Night of the Living Dead*. Totally classic. You're going to love it."

Brynn let out the smallest of sighs even though she wasn't the least bit put out. She'd never been a movie buff, but she had to admit, there was something kind of nice about being curled up on a rainy summer night with margaritas and popcorn. And a hot guy.

Whom she might or might not hate. Leaning toward not.

Brynn's jaw dropped open as the opening credits rolled. "Tell me this movie isn't in black and white."

"It's from 1968, Princess, of course it's in black and white."

Brynn slumped farther into the couch and prepared to be thoroughly bored. "I never pictured you as the type to watch old movies," she muttered.

He turned his head, and she felt his gaze on her profile. "Never pictured you as the type to watch them with me, but here we are."

It was almost an exact echo of what she'd been thinking, and for some reason, hearing him say it did something funny to her stomach. Instead of responding, she pretended interest in the movie.

Which, in fact, turned out to be *horrible*.

"That has to be one of the worst things I've ever seen. Zombies? Really?" Brynn said after the misery ended.

He shook his head. "Never gets old."

"How many times have you seen it?" she asked, turning to face him. "You were *quoting* it, for God's sake."

"Admit it, you liked it."

I liked that you liked it. Okay, this was getting ridiculous. It was *Will*. Just a few weeks ago she was trying to run him out of town and refusing to give him store-bought cookies, and now she was freely offering *her* cookies.

"It was awful," she said, picking out a half-popped kernel from the empty bowl. "I get that it was like a big deal way back when they barely had movies, but I didn't get it."

"So you wanna watch another one?" he asked, standing and stretching as though she hadn't spoken.

His gray UW T-shirt rode up as he extended his arms above his head, and Brynn's eyes lingered on the strip of flat abs he'd just exposed.

"Or we could do something else," she purred slyly.

His eyes briefly ran over her, and did that hot, glowy thing that got her going *every* time. "What did you have in mind?"

Brynn pretended to fiddle with her tiny shorts. "Well, it's no zombie movie, but…"

He pounced on her like something stalking its prey and she giggled as he went straight for her neck. "What is it with you and doing it on couches?"

"We haven't broken this one in yet," he said, accidentally-on-purpose letting his hand run over her breast.

Brynn gave a little moan, and moved to accommodate his weight on top of her. "So true, how dare we have any uninitiated furniture!"

He dipped his head toward hers, pausing when his lips were just an inch from hers. "How about I kiss you and then we watch *The Birds*."

"How about you *do* me and then you can watch whatever movie you want while I fall asleep."

"Deal."

But before he could kiss her, the jarring noise of a cell phone blasted from the coffee table. Will let out a little groan before reaching out to grab it. Brynn fully expected him to silence it and get back to, well, her, but instead he looked at the screen with a thoughtful expression before answering it.

"Soph, what's up?" he said, holding the phone to his cheek as he pushed away from Brynn.

Her stomach clenched in panic. He was talking to her sister? While they were in the same room? Hell, in the same house?

Brynn frantically scrambled to sit up, clamping a

hand over her own mouth as though to keep herself quiet, even though she had absolutely no intention of letting her sister know that she was in the same vicinity as Will Thatcher.

"Not up to much, just watching a movie..." he said.

Brynn let out a little sigh of relief. He hadn't quite said he was alone, but neither had he volunteered that he had lady company.

"They're not gore," Will was saying. "Why do you people keep calling them that?"

Brynn's eyes bugged out at what he'd just let slip and she clamped a hand on his arm in warning. He glanced at her with a shrug and she shook her head vehemently.

Will merely tilted his head as though to indicate he didn't understand, and Brynn's temper spiked slightly. He knew exactly what she was after, and was intentionally being difficult. It wasn't like Brynn wanted to keep secrets from her sister, but this thing with Will... If anyone found out, she would never live it down.

She hadn't even told her family about her new hairstyle yet, much less her new boy toy. And they'd *never* be hearing about that tattoo.

"I didn't mean anyone specifically, I just meant girls in general called the classics gory," Will said into the phone. Brynn sent him a look of relief, but he didn't look at her, and his eyes had definitely lost the sex-haze of a few seconds ago.

"Yeah, dinner on Friday sounds great, Soph. Text me the details. I've gotta go, 'kay?....and yeah, of *course* it's a woman."

Brynn tensed again, but Will merely said a brief good-bye to her sister and hung up the phone.

They both fell silent for a few painful seconds, although for the life of her, she didn't understand why.

"I take it you didn't tell your sister about us?" he asked.

"Us" felt like a strong word, but the tension in Will's voice had her wary, so instead Brynn demurred. "I haven't really told my family about any of this. They knew I took some time off, but not all the other stuff."

"And what is the other stuff, Brynn?"

"You know, the clothes, the hair...the new car...you."

The last word came out quietly, and she began to feel the tiniest speck of shame unfurl in her chest. She was treating him like a dirty secret to be hidden in the closet when respectable company came over.

Which he kind of was.

"Look, I just don't want other people in my personal life right now, okay? It's nothing against you."

His eyes made a liar out of her, but he didn't say anything more about it. But neither did he go back to the flirty, kissy Will, and she panicked a little at his withdrawal.

"How about that movie?" he said, standing abruptly.

"Will," she blurted, standing to grab his hand. "What's going on?"

He took a deep breath and searched her eyes for what felt like an eternity before very slowly the anger faded from his face. "Nothing's going on, Princess. Just a little blue balls is all."

Brynn refrained from mentioning that he didn't have to answer the phone when it rang, but instead she let herself wiggle closer, intentionally rubbing braless breasts against his torso. "Oh yeah? Think we can find a way to fix that?"

He very gently put hands on her shoulders and moved her back a few inches. "Actually, I think I need a minute. You know, to recharge. You think you can stomach another movie?"

Brynn swallowed in confusion. She was offering sex and he wanted to watch old movies? "Um, sure. Or I could go..."

Will was already nodding. "Sounds good. I'll grab your coat."

Ten minutes later, Brynn was standing in her own kitchen, feeling confused.

Once again, Will Thatcher had thrown her a curveball. Something had definitely just happened.

But once again, she had the distinct feeling she was missing something crucial.

CHAPTER SIXTEEN

Jealousy is for the emotionally unstable.

—Brynn Dalton's Rules for an
Exemplary Life, #30

Brynn couldn't believe she'd ever had the audacity to think she knew or understood William Thatcher.

She'd pegged him as the quintessential guy—the kind that lived and breathed sex.

But this was twice now that he hadn't taken what she offered. And not only that, but now he wasn't calling her back.

Brynn wanted to think it was all part of his game. That the recent friendliness between them was disguising some scheme to destroy her life. That he had some diabolical plan that involved trying to string her along like a lovesick ninth grader.

Not that anyone had ever tried to string her along when she was a ninth grader.

Well, she wasn't playing along. If he wanted to turn down perfectly good—okay, *fantastic*—sex, then that was his problem.

But on the sixth day of not having heard from him, Brynn began to consider an even worse possibility. What if Will wasn't playing games at all?

What if he was just...done?

It wasn't like he was known for long-term relationships. What had made her think that she could keep his interest?

And why did she care? Wasn't the entire point of a fling that it wasn't supposed to last? It wasn't like she was looking for commitment from the guy. And whatever this thing was between them had an expiration date in a couple weeks anyway when she went back to work, went back to blonde.

Went back to boring.

Brynn scowled and scrubbed harder at the bathroom mirror she was trying to get streak-free as the unbidden thought popped into her head. Her normal life wasn't *boring*, it was just structured. And if these past couple weeks of carefree living had been some of the best of her life, it was simply because she'd needed a break.

It certainly had nothing to do with a certain six-packed neighbor.

Brynn's phone rang, and even as her brain ordered her not to drop everything and dash at the phone in hopes that a certain jackass was calling, she found herself scampering just a little bit back to her nightstand to answer it.

But the name on the phone wasn't his.

"Hey, Soph," Brynn said, forcing her tone into a bright voice.

"*Hey, Soph?* You dodge my calls for weeks, and I get a *Hey, Soph*? I thought you were *dead*. Or pregnant. Or had some sort of weird rash like that one you had in seventh grade—"

"Gee, I can't imagine why I haven't picked up the phone before now." Brynn caught her reflection in the mirror above her dresser and wandered closer to inspect her skin for new wrinkles. There were two.

"So what gives?" Sophie pressed. "Mom is completely freaking out. Dad thinks you've turned into a liberal and are too scared to tell them about it."

Brynn rolled her eyes even as she felt a twinge of guilt. Her parents were the slightly stiff, semi-neurotic, supercontrolling type. But she'd always had a great relationship with them. Probably because she'd always done everything they'd wanted her to. Hell, probably because she practically *was* them.

But telling them that she was taking some time off from work and needed a "mental break" without any kind of explanation hadn't been considerate.

Brynn had always been the quiet, *deal with your own shit* type of coper, but at the underlying concern in her sister's voice, she found herself seeking a little validation that she wasn't totally losing her mind or irrevocably screwing up her life.

"Soph...have you ever felt, you know...lost? Like you don't know your purpose in life?"

There was a moment of silence on the other end. Finally Sophie responded. "Yeah, Brynn. I totally do. In fact, I even have a name for it. I call it my twenties."

Brynn let out a relieved laugh. Of course Sophie would get it. Brynn might have had the rough childhood while Sophie was a perfect little angel, but somewhere along the line, they'd gone and switched places. Sophie had gone from good grades, good schools, good hobbies, to, well...

Their mother had called it "insane free spirit."

Not that Soph had gone drugs or hippie or anything. She'd just sort of been a floater. Bartending gigs here, waitressing jobs there. It wasn't until she'd met Gray and been mistaken for a hooker—true story—that she'd finally decided to grab her life by the balls and figure shit out.

But Sophie's crisis had led her straight to the love of her life.

Brynn was suspecting *hers* would lead her right back to where she'd started.

"What's going on, Brynny? How come you're avoiding everyone?"

Not everyone. But she could hardly tell Sophie that in her time of need she'd turned to an enemy instead of a friend. Even if she wanted to explain it, she couldn't. Because she still hadn't figured it out for herself.

"I just needed some space, you know? After James..."

"I have tampons with more personality than James."

Brynn winced. "Eeew."

"Seriously, though," Sophie continued. "Take as long as you need to lick your wounds or whatever, just know that everyone thinks you're better off without him."

"Everyone?" Brynn prompted with a knowing smile.

A beat of silence. "Well, okay, just me. Mom and Dad loved James. And Gray says he's 'upstanding,' although if that's not a condemnation, then I don't know what is."

"Yeah, it's really *upstanding* to leave your girlfriend for another woman," Brynn grumbled.

"I am sorry about that part," Sophie said in a softer voice. "That must have stung."

"Yeah. But...not as much as you might think, you know? Mostly I just can't figure out why he went for someone so completely wrong for him. This woman's a total train wreck. I mean, he won't even let people drink water in his car, and this woman has fruit punch in a flask."

"Fruit punch? Who let her out of the penitentiary?"

Brynn wandered over to the window. "You know what I mean. They just don't...match."

"That's the way it works sometimes, Dalton. But that doesn't mean that you cut out your family."

"I know," Brynn said, her eyes inadvertently scanning the windows in Will's house for any sign of movement. "I'm sorry. Drinks on Friday?"

"Definitely. I'll come over there since you live in a boy-free zone."

Not as boy-free as you might think.

For a crushing second, Brynn had the urge to tell Sophie everything. And by everything, she meant Will. About that night three years ago. About the multiple nights recently. But, most important, about the nights that weren't about sex and that weren't about fighting.

But there was always the risk that Soph would slip up and say something disastrous to Will that would give him the wrong idea and send him running. Some things were simply destined to be secrets. She and Will were one of them.

Realizing that staring at his windows wouldn't reveal

anything going on inside Will's head, she started to turn away from the window when her eye caught on movement in his driveway. Brynn frowned at the unfamiliar vehicle. She didn't know the first thing about cars, but this one was dark red and unremarkable. Rental-car variety.

It definitely wasn't Will's car and neither was it a delivery truck. Will had a visitor.

Brynn made the requisite *mm-hmm* noise as Sophie chirped on about some gloriously cheesy dip she would bring over on Friday, but her eyes were locked on that car.

Correction. Her eyes were locked on *who* was getting out of the car.

Will didn't just have a visitor. He had a gorgeous, twentysomething, leggy, big-boobed brunette visitor.

Brynn had been in enough yoga classes to know a good female butt when she saw one, and this woman had cornered the market on tight and curvy. The slim gray pencil skirt and fuck-me heels didn't hurt either.

The woman moved toward the trunk of the car, and Brynn shifted to the other window to get a better view, just like any stalker worth her salt would do.

Brynn's jaw dropped.

The woman had a *suitcase*.

"Soph, I gotta go," Brynn said abruptly.

"Um, okay?"

"Sorry, I'll call you later. Actually, I probably won't. But come over around seven on Friday."

"But, Brynn—"

Brynn hung up, tossing the phone on her perfectly made bed before dashing to the closet. She didn't know what the plan was, but when she did figure it out, she needed to look . . . well, better.

For the first time since the start of her whole identity crisis, Brynn felt totally at a loss as to what to wear. On one side of the closet she had her massive collection of old-Brynn clothes. Classic cuts, cardigans. Lots of taupe.

On the other side of the closet was her smaller collection of off-the-deep-end attire. The leather pants. A skirt that looked like ripped ribbons. A bustier that could have qualified as another layer of epidermis. She chewed her lip and slowly eyed one option after the next.

Compared to Will's supermodel houseguest, she'd either look like a teenager going through a "phase," or Pollyanna.

Worst of all, she wasn't even sure that it mattered. He'd stopped calling even before the brunette had shown up.

Letting out a growl of frustration, Brynn grabbed a pair of tennis shoes and stormed out of the walk-in closet.

The ratty shorts and T-shirt she was wearing were *fine*. Will Thatcher didn't deserve anything better.

Halfway through tying the laces on the second shoe, Brynn's fingers faltered. What business did she have charging over there? She certainly hadn't been invited. And she didn't *technically* have a reason to go over.

What's the plan, Brynn?

The smart option was to let him be. He'd moved on to the next piece of ass, exactly as she'd known he would. Exactly as she'd *hoped* he would. Eventually.

And yet...

Brynn gave a slow smile as a plan began to formulate.

It was time to give Will Thatcher some of his own medicine.

* * *

"What can I get you?" Will asked. "Water? Iced tea? Beer?"

"Water for now," Jenna said, plopping onto his bar stool and pulling her long dark hair into a messy ponytail. "Planes always dry me out."

Will poured a glass of water for Jenna before helping himself to a beer. Sure, it was barely past noon on a Sunday, but when dealing with Brynn Dalton—or in his case, *not* dealing with her—a few vices were allowed.

"Rough day?" Jenna asked, jerking a chin at the beer.

"Rough week," Will said, taking the stool next to her. "But you didn't fly across the country to hear about me."

He gave her what he thought was a winning smile, but Jenna leveled him with a direct gray stare. "It's like I told you that weekend in New York. Don't even try to use your charms on me. I have no qualms about crushing your balls if you annoy me."

"Ah, I'd forgotten. No charm, then," he agreed. This is what he liked about Jenna. She was reliably bullshit-free. She didn't dish it out, didn't accept it.

She was the poster child for *what you see is what you get*.

And what he was seeing was a whole lot of hotness. It had surprised him not at all when he'd learned that Jenna had spent a few years as a model, followed by a lounge singer, followed by any other assortment of jobs, all of which mostly required her to look good.

She should have been his dream woman.

Except she wasn't.

"Rumor has it you've decided to start using your brain instead of your boobs to make a living?" Will asked, easily adapting to the candid conversation she tended to favor.

She lifted a shoulder. "Had to do a little winking and wiggling to get there, but yeah, I landed an editorial position at *GQ*. Mostly it's just a lot of telling other people when their shit sucks."

"So...your dream job."

Jenna shot him her slow cat smile. "Precisely. What about you? Still cranking out new business ideas faster than you can crap?"

Will fidgeted with the bottle. "Taking a little break from the creative side for now. Letting the existing projects ride."

Jenna's gray eyes narrowed on him. "You don't seem the type to let anything ride."

Will hesitated. Just because they'd grabbed dinner a couple times while he was in Manhattan or she was in Boston didn't exactly make them confidantes.

Still, a little female advice wouldn't hurt.

Jenna let out the tiniest of sighs. "Oooooh boy. Listen, I have two brothers—one being a *twin*—and way too many ex-boyfriends. I know when a guy has woman troubles. Out with it."

But before Will could open his mouth, there was god-awful noise coming from his backdoor.

"Um. Is that 'Jingle Bells'?" Jenna asked in confusion.

Will couldn't hide his smile, even as he told himself to be annoyed.

Apparently a certain neighbor had spotted Jenna.

"Yeah, that's 'Jingle Bells,'" he said. "Or at least it's trying to be."

"*....OH WHAT FUN, IT IS TO RIDE...*"

"Ignore it," Will said, his smile turning into a full-out grin. "It'll be more entertaining this way."

He felt a surge of relief that he'd pulled the blinds on the glass door earlier. Brynn wouldn't be able to see in, and it would drive her absolutely up the wall.

An obnoxious tapping noise began along with the Christmas carol, although it wasn't even remotely in rhythm, and Will happily took another sip of beer. This was great. Perfect, even.

Jenna, apparently, had other ideas. She was on her high heels and moving toward the back door before he could stop her.

"For God's sake, someone should put that hyena creature out of its misery." She jerked open the back door, and it was quickly apparent that the hyena comparison was strangely apt.

He'd seen wild Brynn, he'd seen stuffy Brynn, he'd seen fancy Brynn…

But he'd never before seen disheveled Brynn.

And she was breathtaking.

Her clothes didn't match, only one tennis shoe was tied, and there wasn't a speck of makeup on her face. Adding in the fact that there was just the tiniest line of blonde roots starting to peek through the new dark. Something he'd thought he wouldn't see until the apocalypse.

"Whatcha doin' here, neighbor?" he drawled.

Brynn's intense scrutiny of Jenna made it pretty clear what she was doing there, but he wanted to poke at her all the same. Clearly, he should have considered this route earlier. Will hadn't invited Jenna to stay with him with the intent of giving Brynn a jolt, but he should have. There was nothing like another woman to spur a female into action.

And he'd been waiting a full week for something to spur Brynn.

He'd assumed it would be her hormones. But…jealousy worked too.

Without warning, Brynn turned wild blue eyes on him, and had he not been sitting down, he would have taken a step backward.

"Oh, you know, just came for some coffee," she said in a slightly manic voice.

He gave a cocky smile, even as he watched her warily. "Sure, help yourself."

But Brynn had already spun back toward Jenna as she stuck out a hand. "I'm Brynn. Will's…"

She broke off completely, and Will hated that he was practically holding his breath to hear what she filled that gap with. Boyfriend? Lover? Friend?

"I know who you are," Jenna said in her usual husky voice. "We're practically related."

Brynn's head snapped back a little in surprise, and her study of Jenna was more curious than confrontational.

Too bad. Will had a feeling he'd just had a near-miss on a really hot catfight.

"Oh my God," Brynn said as she met Jenna's eyes. Eyes that she should now be registering as familiar. "You're Gray's sister."

Jenna shot a finger pistol at her. "You got it. My brother and your sister are hitched."

Brynn let out a low moan before reaching up toward her disheveled hair. She dropped her arm almost immediately, as though realizing it was too late to save her hair. And her dignity.

Still, he had to give her credit. Instead of slinking off,

she straightened her shoulders and took a deep, steadying breath.

"Sorry about that," Brynn said with an embarrassed smile. "None of this would have happened if Sophie and Gray had gotten married normally with bridesmaids and whatnot instead of eloping in Vegas."

"Yeah, clearly it's *Sophie* who's to blame for this situation," Will said blandly.

Brynn glanced over her shoulder at him, and though there was a remnant of heat there, she mostly just looked confused.

He started to crack, just a little. He'd wanted her to learn how to come to him and to learn to ask for what she wanted. But perhaps he was expecting too much from a woman who didn't even *know* what she wanted.

"You're staying here?" Brynn asked, her voice still wary, as she turned to Jenna.

"Yeah, Gray and Sophie don't have an extra bedroom, so Sophie asked Will to put me up for a few days. I actually think she tried to ask you first, but..."

"But I wasn't picking up my phone," Brynn said with a little groan.

Jenna shrugged.

"Well, welcome to the neighborhood," Brynn said too brightly. "If you need anything, I'm just next door."

Will barely registered that Brynn was no longer in his house before he saw her streaking across the lawn like a tattered little bunny.

Jenna headed toward the fridge. "I think I will take that beer now. And not that I want to get in the middle of any of this, but some advice from a woman...if you don't go after her right now..."

But Will was already moving toward the door. He paused briefly, and turned to Jenna just as she popped the cap on her beer. "Look, I hate to go all soap opera on you, but if you could keep this kind of quiet..."

Jenna held up a hand. "Trust me. I don't even know what I'd say."

And then Will was moving toward Brynn's house, automatically stooping down to pick up the stupid little fake rock in her backyard where he knew she kept her key. He'd bet his life that she'd have locked the door to wallow in her embarrassment in solitude.

He let himself in the back door without remorse, and was slightly surprised not to find her eating peanut butter out of the jar, or scarfing chocolate chips, or whatever it was that women did for comfort.

Will moved quietly toward the stairs, smiling a little when he heard the distant sound of water running. Of course Brynn Dalton wouldn't wallow in embarrassment with sugar or booze or dairy products. She'd hop in the shower to wash the embarrassment away.

She'd left the door open, and the vast amount of steam revealed that she liked her showers piping hot, just like he did.

He had the fleeting urge to pull back the curtain and mime stabbing motions. How often did a horror-movie buff come across the opportunity to surprise a woman in a shower à la *Psycho*? Somehow he didn't think that would help his cause. At all.

Instead he silently lowered himself to the toilet seat as he mulled over what to say.

Want any company in there?
Jenna's just a friend.

Why don't you want anyone to know about us?

But he wasn't playing his cards until he could get a peek at hers. So instead he simply said, "Hey."

He braced himself for a scream. Maybe a bar of soap flying at his head. But instead there were so many beats of silence that he thought she must not have heard him.

"I thought I locked the door," she said finally.

"Yeah, about that... You know the fake rock trick only has a minute chance of working if it actually has other rocks to hide among. A lone rock sitting next to your flower pots is pretty much carte blanche for burglars."

"Or cheating perverts."

He raised his eyebrow at that. "Now hold up a second. If I were a pervert, I totally would be sneaking a peek at the nakedness behind that curtain. And as for cheating... don't you have to be in a relationship for that?"

He leaned forward, resting his forearms on his thighs as he waited for her to respond.

Finally he heard the curtain slide open, and Brynn's face emerged, sulky, dripping wet, and painfully pretty.

"Are you sleeping with her?" she asked.

He could have punished her. Perhaps *should* have.

Instead he shook his head.

"Are you planning on it?"

He shook his head again.

Brynn licked a bead of water from the corner of her mouth as she pushed dripping water away from her face. She glanced at the ground. Glanced at him.

"Wanna come in?"

Will didn't have to be asked twice. It was only after he'd shucked his clothes in record time, and was in the process of worshipping every inch of her wet body, that a nagging thought crept in.

She'd never answered his question about them being in a relationship.

CHAPTER SEVENTEEN

Never kiss and tell. Not even to girlfriends.

—Brynn Dalton's Rules for an
Exemplary Life, #27

"I still can't believe you've been having this whole delicious crisis without me," Sophie said as she pulled her cheesy spinach dip out of the oven.

"That was kind of the point," Brynn muttered as she wrestled with a wine cork.

Sophie grabbed a carrot stick and dunked it in the dip before jabbing it in Brynn's direction. "But you dyed your hair. And your pants are *red*."

"Wow, really living on the edge," Jenna drawled from where she was assembling a salad.

Sophie shot her sister-in-law a look. "Believe me, for Brynn, this is the equivalent of a tattoo."

Brynn nearly fumbled the wine bottle and Sophie looked at her sharply before her mouth dropped comically open. "You didn't!"

Sophie pounced in Brynn's direction, already reaching for the hem of her shirt as though to disrobe her then and there, looking for a mark.

"A tattoo? Mom and Dad will freak!"

"Mom and Dad aren't going to *find out*," Brynn said, grabbing a wineglass and using it to fend off her sister. "And if you want some of this delicious red, I suggest you promise to keep your babbling mouth shut."

"Fine, fine," Sophie said. "But I want to see it."

"It's not for public consumption," Brynn said primly as she poured three wineglasses. "It's for me."

"Just you?" Jenna said, smoothly plucking a wineglass out of Brynn's hand and giving her a long look.

Brynn narrowed her eyes just slightly on this gorgeous woman who was her brother-in-law's baby sister, her sister's new best friend, and ... Will's houseguest.

She should like Jenna. She didn't have any reason not to like Jenna.

But she didn't have to like that Jenna looked like a Victoria's Secret model and was sleeping down the hall from Brynn's man.

Nor was Brynn crazy about the fact that Sophie and Jenna were so buddy-buddy. It had always been just Brynn and Soph, and now there was a newcomer who had New York written all over her designer clothes and smug attitude. And did the woman even have pores?

The sad fact was, Brynn was jealous. Brutally so.

Not just because everyone in Brynn's life seemed to be a card-carrying member of the Jenna fan club (to which

Brynn hadn't even been invited), but because Jenna was
so damn *confident*.

Brynn wanted that.

But then, Jenna probably hadn't ever sat alone at a
lunch table, or been asked by the popular kids to hand out
party invitations to *a party she wasn't invited to*.

Jenna probably hadn't had to transfer schools because
some immature jerk spread rumors that she'd made a "fat
sex tape."

Kids could be cruel.

But she bet they hadn't been cruel to Jenna.

"So how long are you staying with Will?" Brynn
asked, taking a small sip of wine and deliberately avoiding Jenna's question as to who else might have seen
Brynn's tattoo.

"I fly out Tuesday morning. Just came in to check up on
the brothers, and escape the wretched summers in the city."

"Ah yes, New York," Brynn said, helping herself to
some of Sophie's dip. "You've lived there awhile?"

"A few years. I've moved around quite a bit, but New
York seems to be the one that fits. For now."

"But all your family's here...You must have a
boyfriend there?"

Brynn hoped nobody would notice that her knuckles
were white around her glass.

*Just tell me you haven't slept with Will. Tell me he
didn't lie to me.*

To Brynn's surprise, Jenna's features softened slightly
for a moment, and she went from edgy sexpot to vulnerable girl.

Sophie gave a little cackle. "Jenna's in love with a New
Yor-kah and she hates to admit it."

"Your New York accent is terrible," Jenna said. Her feet shifted imperceptibly, almost as though she was nervous. "He's just...he's a good guy. I don't know that I'm in love."

Ah. Jenna's eyes flicked to Brynn for a moment, and for some reason something clicked between them, as though they were on the same page. Somehow Brynn knew that Jenna *was* in love. But she didn't know if the guy was in love with her.

And without that validation, she wasn't admitting anything. Not even to herself.

Brynn couldn't blame Jenna. Especially not after what had happened with James. Although in hindsight she was thinking she *reaaaaallly* should have been more upset about that. Instead it had taken her all of a haircut, a new pair of pants, and sex with an enemy to snap her out of it. In about a week.

"I'm sleeping with Will."

Brynn immediately slapped her hand over mouth as soon as she said it, her eyes automatically flying to sister. Sophie slowly straightened, the chip she'd been dipping forgotten. Brynn searched Sophie's face, but while her already big eyes were extra huge, she didn't look completely surprised.

She looked worried.

"How long has this been going on?" Sophie asked, fixing a fake smile on her face.

"Since, you know...this," Brynn said, waving a hand over her hair and her uncharacteristically skimpy attire.

"Is it serious?"

"No. God no. It's Will. I don't even think it's *safe*, it's just..."

"Hot?" Jenna volunteered.

Sophie winced. "Sick, it's like you're talking about my sister and brother."

"Says the woman who's banging *my* brother," Jenna said. "And they're totally hot for each other. I've seen it in action. It's like...well, I bet you guys have great angry sex, don't you?"

This last question was directed to an off-balance Brynn, who was rapidly regretting sharing what was supposed to be her ultimate secret. Although her reasons for insisting it be a secret were getting harder and harder to remember. Particularly when she was talking to his best friend, and a woman who apparently knew and liked him well enough to stay in his house.

Especially when it was getting harder to remember why she didn't like the guy.

Still, Brynn hadn't lost total perspective. The guy might have surprised her recently, but he still was the antagonist to nearly every single item on her life list.

He didn't believe in commitment.

Didn't believe in settling down.

He'd never had the same job for more than two months or stayed in the same city for more than a couple years.

He never even kept the same car for more than six months.

Brynn Dalton was all about stability.

Will Thatcher was not.

"It's just a fling...thing," Brynn said after catching the knowing look Sophie and Jenna exchanged. "I think it's pretty much over anyway."

Sophie tapped her fingernails on the counter thoughtfully. "You know, Gray tried to tell me from day one that you and Will's dislike of each other was really sexual tension, and I ignored him. I mean he's not exactly an of-the-people type of guy."

"Hear, hear," Jenna said.

"But he was right, wasn't he?" Sophie asked Brynn. "All the bickering was just foreplay."

"No," Brynn said vehemently. "I can assure you that the bickering was, in fact, bickering, which was based on dislike. The sex stuff...that's just extra. And recent."
Kind of.

Jenna topped off their wineglasses. "You could totally be the main character in one of those girly self-discovery movies, you know? I can see the trailer now...good girl gets dumped, chops off her hair, falls for the bad boy, and learns what an orgasm is."

"I knew what an orgasm was well before Will, thank you very much."

Jenna wiggled her eyebrows. "But I bet he's better."

Sophie made a gagging noise. "Enough. I refuse to let you ruin my delicious cheese dip with details. But Brynny, in all seriousness...where is this going?"

Brynn took a deep breath. "It's going nowhere. That's kind of the point."

A strange, unreadable expression crossed Sophie's face. Sadness? Disappointment? "So it's really all about an itch that he's helping you scratch? You don't care for him? Not at all?"

The question sent a little jolt in the direction of Brynn's heart, but she forced herself to keep the question and answer at the head level.

"Soph, I know he's your friend, but we're horrible for

each other. And while he's not quite as miserable as I always thought, he's not a good long-term prospect."

"Why not?" Jenna asked.

Back off, missy. You may be his current roomie, but I've known him my whole life.

Except *did* Brynn know him? Really? Everyone but her seemed to be on to something that she wasn't seeing. *Or that you're not letting yourself see.*

"I'm nothing but a game to him," Brynn said quietly. "He's disliked me since high school, and that dislike has only been fueled by the fact that I'm one of the few women that wouldn't let him into my pants."

Except that one time . . .

"What if he *did* care?" Sophie said casually. "Hypothetically."

Brynn shook her head. It didn't even compute. "Has he had a serious girlfriend ever? Or even a woman he's been faithful to for more than a couple weeks?"

Sophie became suddenly fascinated with the dip, and Brynn pounced on her. "See? You know exactly why someone like me would never be with someone like him. I want a ring, and babies, and a white picket fence. He wants none of those things."

"And yet he moved to the suburbs," Jenna emphasized.

"Next door to *you*," Sophie added more quietly. "There's got to be a reason for that."

Brynn rotated her shoulders in irritation. "Yeah, and I'm sure there was, but not in the romantic way you guys are trying to make it out to be. He and I started this game back when we were fifteen. He's come back because it's time to finish it."

"I wonder who wins," Jenna added thoughtfully.

Brynn swallowed around what felt suspiciously like a lump in her throat. "I'm beginning to think neither of us."

* * *

Brynn was somehow unsurprised to find Will rummaging around in her kitchen at the crack of dawn on Monday morning.

She blinked sleepily at him, gratefully accepting the mug of coffee he handed over.

"How'd you get in? I moved my key."

Will grabbed a plastic brown blob off the counter and waved it at her. "The fake-dog-poop key holder? Really?"

"What? No burglar is going to risk picking up a pile of poop to see if it's fake."

"He doesn't have to, he can just give it a whack with a stick and hear metal rattling against plastic."

"Damn," Brynn said, slumping into her kitchen chair as she tried to blink off the fog of sleep.

"Maybe you should just forgo the spare-key route," Will said as he rummaged in her cupboards for a box of cereal. "Something tells me you've never forgotten your key in your life."

She didn't deny it. "I like to be prepared."

"Shocker." Will held up the box of cereal. "Whole grain, organic, no sugar?"

"It's healthy," Brynn said.

Will shook his head and poured some into a cereal bowl before pulling the milk out of the fridge. "Wow, nonfat. Really living on the edge."

Will unceremoniously handed her the bowl, and her

gaze caught on the fine hairs of his forearm before traveling up to where his navy T-shirt strained around his bicep.

She tore her eyes away and accepted the cereal even though she wasn't hungry. At least not for food.

"You know, I had high hopes for you when you first started on this kick," he said, grabbing his own coffee mug and joining her at the table. "You were all leather and dark hair dye and tattoos. But I've gotta say, you're totally posing."

Brynn munched on her cereal. "What were you expecting? Motorcycles and genital piercings?"

His coffee cup paused halfway to his mouth. "Keep talkin'."

She ignored this and jabbed her spoon at him. "A vacation from oneself is entirely relative. For some people, 'edgy' might be skydiving. For others, it's something as simple as going to a restaurant and dining alone."

"And for you, it's what...skipping a day of flossing?"

Brynn made a face and scooped up another spoonful of cereal. "Please. I would never skip flossing. But I did go rock climbing the other day."

She heard the smugness in her tone, and didn't care. It had been exhilarating, and completely unlike the safety of yoga.

Will raised an eyebrow. "Really? Where?"

She shifted slightly. "Nearby."

"I've gone rock climbing a few times with a friend. I might know the spot."

She purposefully ate a too big bite of cereal so she wouldn't have to answer.

"Brynn..." Will said in a low voice, leaning toward her. "Was this 'rock climbing'...indoors?"

She gazed back at him, stubbornly refusing to answer.

Will sighed. "You went to the flagship REI store and did it there, didn't you? You know, scaling a fake rock at a sporting-goods store is meant to be *training* for rock climbing, not *actual* rock climbing."

Brynn waved this away. "It's like I said . . . it's all relative."

He shook his head in exasperation. "Hurry up and finish that, would you. We need to get on the road."

Brynn froze. *Get on the road?* "Could you be more specific?"

"Not without ruining the entire point."

"What point?"

He reached over and ruffled her already mussed hair. "Furthering your understanding of spontaneity. You've come along nicely from your previous paralyzed self, but you have miles to go before we can remove 'uptight' and 'rigid' from your personality profile."

"I have plans today," she said, scowling up at him.

"Exactly the problem. You have absolutely no idea how to take even the most tepid of getaways. Screw the plans." He stood and rinsed his coffee mug before putting it in the sink. "Where do you keep your luggage? And no proper suitcase. I want your oldest, ugliest duffel bag."

"But I don't have an old duffel bag," she said in confusion. "They're bad for your back. The wheeled suitcases are really much better—"

He threw up his hands. "Fine. Where's your fancy suitcase?"

She was apparently still addled by sleep, because she heard herself directing him to her luggage as she finished her cereal and coffee and tried to figure out what he was up to.

Brynn frowned when she realized he hadn't come back into the kitchen. "Will?"

She went looking for him and she walked in on her worst nightmare. "What are you doing?" she wailed, dashing toward her suitcase. "Everything will be a wrinkled mess."

"Kind of the point," he said with a grin, elbowing her out of the way and dropping a wadded-up pair of jeans into her designer suitcase. "Get some socks. The warmish kind, it's supposed to be rainy and cool."

"Just my kind of vacation," she muttered. Still, she did as instructed, pulling out a few pairs of her comfiest socks. She started to reach for her more comfortable bras and panties, but he stopped her.

"Uh-uh. The sexy stuff."

Brynn narrowed her eyes. "You're packing my oldest jeans, rattiest sweatshirts, and tennis shoes, yet you want me to bring silk and lace?"

He dropped a baggy sweater into the suitcase—unfolded—before advancing on her, backing her into the dresser. He backed her into things a lot. She liked it.

"Actually, how about we forget the silk and stockings," he said, dipping his head to nuzzle her neck. "Let's go with…nothing at all."

"Ah, so it's *that* kind of vacation," she said, letting her head dip back so he could have better access to her collarbone.

His thumbs grazed over the center of her breasts, finding her nipples hard and aching beneath the silk of her nightgown. "Definitely that kind of vacation," he agreed.

He moved his mouth to hers, but she ducked before he could make contact.

"Haven't brushed yet," she muttered.

Will paused and let out a soft laugh. "My little wild child. Fine, go brush. But *no flossing*. We've got to get going."

"Going where? And you said this was a spontaneous trip. Surely it can be delayed a few minutes."

"Just…go get in the shower, would you?" he said, jerking his thumb over his shoulder toward the bathroom. "I'll finish packing."

"I don't think you can call it that," she said as she watched him put her dirty shoes on top of a white shirt. Disaster.

"Your five minutes are counting down."

Her jaw dropped. "Five minutes? I can't get ready that quickly."

Will shrugged without looking at her. "Guess I leave without you."

Brynn's eyes narrowed, unsure of whether she believed him or not. She decided she didn't want to risk it, and scampered toward the shower, then showered in record time.

Will Thatcher had planned a romantic getaway with her.

The thought made her smile more than it should have.

CHAPTER EIGHTEEN

The best vacations are the cultural variety.

—Brynn Dalton's Rules for an
Exemplary Life, #2

You weren't kidding about the cold and the rainy."

Will sucked in an appreciative breath of cool ocean air. "But cold and rainy by the sea is much better than cold and rainy in the city, is it not?"

Brynn watched a seagull swoop low over the dark gray water before disappearing into the mist. With the exception of the crashing surf, the seagull was the only moving thing she could see for miles.

"It's wonderful," she breathed, bracing her forearms on the deck railing and taking it all in.

Will mimicked her posture. "I thought you might like it."

She glanced at him out of the corner of her eye, watching the way his blue eyes soaked in the quiet, peaceful nature scene just as hers had. "I admit I'm surprised," she said lightly, bumping him with her hip. "For all your yammering about adventure and rebellion, I was expecting a casino or a nudist colony or something."

"How about a nudist colony for two?" He wiggled his eyebrows.

"Depends if you can figure out how to get that huge fireplace in commission."

"Of course I can. I was a Boy Scout."

"You were?"

The corner of his mouth tilted up. "Definitely not. But I do always carry protection. Wanna see?"

"I'm pretty sure condom supply is not what they're teaching in Boy Scouts these days."

Brynn tilted her head up and felt the beginning of drizzle against her cheeks. Normally she would have been ducking for cover at the first sign of moisture in the air, but today she just stayed, loving the coolness against her face.

When she finally straightened, she found Will watching her with an unreadable expression. The look was oddly intense, and she forced a smile to lighten the moment even as she wanted to beg him to kiss her in the rain with the Pacific Ocean crashing noisily in the background.

With every additional moment she spent with Will, she feared more and more that there was nothing easy and casual about what they were doing. Every look, every kiss hinted at more.

And it scared the crap out of her.

"Tell me you brought some food in one of those huge coolers," Brynn said, trying to lighten the strangely intimate mood.

The old, easy Will returned instantly as he pushed back from the rail and headed inside. "Of course I brought food. Nothing organic, though, and I don't want to hear one peep about preservatives or nitrates."

"Exactly how long have you been planning this?" Brynn asked as she trailed after him.

For all his yammering about spontaneity, it was clear that Will had put a decent amount of thought into this little getaway. By the time she'd hurriedly showered and dressed that morning, he'd already loaded her suitcase into his car along with a couple of coolers and his own black leather bag.

The car ride had been complete with a road-mix sound track and a thermos of hot chocolate, and the guy hadn't once looked at a map to know where they were going. *Spontaneous my ass.*

Brynn had never heard of Moclips before now, but from the looks of it, it was one of those cute Washington coastal towns that she'd always meant to visit on a whim. Instead, she'd ended up going on elaborate vacations that took eighteen months to plan.

Even the house they were staying in was perfect. From the outside it had looked sort of rustic and plain, but the owner had obviously spared no expense on the inside. Granite countertops in the kitchen, rich dark leather sofas in the living room, and the biggest fireplace she'd ever seen.

She hadn't seen the bedroom yet, but she'd bet big money that there was a big bed.

"How'd you say you found this place?"

Will opened one of the coolers and pulled out a couple of sandwiches. Brynn's fingers fumbled a little as she opened the sandwich he gave her and found her favorite combination of all time: turkey, cucumber, and Brie.

It's not a sandwich that one accidentally threw together. And she was reasonably sure that she'd never told him her favorite sandwich. And yet he'd known.

Her spine tingled a little in warning.

"One of my biz-dev guys bought the house for next to nothing a few years ago and fixed it up. There's been an open-ended invitation for a while, but I've never taken him up on it."

"You say that like it's supposed to mean something to me," Brynn said around a mouthful of sandwich. " 'Biz-dev' ... ?"

"Business development," Will said, unwrapping his own sandwich. Brynn had the odd urge to know what kind it was. To know him like he apparently knew her. She pushed the urge aside. Flings didn't need to know each other's food preferences.

She shook her head. "Business development? Could you be any more vague?"

He gave her a funny look. "Sounds to me like you might actually be interested in my career, Princess."

Brynn lifted a shoulder, feeling oddly embarrassed. "I'd be interested if you had one."

For a second Will looked completely stunned, and then his face registered something else entirely as he set down his untouched sandwich and stared at her. "You think I don't have a career?"

The crushed expression on his face paralyzed Brynn. *My God, I don't know him at all.*

"I, um...I guess I never thought about it. I mean, you obviously have money, but you never seem to work. I figured it was from an inheritance or taking a shortcut somewhere."

He leaned back in his chair. "Taking a shortcut?"

The sandwich that had a minute ago tasted like heaven kept wanting to get stuck in her throat. Why had she taken the conversation in this direction? "I mean, you move all over the place whenever you want, you don't wear suits, you don't work nine-to-five..."

"Well, gosh, if I don't have tassels on my shoes and a company-sponsored 401(k), then I must be an unemployable slacker, right?"

"No!" *Maybe.* "I guess I just never understood what it is that you do. How you make your money..."

His eyes snagged hers and held. "You could have asked."

"But...I couldn't have, not really. I mean, when? Amid all that fighting and trying not to kill each other?"

"And what about the past two and a half weeks, Brynn? Have we been fighting then?"

"No...but we both know it's a temporary reprieve," she said, her words all coming together in a rush. "It's not like we entered this thing with a get-to-know-you goal in mind."

His steady gaze told her what she'd been beginning to suspect. *I already know you.*

It was *she* who was clueless. She who was in unfamiliar waters.

The playing field wasn't nearly as level as she'd thought. And she didn't like it one bit.

"So tell me, then," she said, lowering her voice. "What is it that you do?"

Will shook his head. "Eat your sandwich. I'm going to change my clothes, and then we'll go for a walk on the beach."

He was already moving toward the bedroom, where he'd put their bags, when she reached out a hand to grab his wrist. "Will, talk to me. I want to know—"

"No, you don't, Brynn. You think you care now, but in a week, when this is all over, you won't care whether I'm a billionaire or a bankrupt bum who drinks beer all day in his underwear."

"Well, at least I'd get a good view from my window," she said, trying for teasing.

He pulled his arm out of her grasp and walked away.

Brynn picked up the sandwich and took a mechanical bite even as her eyes stared unseeingly straight ahead at the dopey sailboat artwork. She'd been through a gamut of emotions over the past few months, but this was the first time that she felt good and truly ashamed.

She'd put endless energy into making sure she only saw Will as a callous womanizer with no care beyond bra cup size.

But it was *Brynn* who was the real user in this entire thing.

She'd been treating him like a glorified booty call. The sandwich turned sour in her stomach as she thought of all the times she could have asked him something about himself. *Anything* about himself.

But she'd been too busy looking for her next lay, worrying about *her* life, and getting riled up every time he wasn't at her every beck and call.

She thought he'd wanted it that way, just as she had.

Obviously she'd been wrong.

"You ready?" he asked, coming out of the bedroom wearing faded jeans and a pullover fleece instead of the shorts and T-shirt of before. "You should grab a sweater or something. It's colder along the water."

Brynn hadn't even eaten half of her sandwich, and he hadn't eaten any of his, but neither of them seemed to care. Brynn dug in her suitcase for a sweatshirt, eager to join him before he changed his mind and went on a walk without her. Or worse, before he turned around and headed back home to find someone who cared about his work life. Or any part of his life.

They walked in silence down the long winding staircase toward the beach. The rain had died down to a faint mist, but the wind had picked up, whipping around them, carrying away the words they weren't saying.

Will leaned down to take his shoes off, and Brynn did the same, despite the fact that the wind was cold, and the wet sand would be even colder.

It *was* colder, but it was also delicious, and Brynn curled her toes into the damp, chilly sand and took in a deep breath.

"I'm surprised you're not freaking out about hypothermia, or bugs, or stepping on glass."

Brynn gazed out at the gray, whipping ocean that was so comforting in its intense monotony. Routine could be powerful. But it didn't have to be dull. She would do well to remember that when she went back to her real life. "I'm not afraid of anything right now."

Will silently extended a hand toward her, and she took it. He twined his fingers with hers in a way she usually associated with romance and sweetness.

Not Will's usual cup of tea. But perhaps he'd changed.

Or perhaps she'd been blind.

They walked hand in hand down the deserted beach, far enough to the water that the sand grew firm beneath their feet, but not close enough so that the frigid Pacific waters nipped at their toes. Brynn didn't know how long they walked, silently, hand in hand.

And it was the calmest she'd felt in weeks. Maybe months. Hell, it was the most at peace she'd felt in *years*, and she was experiencing it with the person she'd always associated with chaos and crassness.

She almost found herself wanting to confide in him. To explain that she didn't mean to be so damn focused on doing everything right, but that she was afraid that if she stopped trying, she would be an outcast.

She waited for the usual sense of justification that came from recalling the miserable childhood memories.

Waited to feel the usual sense of recommitment to making sure she never gave anyone anything to criticize.

However, this time, the memories felt stale...like maybe it was time to let them go...

But she couldn't. Not yet. Those memories had shaped her. Without them...

She didn't even know what she'd be. *Whom* she'd be.

Eventually they came across a more populated part of the beach where a rowdy group appeared to be attempting a clambake, even though the weather wasn't cooperating.

In silent agreement, they turned around and began heading back toward the house. By the time they made it back to their shoes it had started to rain, and between the gritty sand and the continual drizzle, Brynn had a heck of a time trying to put her impractical ballet flats back on.

"Fuck it," Will finally muttered. He grabbed her shoes from her hands and thrust them at her before scooping her up against his chest, one arm hooked beneath her knees in the classic Rhett Butler style.

"Why, William Thatcher, I didn't know you had these kinds of moves," she said, trying for coy and failing miserably.

"There's a lot you don't know about me."

It was a blatant reminder of their disastrous conversation from earlier, and Brynn's smile slipped. But Will was apparently ready to forgive and forget, because instead of lapsing into a male sulk, he stamped a hard kiss on her mouth.

Brynn knew what he was offering—forgiveness—and she grasped at it eagerly, hooking a hand behind his neck and keeping his cool lips locked against hers as she slipped her tongue into his mouth and took the kiss deeper.

Their tongues waged a hot, wet war as they kissed as furiously as they'd ever argued. Their teeth bumped, and his stubble burned her chin, but she didn't let go, not until they were both gasping for air and bursting for more.

Will pulled back with a muttered oath, and he began taking the steps two at a time. She squirmed to be put down when they reached the back door, but he held her still, somehow managing to open the sliding door with his elbow and hip. Will headed immediately for the bedroom, and every part of Brynn throbbed in anticipation.

He gently set her on her feet in the bathroom, and she

reached eagerly for the hem of his fleece. Will stilled her hands.

"You can shower here. I'll use the second shower."

He didn't meet her eyes as he left the bathroom, and Brynn stood there for several seconds, before she realized she was frigid, and the sand was starting to make her feet itch. Numbly, she stripped, leaving her clothes in a messy pile as she stepped into the open-styled stone shower.

She stood there for long minutes, letting the hot water rush over her, even as she wished it was Will's deft, capable hands doing the warming.

What was the point of a weekend getaway with sexy lingerie if a guy turned down a prime opportunity for shower sex? And she knew his preferences by now. Will *loved* shower sex. Loved when she sank to her knees and took him in her mouth...

Brynn let out a frustrated groan as she shut the water off and snatched one of the fluffy blue towels.

She took her sweet time drying her hair, not only to ward off the chill, but to try and gather her thoughts. What the hell was going on here? They'd been angry, they'd been frustrated, and they'd been hot for each other, but they'd never been *this*. She'd never felt uneasy around him.

And he'd never been wary.

She sensed they were circling something that was both precious and fragile, but damn if she knew what it was.

Pulling on a pair of wrinkled pink-and-white PJ pants and a fuzzy white sweater, she wandered out into the main living area. She was pretty sure she'd seen wine in his arsenal of supplies. Perhaps that would help.

Brynn froze at the scene in front of her.

He must have been a Boy Scout after all, because the fire was huge and crackling. The scene in front of the fire was even more intriguing. Wine. A cheese plate. And a thick, soft-looking blanket that practically advertised *writhe on me*.

But it wasn't any of that that made her breath catch.

It was Will, blond hair darker than usual for being wet as it fell across his forehead. Like her, he was clad in PJ pants, but unlike her he'd forgone the shirt, as though he knew that his abs were her Achilles' heel.

And then she saw his eyes, and her heart dropped an entire foot to her stomach.

He's scared.

Brynn moved slowly toward him, stopping when they were scant inches away, but not touching. Wordlessly, she reached for his hand. Put it against her cheek. *I'm scared too.*

His eyes closed and he let out a shuddering breath. When they opened again, they were more like the Will she'd come to know, although there was still something odd about his expression. Something she didn't know how to read.

His other hand moved up to cup her face as he slowly moved his face toward hers, giving her a chance to run away. To take them back to their usual frenetic pace instead of this slow, dreamy firelight seduction.

And even though every instinct was yelling *mistake*, Brynn wanted to know him like this. Just once, she wanted to know this part of Will Thatcher before they were gone from each other's lives.

They kissed each other slow and sweet, as their lips teased and explored, tongues barely touching as they breathed in each other's scent, listened to what made the other person's breath catch. He continued to hold her face in the most gentle of caresses and Brynn felt the inexplicable urge to cry.

When he finally lowered her to the blanket, she waited for him to speed it up, to take them somewhere fast and safe, but he refused to be hurried as he ran a hand lovingly along her side, his palm just barely brushing the places that she wanted him to touch.

"Brynn," he said quietly. "Brynn, I..."

She grabbed his hair, pulling his mouth down to hers before he could say something that would destroy her. Destroy them both.

A hot hand slid up under the back of her sweater, his palm pressing into the damp hollow at the base of her spine, tilting her up to him, even as he kept the kisses slow and drugging.

"Let me make love to you," he whispered against her lips.

Brynn nodded, helpless to do anything else but accept whatever he was offering.

She lifted her hands over her head as he slowly pulled the sweater up and off, before pulling back slightly and looking down at her.

"You're beautiful," he said quietly, moving a hand beneath her breast and lifting her slightly. "Perfect."

"I'm small," she said nervously.

He showed her what he thought of that by lowering his head slowly and swiping the flat of his tongue against her nipple, making her gasp.

"Perfect," he said again, before giving the other breast the same treatment. Back and forth he went, licking and nibbling until she was making small keening noises she didn't even recognize. He glanced up at her then, waited until she met his eyes and then closed his lips around her nipple and sucked hard, her hips bucking up against his as she said his name.

"Again," he said, raking his teeth over her nipple. "Say my name again."

"Will," she said, her voice breaking slightly.

He slowly moved down her body, kissing every one of her ribs before slowly sliding her pants off. He smiled in gratification when he saw she was completely naked.

"No underwear," he said gruffly.

She licked her lips and looked down at where his face hovered above her hips. "Seems someone forgot to pack them."

Will slowly pushed her legs apart, sliding his hands beneath her butt and meeting her eyes once more. "It was so I could do this."

And then his mouth was on her, loving her in a way that she'd always thought was depraved, but felt so damn *right*.

Brynn had always been too distracted by the intimacy of the act to lose herself in it before, but Will wasn't accepting anything but complete capitulation as he sucked and stroked and licked in exactly the right way.

Brynn felt his hand shift, his thumb slipping inside of her before he pushed the flat of his tongue against the sensitive nub of nerve endings, licking her in small, tight circles until she was helpless to do anything but rotate against him.

Together they found the perfect rhythm until Brynn broke into a million pieces, grasping at the blanket beneath her as her hips arched up against his wet mouth.

As the fireworks turned into tiny aftershocks, Will planted tiny kisses along her inner thighs before moving back up her body and finding her mouth was his.

"So that's how Will Thatcher makes love," she said dreamily between kisses.

He moved his mouth to her closed eyelids, kissing them each in turn before planting a lingering kiss on her forehead.

"No. This is."

Her legs fell open against the gentle pressure of his hands, and she felt the tip of him against her sensitive opening before he pressed all the way in. Her eyes squeezed shut at the perfection of the moment, and her mind had the fleeting, alarming thought that *this* is where she belonged. Always. He stayed still, waiting for her to open her eyes. When she did, Will gave the tiniest of nods as though confirming her traitorous thoughts. As though confirming that she was his. But then he started moving, and her thoughts were pushed aside by pure sexual pleasure.

She wrapped her legs around his waist, giving herself over to him, but instead of taking her harder, he kept the pace steady and slow until she thought she'd die from anticipation.

Wanting to send him over the edge like he had her, Brynn moved quickly, catching him off guard enough to give her the chance to roll him onto his back.

His eyes widened slightly as she raked nails over his chest before she took him inside her with deliberate precision, watching his face tense as she took him inch by inch.

"Brynn," he said hoarsely.

She allowed herself a small smile, even though she could barely think. "I like when you say my name too."

His hands found her hips, and Brynn began to ride him, refusing to let herself worry about all her sharp angles, or how small her breasts must look.

She only cared about making Will feel.

Only cared about *Will*.

He tried to maintain the tantalizing slowness of before, but she wouldn't let him, moving faster and faster, milking him for everything he had. Only when his eyes squeezed shut in that way that told her he was close did she slide a hand down her belly to touch herself, moving her hand and hips in rhythm until Will let out a hoarse guttural cry, his body arching toward hers just as Brynn exploded for the second time.

Brynn tried to ease herself down gently, but her muscles didn't seem to work, and instead she collapsed awkwardly on his chest.

Will didn't seem to mind, instead wrapping shaking arms around her narrow back, and holding her pressed against his furry chest.

They were both damp and sweaty and panting, and it should have been gross, but instead it was unexpectedly perfect.

Eventually he rolled her off him so she was lying on her side. He pulled the blanket up over her shoulder as he pushed her hair back from her face.

"You hungry?" he asked. "I got some of that stinky bleu cheese you like. And the weird rice crackers that taste like air, except without as much flavor."

She smiled and wiggled closer. "Later. Can we...can we sleep like this? Together?"

His eyes went soft as he eased back down beside her. "Of course we can."

Brynn smiled into his crinkly chest hair and let her eyes close as the aftermath of two fantastic orgasms settled her.

But the subconscious was a wily little happiness-wrecker, and before she drifted off to sleep, she kept picturing Will's face as it had looked when he'd first laid her on the blanket.

Brynn, I...

What had he been about to say?

And why had she been so desperate to make sure he didn't?

CHAPTER NINETEEN

There's no shame in being in love with your career.

—Brynn Dalton's Rules for an
Exemplary Life, #6

"Hey."

Brynn's head shot up from her locker at the unfamiliar male voice.

She nearly dropped her geometry book.

It was him.

She'd seen him several times since that day on the football field. Had felt his eyes on her across the cafeteria, across the courtyard.

It should have been creepy, but it was oddly exhilarating. And not just because he was a junior and one of the most popular guys in school.

It was like he saw her. Knew her.

"Hey," she said back, keeping her voice as level as possible even though she kind of wanted to puke. She'd never been good at talking to guys. Mostly because they'd never wanted to talk except to ask if she was re-lated to Mr. Ed. Or to tell her there was a wait list on the swings.

She'd like to think that most of them had grown out of their meanness by now, but she wasn't taking any chances.

Much better to keep her distance.

Her heart still pounding, she closed her locker and be-gan walking in the direction of class. She realized too late that she was walking in the opposite direction as her ge-ometry classroom, but she couldn't very well turn around now. Not when he was already following her.

"I'm Will," he said, easily matching her pace, watch-ing her face as she walked.

"Congratulations," she said, not glancing up at him.

Stop being a bitch, her mind ordered.

But it was as though her brain was putting up walls, trying to protect her from this too-gorgeous guy who couldn't possibly be interested in her. The dry sarcasm was just there. Keeping her safe.

He let out a little laugh. "And you are…"

She didn't answer. Too afraid that she'd say Dumpy Dalton by accident. Because sometimes preemption was the best defense.

"It's Brynn, right?"

"Ding ding ding, give the boy a prize."

His hand lightly touched her elbow, and she had the strangest urge to lean into this boy she didn't even know.

She swallowed nervously and came to a halt.

"You're nervous," he said softly, giving her a sweet little smile.

Well, duh, the hottest guy in school is talking to a nerdy, quiet freshman, so . . . yeah, I'm nervous.

"Nervous or uninterested?" she heard herself say.

His head snapped back a little, and his eyes were considering, as though to say, so it's going to be like that, then?

She forced herself to meet his gaze, as she silently answered back. Yeah, it's going to be like that. Don't pretend that you're interested.

He gave a curt nod, his expression somewhere between irritation and disdain.

"See you around, Princess."

"Whatever," she muttered, flipping her hair over her shoulder.

She felt his eyes on her back all the way down the hall, and she wanted to turn around and apologize. Wanted to turn back and ask for a do-over. Wanted to explain that she didn't know how to act around a boy who was nice to her.

That she was afraid that it wasn't real.

Finally she worked up the courage to turn back.

But he was already gone.

* * *

It took Will several minutes to figure out what he was looking at.

He pulled himself into a sitting position, wincing a little at his sore back. Apparently, he was past his days of being able to sleep on the floor all night without repercussions. He rubbed one hand over his face groggily as he accepted the mug of coffee that Brynn held out.

He would have been able to tell it from her face, but he didn't have to. Her clothing and the suitcase by the door said it all.

"You're already dressed," he said simply.

She nodded once from where she sat on the hearth. The fire had gone out long ago, leaving nothing but dark, depressing ashes in its place.

The symbolism wasn't lost on him.

He took a bracing sip of coffee as his eyes swept over her put-together face. She'd applied makeup he hadn't even known she'd brought with her. This wasn't the rumpled Brynn on a casual beach vacation.

This was carefully styled career Brynn.

She pressed her lips together before folding her hands and carefully setting them in her lap, her shoulders back and straight, and her sterling posture confirmed what he'd known the second he'd seen her.

The old Brynn was back.

"I got a call from Susan today," she said, her voice steady and even.

Will shook his head to indicate he didn't follow.

"Susan's my partner. She's been covering me while I've been on this little...meltdown."

Will didn't misinterpret her word choice. Meltdown. Not adventure, or vacation, or even rebellion.

It had been a *meltdown*.

Her time had been cut short and now she had to justify it to herself. He got it. Had been waiting for it. Didn't mean he was going to make it easy for her.

Will didn't say a word. Didn't prompt her. Didn't give her a reassuring smile. He just waited.

"Anyway," she said, licking her lips nervously. "Susan's mom had a stroke. She's flying down to San Jose this afternoon and will be in California for at least a week."

"There's nobody else who can cover?"

"Well, there's Dr. Anders, but he's not ready to handle the whole office by himself."

"So what, you just go rushing back? Cut your vacation short?"

She gave a short huff of irritation. "It's a Tuesday, Will. It's time I start being an adult."

His head snapped back slightly at the scorn in her voice, and he remembered her blatant dismissal of his own "work" the day before. Never mind that he had more money than he knew what to do with and had worked his ass off to launch some of the most innovative start-ups in the tech world. Never mind that he'd stepped back and put all of *his* companies on autopilot so that he could help her with *her* life.

"Got it. Better get going, then," he said, calmly setting the coffee mug on the hearth and getting to his feet, not caring that he was buck-ass naked.

She averted her eyes and blushed, and damn if that didn't just about say it all.

By the time Will got out of the shower, Brynn had already put half the stuff in the car and was wrestling with the big blue cooler, which was still heavy because it was still full. Full with food for a long getaway.

Full of hope for something that had just disappeared.

Will shook the maudlin thought from his head as he

wordlessly pushed her out of the way and easily lifted the cooler into the trunk before tossing his duffel on top.

"Ready?"

If she noticed his curt tone, she didn't show it, and she merely nodded before climbing into the passenger seat as he locked up the house. The overcast skies of yesterday were long gone, and the sun was warm and bright on his face as he headed toward the car.

It was an absolutely perfect day for the beach picnic he'd planned, and he opened his mouth to coax her into it.

But then he caught her glance at her watch and give a little sigh. *So no picnic, then.*

Will resisted the urge to slap his fist on the roof of the car before he took a deep breath and slid behind the wheel. He'd known it would come to this, but that didn't mean he had to like it.

Brynn made pleasant, inane conversation most of the drive home, but he couldn't manage more than a few forced smiles and courtesy laughs at her carefully worded stories.

This was dinner-party Brynn. And he *hated* it.

Finally she ran out of meaningless things to say and they rode in strained silence for the last thirty minutes of the trip.

By the time he pulled into Brynn's driveway, his knuckles were clenched around the steering wheel. He'd spent the entire drive trying not to bellow like a wounded bear at her lack of acknowledgment of what had happened last night.

She was going to pretend that it hadn't happened. That *they* hadn't happened.

"You don't have to see me in," she said, putting a bright smile on her face.

His hand faltered briefly as he reached for her suitcase, half tempted to let her get the bag herself and scurry into the safety of her house where she could retreat behind nine-to-five and cardigans. Leaving him free to do...well, shit, he didn't have the faintest idea.

Will yanked her bag out of the car with more force than necessary and waited patiently while she let him inside, both of them all polite manners as they were careful not to touch, not even in the most accidental of brushes.

It was only when he'd set her suitcase by the stairs and turned to face her that he saw a tiny break in her placid reserve. There was the briefest crumpling of her face, and he wanted to believe it was pain, regret, but then her expression went blank again and her spine stiffened with something else entirely.

Impatience.

She wanted him out of her house. Out of her life.

He forced himself to accept what he'd been suspecting the entire day.

He'd failed.

And it *hurt*.

Will allowed himself to meet her eyes—really meet them—for the first time since he'd woken up that morning and seen her with her suitcase.

"Just like that, then?" he asked.

"Will..."

He crossed his arms over his chest and gave her his best derisive, *you don't matter* smile. "I get it, Princess. No room for unemployed boy toys in your real life, huh?"

Her mouth went stubborn. "It's not like that."

"No? What's it like?"

Her silence spoke volumes.

When she finally opened her mouth, he already knew what was coming. "You knew this wouldn't last. We both went into this eyes wide open, knowing it was a fling. Knowing that we're horrible together."

I *didn't know.* The thought felt like it was ripped from the deepest part of him.

"We're good in the only area that matters, though," he said instead, letting his eyes linger insultingly on her chest.

It was exactly the fuel she'd needed. "See that? *That* is why someone like me would never be with someone like you. You're all about the short-term gratification of sex and don't have a clue about how to build something lasting. How to build something that matters."

"You're absolutely right, Princess. Perhaps I should just get myself a journal and start writing a bunch of arbitrary goals that I'll fail miserably at."

"I am *not* failing at my goals." She jabbed a finger at him. "I intentionally set them aside to get some perspective."

"And did you?" he asked in a low voice. "Did you get perspective?"

Come on, Brynn, he silently coaxed her. *Dig beneath that pretty, boring surface.*

She opened her mouth before closing it quickly and staring blankly over his shoulder. His heart sank. She wasn't going to reach for it—wasn't going to reach for *him*.

"So what's next, then? You go back to your boring routine and spend your life covering up your tattoo? Covering up the past few weeks?" *Covering up who you really are?*

"Why are you acting like this?" she asked irritably. "I haven't *once* indicated that this was anything but a phase. I even set an *end* date."

"Which isn't for another six days."

He'd been counting. Carefully.

She shrugged. "What difference does it make? Today or next week…it'll end the same."

He tilted his head back, reading between the lines. It would end with her finding some boring lawyer with a briefcase and him trying to fill the void with an endless string of women who weren't Brynn. Who would *never* be Brynn.

He tried one more time, taking a small step forward. "Brynny, it's okay to just let yourself *be*. Nobody's going to criticize the real you, if *you* don't criticize the real you."

It was the wrong thing to say.

Her eyes shuttered completely, and she took a step backward. "You don't know everything about me," she snapped.

So tell me.

But she didn't.

"Got it," he said with a nod. "So if we happen to be in the yard at the same time, I'll just wave, then? Or do I pretend you're not there?"

She sighed. "Will…"

"How about if we're getting the mail at the same time? Should I compliment the good condition of your front lawn? Because God knows I won't have access to your *other* lawn…"

"Hey!"

"Well, what's it going to be, Brynn?" he asked, keeping his voice low even though his temper was straining. "You're clearly in charge here, so I'd love to know what it says in your little planner about what happens now."

"I thought..." She pursed her lips. "I thought we could just go back to the way we were."

He snorted. "At each other's throats, dripping with sexual tension?"

"It wasn't *just* sexual tension. You've always hated me. It's not until I let you into my pants that you've pretended to be nice."

You stupid little fool.

"Right. Well, thank God I don't have to hide my dislike anymore," he said in a low voice.

"Thank God," she said, her voice faint.

"And you won't either," he continued, pressing her. "All the disdain you've kept carefully at bay the past few weeks can come spilling out."

"I've enjoyed the past few weeks!" she yelled.

She looked as surprised at her outburst as he felt.

"Yeah?" he asked carefully. Careful to keep his voice casual. Curious, rather than desperate.

"Yeah," she said with a shrug. "I also really like butter pecan ice cream, doesn't mean it's good for me every day."

She might as well have stabbed him.

A harsh laugh came out of his mouth. "Okay, then. Got it. This tub of Häagen-Dazs will just get himself back to his own house, yeah?"

His hand went for the handle of the front door when her voice stopped him, a quiet, tentative plea. "One last thing."

Will froze, but didn't turn around.

"Last night . . . the fire, the candles . . . the . . . intensity . . . What was that?"

It wasn't easy for her to ask. He knew that. It also revealed that she recognized a tiny crack in her carefully laid plan.

But the question was too little, too late. He was done helping her find answers. Done providing them for her.

She was on her own.

"Last night is what I like to call the sexual grand finale." He shot her a steady, cool look over his shoulder. "I'm not surprised you dug it. Most women do."

He wasn't the only one that could read between the lines. He saw in her narrowed blue eyes that she caught his implication. *Last night was commonplace. You're not the only one.*

"Well, for what it's worth, it needed some work," she said in a waspish tone.

He gave a careless shrug as he opened the door. "I did the best I could with a subpar partner."

And just like that, they were back to where they started.

Like they hadn't gone anywhere at all.

CHAPTER TWENTY

*Your parents have the right to only
know you as their little girl.*

—Brynn Dalton's Rules for an
Exemplary Life, #52

*N*ow, tell me again why you cut your hair, honey?"

Brynn plucked a fancy olive off one of her mother's trademark hors d'oeuvre platters and mentally patted herself on the back for dyeing her hair back to its natural blonde color before trying to survive dinner with her parents.

If her mother was having this much trouble adjusting to the choppy layers, the dark color might have made her swoon.

To say nothing of the tattoo that her mom would absolutely never see.

One step closer...

"Just wanted a little change," Brynn said as she reached for the pile of cloth napkins and began carefully sticking them through her mother's pewter napkin rings.

But Marnie Dalton had never been one of those mothers who was content to be blissfully ignorant of what her daughters were up to, and neither was she a live-and-let-live personality.

And right now, Brynn was wishing she and her mother had just a *little* less in common, because she knew her mom was seeing right through her.

Right to that tattoo, and right to the stain that Will Thatcher had left on her...well, not her heart. But somewhere.

"Just a change, huh? Just like this little hiatus from your career was a change?"

Her mom had stopped short of calling Brynn irresponsible, but Brynn heard it anyway. She knew that tone from dozens of *I'm disappointed* talks. Only, those lectures had never been directed at Brynn. Sophie had always been the one to drive her mother batty with her refusal to do anything "expected" for much of the past ten years. Only Sophie's marriage to someone as classically conservative as Gray had managed to appease Marnie.

Apparently their mother had decided to channel her meddling energy elsewhere, and Brynn was really wishing she had another sibling right about now. Anyone to deflect her mom's speculative gaze.

"Come on, Mom, haven't you ever needed a little break from yourself?"

To Brynn's surprise, her mom paused in slicing a tomato and appeared to put genuine thought to the question. "A break from myself? I don't think so. I'm not sure what I would need a break from."

Brynn hid a smile at her mom's immodesty. "Is it hard, then? Being so perfect, I mean?"

Marnie raised an eyebrow and went back to slicing her tomato. "You've been hanging out with your sister, I presume. Such sass is usually Sophie's bit."

Actually, Brynn had always been every bit as sassy as Sophie, it had just rarely left her mouth. But Brynn wasn't about to confess to her mother that it hadn't been her sister who'd brought about the more caustic change in Brynn. That it had been Will who'd made Brynn feel the most like herself that she'd felt in years—maybe ever.

Trouble was, it wasn't the self she wanted to be.

Brynn resisted the urge to go to her purse and pull out her trusty notebook. After weeks without looking at it, she'd practically slept with it every night since Will had stormed out of her house a week earlier. Had needed it to remind her that it was time to start making Good Choices.

Her dad came in from the backyard, where he'd been fussing with the grill, planting an absent kiss on the side of her head before washing his hands.

"Chris, what do you think of Brynn's hair?"

Oh Lord.

Like his wife, Chris Dalton was tall, blond, and handsome. Unlike his wife, he didn't give a crap about his daughter's hairstyle.

He dried his hands as he examined her hair. "Looks about the same to me. Pretty as ever."

Brynn beamed at her father as Marnie made a scoffing noise.

"So, Brynnster, I was beginning to think you'd gone and outgrown Sunday dinners with the family," Chris said, helping himself to Marnie's appetizer platter.

As far as guilt trips went, Chris had a lot to learn from his wife, but that didn't mean the comment didn't cause a little jolt of regret at having disappeared from her parents' life for the past few weeks with no explanation.

"Just sort of taking some time to myself, ya know?" *God, I'm lame.*

Her dad nodded. "Sorry to hear about James. We really liked him."

James?

For a second, Brynn's mind went completely blank as though trying to place him. How strange that she'd hardly given the guy a passing thought recently. But of course her parents would assume it was a breakup with a serious boyfriend that would have her turning hermit for a few weeks. They probably imagined her sitting alone eating ice cream in her bathrobe all day.

It was a safe assumption—much better than what she'd actually been doing. She had a vivid mental picture of how warm Will's eyes had looked by the firelight that last night together. It was quickly followed by the disgust on his face the day after when he'd walked out of her life.

Which was your idea. Let it go.

"I guess he wasn't the one," Brynn said lightly. She wasn't even sure to whom she was referring anymore.

"Always thought it was a good match, though," her dad continued. "James was stable, reliable, driven... You had all the important things in common."

All the important things, huh? Just a month ago Brynn

would have agreed. Just a month ago, her dad's words could have come out of Brynn's own mouth.

But now...

"Dad, did you just call me boring?"

His mouth paused in chewing a piece of some fancy deli meat and Marnie's head shot up as they both stared at her. "Of course not," her father said, his face the picture of confusion. "I thought I was complimenting you."

She gave a small smile. In his mind, he probably had thought that. To the Daltons, there was no greater compliment than "reliable." It was the reason Brynn had always gotten along so well with her parents while Sophie had ruffled feathers with every job she'd quit on a whim.

And speaking of...

"Where's Soph?"

Marnie let out the tiniest of sighs. "Not coming. If it's not one daughter avoiding me, it's the other."

Brynn didn't resist the eye roll. "Laying it on just a little thick, Mom."

Still, she was a little surprised that Sophie hadn't mentioned not coming to the Sunday dinner. They usually gave each other a heads-up before leaving the other alone with the parents.

"Did she say why?"

Marnie shrugged. "Something about not being in the mood for fireworks. I can never follow that girl."

Brynn's eyebrow went up. Fireworks? At a Dalton family dinner? The closest they'd ever come to that was when Sophie had completely lost her shit and accused them all of belittling her existence.

It had been a spectacular explosion.

And, sadly, completely justified.

The front door opened and Brynn felt a little jolt of relief. Apparently Sophie had changed her mind.

She got up to greet her sister and dodge any more *James was the best* talks, but she froze when she heard a familiar laugh. And not Sophie's.

Her skin went hot. Then cold.

Oh. Hell. No.

"Will's coming to dinner?" She practically choked out the question, but her parents barely noticed. The entire family had learned to turn a blind eye to Brynn and Will's angry history. Probably because they didn't even have a clue what that history entailed.

"Of course he's coming," Marnie said with a scolding look. "He's always been part of the family. He's been here almost every Sunday since moving back to town."

Her mother left it there, but Brynn heard what was unsaid. *Unlike you.*

So Will had been going to her family's family dinners without her. The thought was unnerving. Had he said anything about her?

But Brynn rapidly realized that her parents were the least of her worries.

Because Will wasn't alone.

Despite what Brynn liked to think of as her exacting standards, she generally tried not to judge other women.

But this one? This one was a bimbo.

The hair was dark brown with too-light highlights, not even *remotely* trying to hide the fact that the color was obviously fake. The long coral fingernails . . . also fake. The spider eyelashes? Fake. The "designer" purse? Fake. The boobs? Definitely fake.

In other words, here was Will's dream girl. It made

sense that he was hanging out with this creature. He'd probably needed to detox from all of Brynn's class and sophistication.

Don't look at him. Don't look at him.

For once, her body obeyed her brain. She didn't look at him. Not once.

Not when he did introductions between her parents and Lily. Not when she shook Lily's hand. Not when her mother cooed that it was so great that Will had found a nice girl.

Brynn's eyes narrowed on her mother at that last bit. There was no *way* her parents approved of this artificial Barbie doll.

But they were all smiles, just like Lily.

Just what the hell was going on here?

This dinner was supposed to be her big comeback to her Real Life. Instead, she was the fifth wheel at her own family dinner, while her parents fawned over their pseudo-son and his all-wrong-for-him girlfriend?

Where did that thought come from?

Lily wasn't wrong for Will at all.

Brynn tried to look at the other woman through different eyes, and was dismayed to realize that she could actually see Will with someone like this. Sure, she laughed just a little too loudly, and her rambling story about how she locked her keys in her car at the mall was a bit, well…mind-numbing. But there was also a sweet openness there.

Something Brynn knew she would never have.

"So how long have you two been together?" Marnie asked as she ushered everyone into the dining room.

"Oh, we went on a few dates years ago," Lily said as

she took the salad bowl out of Marnie's hand as though she were freaking co-hostess. "Then this big jerk goes and moves across the country. But I was thrilled when he called me up this week and wanted to hang out."

Hang out. Brynn knew what that meant. And she took it like a kick to the ovaries. Will was sleeping with this woman.

"Couldn't forget her, huh, son?" Chris said, playing the dutiful fatherly role.

Will let out a low chuckle as his hand found the small of Lily's waist. "Sometimes a guy realizes he needs a little sweetness in his life."

Only years of carefully cultivated maturity stopped Brynn from gagging. She still managed not to avoid looking at Will.

It didn't matter.

It didn't matter that he'd brought a woman here just a week after they'd ended things. Didn't matter that the woman gave Will secret smiles as though she owned him.

This was *exactly* why she'd selected Will for her little fling anyway. She'd known they could both move on without losing any skin in the game.

Although when she found herself sitting across the table from the two of them and watched Lily's hand find Will's leg, it didn't quite feel like nothing.

"So you guys have been dating for…a week, then?" Brynn heard herself saying.

"Technically, yeah. But I haven't been able to get her out of my mind for the last month or so," Will said.

Brynn's spine stiffened and finally, *finally* she let her eyes meet Will's.

They were the same, boring old blue they'd always

been. Except there was a chill in them she'd never seen before. Not even during their biggest spats or their most determined stages of ignoring each other had he seemed so lifeless to her.

"Hmm, well, I can't *imagine* what took you so long to give the pretty girl a call," Brynn said in her most polite tone.

Her dad leaned in under the guise of filling up Will's glass as he gave her a warning, *Brynn*, under his breath.

She ignored her father.

Will's expression didn't change as he met hers coolly. "I've been a little busy the past few weeks," he said mildly.

"Will works like a dog," Lily chimed in.

"Not true, Lil," he said with a self-deprecating grin. "I pride myself on working as little as possible. Sort of a professional slacker, ya know?"

"Oh, I *do* know," Brynn chimed in, giving him her sourest smile. "Still, this month must have been a new record for you. It was what, three weeks without a new girlfriend?"

She was walking on dangerous territory, and she knew it, but she'd be damned if she'd sit here and listen to him blather on about how he'd been thinking about Lily in the time he and Brynn had been together.

"Well, actually, there was someone," he said, letting his voice go low and almost sad.

Brynn's eyes narrowed on him. He was calling her bluff. *He wouldn't dare.*

He arched an eyebrow at her and she took a quick sip of wine, angry that she'd taken them this direction. Of course he would call her bluff. He had nothing to lose.

She had everything to lose.

Well, at least her reputation. And her dignity...

"Lily, did Will tell you that he moved in next door to Brynn?" Marnie asked when Will failed to finish his sentence. "It's so lucky for us to have our daughter and close friend so close together. Not that either has invited us over, of course..."

Lily gave her a bright smile. "I think it's so great that you have been good friends for so long. High school, right?"

Marnie gave a nervous laugh. "Well, actually, it's our younger daughter, Sophie, who's always been thick as thieves with Will. But Will and Brynn were closer in age, so they've also been..."

Her voice trailed off as she gave an absent wave of her hand, before busying herself with passing the salad around. Apparently even Marnie's obsession with social niceties wouldn't extend to outright lying and pretending that Will and Brynn had ever been *friends*.

"So what do you do, Brynn?" Lily asked politely.

"I'm an orthodontist."

Will pretended to suddenly fall asleep before jerking himself upright. Brynn ignored him but didn't miss the fact that her dad was hiding a smile.

"And you?" Brynn said, stabbing a piece of cucumber and giving Lily a bland smile.

"I'm a website developer," Lily said. "It's actually how Will and I first met. He hired my firm a few years ago to build the Airamore microsite."

"Airamore, that's the virtual travel agent company you sold for an obscene amount of money, right?" Chris asked.

"That's the one," Will said.

Brynn's stomach felt oddly hollow, although she didn't know if it was from the fact that she'd wrongly assumed that Lily's profession would be along the lines of a "dancer," or if it was because she clearly didn't have the faintest clue about what Will had been up to all of these years.

And apparently she was the only one.

"So an orthodontist, that's so cool," Lily said.

Brynn swallowed a sip of wine and gave a tight smile. Lily apparently had noticed her discomfort and was trying to draw Brynn back into the conversation. Could she be any nicer?

"It's, um...it's..."

Tell her that being an orthodontist is thrilling. Fulfilling. That it's everything you ever wanted.

"Being an orthodontist is actually a little bit boring," Brynn heard herself say.

Lily gave her a sympathetic nod, but the rest of the table had fallen silent. Brynn didn't have to look at her parents to know that they were stunned. Brynn had decided she wanted to be an orthodontist when her recently removed braces had revealed a row of perfectly straight teeth. She had been sixteen. And never once since that day had she wavered from that course as she carefully ensured she was taking all the right classes and all the right internships to lead her in that direction.

Nobody had been surprised when she'd graduated at the top of her class. Nobody had been surprised when she'd opened her own thriving practice.

They apparently *were* surprised to learn she didn't like it.

But nobody was as surprised as she was.

It's just a phase. You just haven't gotten back into the swing of things.

Marnie opened her mouth as though to question Brynn further, but Will was faster. Only he didn't direct any questions toward Brynn. Instead, he directed conversation to Marnie and Chris's upcoming European cruise.

He had saved her.

Dammit. He'd known she wasn't ready to have that talk with her parents, and he'd helped her out. She felt a spark of anger. He shouldn't presume to rescue her from anything. He didn't even *know* her.

Except, apparently, he did. Because she really, *really* hadn't meant to say that she didn't like her job. And she sure as hell hadn't wanted to talk about it. And he'd known that.

Brynn scowled as she mechanically shoved salad into her mouth. She did the same through the main course, speaking up only to answer direct questions, and even then, she kept her answers as short as possible.

The four of them seemed to get by just fine chatting along without her, but as Marnie dished up strawberry shortcake, Brynn's reprieve was apparently over.

"Brynn, honey, have you put any further thought into that housewarming barbecue you keep talking about? You've been there a few months now, and it might be a great way to meet people…"

"Meet men, you mean," Brynn interrupted. "I know that matchmaker tone."

Marnie gave Lily a woman-to-woman smile. "Brynn just came out of a long relationship. We want to get her back on the horse."

"How do you know she hasn't already started riding again?" Will asked.

Brynn made a choking noise, and Marnie's cheeks were definitely pink with embarrassment. Brynn's poor father looked like he would rather be waterboarded than remain at the table.

Marnie recovered quickly. "Oh, well...you know Brynny, she's not the type to go rushing into anything. That's why she took some time off work. To reassesses, to heal..."

Brynn heard what her mother was saying, but she only had eyes for Will. And if looks could kill...

"Well, you know what they say about hair of the dog," Will was saying. "If it's a guy that did the damage, maybe it was a guy that did the repairs."

"Will, I think maybe this is a little inappropriate," Lily said, looking chagrined on Will's behalf. Even Fake Boobs had more sense of propriety than Will.

But it was too late. Already her mom was looking at her speculatively. "Brynn Elizabeth Dalton, have you been seeing a *man* these past few weeks?"

"No!" Brynn said, feeling her face go hot. "You're believing *him*?"

"Well, he does live next door, sweetie, and I can see how you might want to hide from your parents for a little while if you were having a little...oh, what do they call it..."

"Yeah, what do they call it?" Will asked with false curiosity. "One could say...a fling?"

"Yes, a fling!" Marnie agreed in delight. "Because, Brynn, your father and I are quite modern, and we would completely understand if you..."

"We would understand, and *we wouldn't need any details*," Chris said with a pointed look at his wife.

Marnie winked at Brynn. She mouthed, *Later*.

Brynn mouthed, *Never*, right back.

And where the *hell* was Sophie? Of all the nights her sister ditched her, it was the one where her mother apparently wanted to talk sex. And Will looked like he was about five seconds away from telling her parents that they'd screwed like bunnies.

What's the big deal? her subconscious demanded. Sophie already knew, so Gray likely did as well. What would it matter if her parents found out? They *loved* Will—they'd probably be thrilled.

The problem was her.

Brynn knew what she wanted. She went after what she wanted. Everyone knew that about her.

And Will had never been part of that plan.

She slowly forced herself to meet Will's eyes, daring him to rat her out. He held her gaze with a faint mocking smile.

Once again, it fell to poor Lily to try to keep the conversation civil. "You know, Brynn, as a lone female in a male-dominated field, I know loads of guys who'd flip over you. Let me know if you want me to set you up on a date or something."

I'll do that. Just as soon as I start watching Star Trek *and eating* SPAM *and painting zebra stripes on my fingernails*...

Will was making a rude *tsk*ing noise. "Now, Lil, you wouldn't know this because you just met Brynn, but she has a *very* exact type."

"That's true," Marnie said as she began pouring coffee.

"Doctors, dentists...the occasional lawyer..." Will was saying.

"You make me sound like a total snob," Brynn snapped.

For several seconds nobody said anything. Neither parent defended her. Nobody rushed to confirm that she wasn't a snob.

"Got it, so I'm a total bitch, then," she said, pushing her dessert plate away.

Her parents glanced at each other in confusion. "Brynn, nobody thinks that. And it's true that you've always been picky, but..."

"Not always," Will said under his breath.

Brynn fiddled with her spoon, her fingers itching for something with sharper edges that she could lodge in his solar plexus.

"Actually, Lily," Brynn said with a forced smile at Will's dinner date, "I *could* stand to expand my social circle a little. I'd love to meet one of your friends."

She resisted the urge to issue Will a smug smile. Two could play at this game.

But he looked completely unperturbed. As though the thought of her dating someone else didn't bother him in the least. Just like him bringing Lily here shouldn't bother Brynn in the least. Except it did.

In hindsight, Brynn would wish that she hadn't gotten so lost in her own musings that she'd failed to study Will's face closely enough to know what was about to happen. That she might have had a chance to stop it.

But her guard was down, and she didn't see the change in expression from pain-in-the-ass to downright asshole.

"Well, best of luck getting back out there, Princess,"

Will said, raising a glass to her in a mocking toast. "Tell me, how many dates will it take before the poor guy gets a peek at your tattoo?"

A wave of red washed in front of her eyes as she tried to tell herself that that had not just happened. That she hadn't heard Will mention her tattoo out loud. In front of her parents. In front of his new girlfriend.

Her mother snorted. "Will, don't be ridiculous."

Brynn started to reach out a hand to him. To plead. To beg. But he wasn't looking at her. Instead he was turned toward her mother, his face all boyish innocence as he widened his eyes dramatically.

"Oh, it's great, Marn," he said. "It's this cute little saying that sort of runs a sweet line from her crotch to her butt. See, I saw it up close when we—"

Brynn didn't remember tossing her strawberry shortcake at him, but she would remember everyone's stunned reaction to the goopy red dessert as berries slowly dislodged from his chest and dropped into his lap.

Without taking her eyes off his shocked face, she very primly dabbed her mouth before offering him her napkin with a sweet smile, then making a calm exit from the room. She paused only long enough to grab her purse before walking out the door.

For the first time she could remember, Brynn had just willingly turned her back on her dignity.

Because she had something much stronger to fuel her.

And anger and betrayal were one potent combination.

CHAPTER TWENTY-ONE

Falling in love is no excuse for behaving irrationally.

—Brynn Dalton's Rules for an
Exemplary Life, #14

"Can I take you out again?"

Brynn looked up at the handsome man standing on her front porch and wondered why she didn't feel more than an indifferent hum.

Evan McCain was perfect for her. Handsome, successful, conventional. A lawyer. Stable. But the first date, which was perfect on paper, had been merely pleasant. All of her usual criteria were fulfilled, but she couldn't seem to muster any excitement about a future date.

She studied his classically attractive face, and assessed. Her parents would love him—he was the ultimate son-in-law material. Her friends would approve. He'd fit in perfectly at her cousin's elaborate dinner parties.

Sophie would be the only one less than impressed. She'd write him off as "too perfect," which had never made sense to Brynn. What was better than perfect? Brynn had never understood why Sophie craved unpredictability, passion, and change. It was so messy.

But for the first time in her adult life, Brynn was beginning to wonder if her sister might be on to something. Perhaps Brynn was missing out on some crucial factor by only dating men who fulfilled her carefully configured checklist of required qualities.

She thought briefly of Will, but immediately pushed him away. Talk about a man who had none of her required qualities. Well, except for the looks, of course. Will was definitely handsome, if you liked the obvious, male-model thing.

Brynn hadn't seen him since the depraved scene on his kitchen floor a month before. He'd called a couple of times, but she hadn't picked up. He was probably calling to gloat that he'd found her underwear, which they'd been unable to locate during the awkward morning after. Brynn wasn't adept at spontaneous sexual encounters, and she certainly had no idea how to handle the aftermath of this particular mistake.

She was ashamed to admit that she'd even lied to her family about having work on Sunday nights in order to avoid seeing Will at dinner.

"Brynn? Have I lost you?" *Evan asked with a gentle smile.* "How about next weekend?"

Oh, what the hell. *The guy might be as exciting as Wonder Bread, but she was sick of being single.*

"Sure!" *she agreed with more enthusiasm than she felt.* "How about Friday?"

Evan gave a quick victorious grin, perfectly masculine

without being chauvinistic. It should have been appealing. Hell, even a month ago, it would have been appealing. Damn weddings and their false promise of romance—look at where all the talk about lifelong vows had gotten her. Up against the wall of Will Thatcher's bachelor pad.

"*Kiss me?*" *she said suddenly to Evan. He looked slightly surprised at her forwardness, but plenty willing.*

She regretted her impulsive request as soon as Evan's head dipped toward hers. But maybe the kiss of another man would banish the demon of that man. She tried to lose herself in Evan's kiss, she really did. But the harder she tried, the more she realized it wasn't right.

When they finally broke away, he too seemed aware at the lack of chemistry.

"*You're sure about Friday?*" *he asked.*

Brynn forced a smile. "Of course! I look forward to it."

He gave her a small smile, looking a lot less interested than he had before their lackluster kiss. He made some noncommittal comment about double-checking his schedule and calling her.

Brynn had given enough polite brush-offs in her dating career to recognize when she was receiving one, but she couldn't bring herself to care that this was probably the last she'd see of Evan the lawyer. She couldn't blame the guy—from the way she'd kissed, he probably thought she was frigid.

She sighed and let herself inside, anticipating a hot bath, a good book, and a cup of tea.

The sight of the man sitting on her couch had her screaming like a banshee and dropping her purse. "What the hell are you doing here?"

Will held up her latest issue of Cosmopolitan *without glancing up from the magazine. "Did you know," he said, "that the average American woman has seven sexual partners in her life? Isn't that interesting?"*

Brynn took a deep breath to steady her pounding heart.

"Which notch is Evan on your bedpost?" Will asked thoughtfully. "Five? Fourteen? Thirty?"

"You were spying on me?"

He shrugged. "Open window, perfect hearing. Very awkward."

Brynn let out a snarl. "Get out of my house. How did you even get in here?"

He sighed as though she was being an unreasonable child, and reluctantly set the magazine aside after dog-earing a page. "If you must know, your mother gave me a key. I stopped by to fix their computer and she asked if I could drop off the pie dish you left at their house."

"My house isn't even remotely *on your way home. You mean to tell me that my mother expected you to drive all the way out here for a six-dollar pie dish?"*

He merely watched her, somehow managing to look both amused and disinterested. "No. I volunteered," he said simply.

"Why would you do that?"

"To spy on you and Romeo, of course. Who was he? Accountant? Chiropractor? Does he supply the retainers for all your snaggletoothed teens?"

Brynn gave a small, secretive smile as though the thought of Evan got her juices flowing. "He was a lawyer. Very rich. Very *handsome."*

Will snorted, and followed her into the kitchen. "He sounds absolutely riveting. How was the kiss?"

"*That's some pretty thorough spying,*" she said in response.

Brynn pulled down two wineglasses even as she told herself that he would absolutely not be staying. "*Why are you here? And no more crap about my pie dish. I'm not really in the mood for company. I'm tired, cranky, and sort of…*"

"*Horny?*"

"*I was going to say* pissed *that you're in my home, unexpected, without asking. If you've come to apologize about our… episode, let's get it over with and then you can leave.*"

He frowned and stepped closer. "*Why the hell would I be apologizing? I don't apologize for fucking, Brynn. Not when the woman is as willing as you were.*"

A blush crept over her face. She *had been* willing. More than willing.

"*You're not seeing him again,*" Will said.

"*What? Who?*"

"*That idiot who was stupid enough to leave after one kiss.*"

"*The Neanderthal routine doesn't suit you, William. What can you possibly care about who I date?*"

The expression that flashed over his face might have been hurt, but it was gone before she could identify it. "*Did that night mean so little to you, Brynn? You're already looking for your next conquest?*"

She looked at him more closely. "*Aren't you? Wasn't what happened between us just the latest move in the power game we play?*"

And then she saw it again. It wasn't just hurt. It was vulnerability. Had that night mattered to him? Did she matter to him?

"Never mind," he said roughly. "I'll be going. I didn't mean to intrude upon your post-date euphoria."

The moment had passed and damn if she didn't want it back. "No, Will, wait." She reached out a hand but stopped before she touched him. "Can't we just...can't you..."

"What?" he asked, watching her intently. "What do you want?"

"I...I just wanted to make sure that you hadn't told anyone about us."

His eyes went colder than she'd ever seen them. "No. Not a soul. You weren't worth the bragging rights."

That stung, but she didn't let herself swipe back. "You should go. And I'm sick of skipping my own family's dinners so that we can avoid each other. Maybe you could miss one once in a while?"

Will gave her a disgusted look. "Exactly how old are you, Brynn?"

She blushed but stood her ground. "Look, I know it's immature, I just...I can't see you after knowing that we..."

She shuddered a little at the intensity of the memory, and saw immediately that he misinterpreted the reaction as disgust.

"All right. If that's what you want."

His voice was so dead that she almost panicked. Almost begged him to take her again. But instead she gave a businesslike nod. "Good, then we're agreed. It doesn't have to be forever. I just need a little space."

"Baby, I'm about to give you all the space you need," he said with a blank expression.

"What's that supposed to mean?" she yelled at his retreating back.

*But her only answer was the resounding slam of her
front door.*

* * *

Brynn barely remembered the drive home, but by the time
she made it up to her bedroom with the intent of taking
a bath to soothe her rage, she had several missed calls,
which she'd ignored.

There were three from her mother, each with an ac-
companying *We still love you, but are you doing drugs?*
voicemail. There were two missed calls from her sister,
which meant Sophie had been updated on big sister's
meltdown and wanted all the gritty details.

There was even a typo-ridden text from her dad saying
that his college roommate had gone into psychiatry if she
ever needed someone to talk to.

And one missed call from Will. But no voice mail.

It didn't even occur to her to hit redial. What could
possibly be said?

Brynn turned on the hot water in the tub before bracing
her hands on the vanity and taking a deep breath as she
stared at the mirror. She looked...awful.

Hair that was shorter than it had ever been before and
sticking up and curling in weird places. The fact that it
had been dyed back to her usual blonde should have been
calming, but combined with the layered cut, it was all
wrong. It was like old Brynn had collided with the new
Brynn, who had in turn tried to go back to old Brynn,
only...

She couldn't go back.

Her eyes had a wild, unhinged look that she didn't recognize, and her white blouse had pink spots from where she'd gotten blowback from the strawberry grenade she'd tossed at Will.

Her mind kept flitting back to that moment when she realized what he was going to say.

On one hand, she regretted her reaction. She could have just let it go. Given it no more reply than a rolling of the eyes, and let her parents assume it was merely round two thousand eight hundred and ninety-one in the saga that was *Will and Brynn hate each other*.

But oddly, calm had never once entered her mind.

And given a time machine, she wasn't sure she could muster up a calm reaction if she got a do-over.

Because in that moment, she hadn't been feeling calm, or annoyance, or even rage.

She'd been hurt.

Which was stupid, really. She'd known the minute she'd knocked on Will's door and asked him to have a fling that it was irresponsible. She had known on some level that having your worst enemy accompany you to a tattoo parlor was begging for trouble.

But then in some strange, unexplainable little bubble of time, she'd trusted him. Trusted him to decide what permanent brand she was putting on her body. Trusted him not to tell anyone.

Some detached, obviously moronic part of her had thought it was *their* thing. A forever marker of their ill-fated but somehow necessary time together.

And he'd thrown it in her face.

Swallowing around a lump in her throat at the ache, she dumped some of her favorite honey-almond bubbles into the steaming water and let it foam enticingly before slowly beginning to disrobe in wooden, mechanical movements.

Her eyes caught on her reflection in the mirror as she shimmied out of her skirt, and she sucked in a breath at the sight of the tattoo. Her fingernails raked over it lightly, wishing she could scratch it right off and be done with it. Be done with its memories. Her fingernails scratched harder. God, what had she been *thinking*?

"I don't think it works like that."

Brynn let out a screech at the unexpected voice as she threw her arms over herself, futilely trying to cover the essential areas. Not that it mattered. Will wasn't even trying to look at her more interesting parts.

And if Will Thatcher was passing up an opportunity to stare at her boobs, they were really and truly over.

Hot blue eyes gave her a pitying look as she grabbed for a towel and wrapped it around herself. "I don't know why you bother. It's nothing I haven't already seen, and the novelty's worn off. Not all that impressive to begin with, actually."

Brynn's chest heaved in agitation as she debated just how bad a murder charge would be. "Get out."

She didn't bother asking how he'd gotten *in*. He seemed to think that being neighbors was akin to being roommates. Will merely leaned against the doorway, clearly having no intention of going anywhere until they had this out.

She didn't even know what *this* was.

"Why'd you do it?" she asked. To her horror, her voice broke as she blinked back big pathetic tears.

Brynn saw his fist clench and unclench as his expression softened for a split second. She thought he might apologize. Maybe even reach for her.

But then his hand clenched into a fist and the shutters went down. "Why'd I do what? Tell Mommy and Daddy their daughter got herself a little ink?"

She swallowed. "That. And you let them think..."

"That we fucked?"

Brynn winced and gave a little huff of dismay. But one look at Will's angry face told her it was the wrong thing to do.

"What's wrong, you embarrassed? Embarrassed that you got caught banging someone without a 401(k)? Embarrassed that you did something the country club would frown upon?"

He advanced on her, but Brynn stood her ground. Had no choice, really, unless she wanted to back up into the tub.

"It was supposed to be our secret," she said, keeping her voice low and calm.

His face contorted in disgust. "And who decided that?"

Brynn blinked. "We did."

"No, we sure as hell didn't!" he exploded, throwing his arms in the air.

She stared at him in stunned silence. She didn't know what was more shocking, the fact that the usual implacable Will was having an outburst, or what the outburst itself suggested.

"What are you talking about?" she said, frowning in confusion. "We decided three years ago after that... mistake...that we wouldn't tell anyone."

"Did we really? Because that's not the way I remember it."

"But—"

He didn't let her finish. "The way I remember it, a woman I'd known forever showed up on my front porch, screwed my brains out, and then promptly swore me to secrecy like I was some sort of humiliating disease."

Brynn scoffed. "Don't even try to make it sound like you wanted to go public. You've always hated me."

He didn't respond, but his eyes were fierce as he moved even closer. This time, instinct *did* have Brynn stepping back until her heels hit the tub. Her heart began to pound. She'd seen a lot of versions of Will over the years, but never this one.

The man was livid.

And she had no idea why.

"Will, let's just calm down a sec. Let me put some clothes on and we can discuss this like rational adults."

He let out a harsh laugh. "Do you even hear yourself? A guy is standing here trying to tell you something and all you want to do is be rational."

Brynn licked her dry lips, all instincts on high alert. "Fine. What do you want to tell me?"

His eyes roamed over her hair, his chin resting against his chest briefly in defeat before he raised his head again. "Just forget it."

Before she realized what she was doing, she reached out a pleading hand. "Wait, I want to know—"

He backed out of her reach. "No, you don't, Brynn. You really don't. If you did, you would have shown some sort of reaction when I showed up with *another woman* at your family's house tonight."

"Well, I certainly showed emotion when you sold me out to my parents!"

His hands found her shoulders and gave her a little

shake. "And what was it you were feeling, Brynn? Anger? Embarrassment?'

Hurt.

She took a breath. Then another. And then said it. "It hurt."

His lips twisted slightly. "It was supposed to."

She shouldn't be surprised, but it still felt like a slap in the face.

"Why?" she asked in a small voice.

He ignored her question. "What exactly are you so scared of, Brynn? That all your friends will turn their backs on you because you didn't marry a doctor? My God, do you really think a *friend* would even care?"

"No," she said in a small voice.

"Then why? Why don't I even get a chance?"

"Because guys like you aren't interested in girls like me!" she exploded. "Not for keeps, anyway!"

His jaw dropped slightly. "What the hell are you even talking about? What do you mean guys like me?"

She rolled her shoulders restlessly. "You know. Popular guys. And then the not-so-popular girls."

Will stared at her for several seconds. "Hold up. Did we just take a time machine to high school? God, is that why you always date boring nerds? Because they won't reject you?"

A time machine to before *high school, actually*, she thought. But she'd already said way more than she'd wanted to. "Can you please just…leave?" she asked weakly.

"Not until you explain. Are you pushing me away because you're holding on to some shitty memories of when you were a little chubby and awkward?"

She sucked in a small breath. "You don't know anything about it."

"Damn straight! Because you never told me."

"Because it's painful," she said. She waited to feel righteous. Waited to feel justified in her confession. Instead, she felt...small. And a little pathetic.

"Look, Brynn...don't let a few ancient insecurities ruin this."

"There's nothing to ruin."

"Bullshit," he said plainly.

Her hair was sticking to her neck and it was getting increasingly harder to breathe. Why the hell was he pushing this? She needed him out. She needed space. She needed...

"We're not right for each other," she said, tightening the towel around her and forcing herself to take deep, even breaths.

"Why not?"

"Because you're all charming and easygoing, and everyone loves you just by looking at you, and you're going to wake up one day and realize that you don't want me."

Will threw his hands up in the air. "Dammit, Brynn! You're not Dumpy Dalton anymore!"

A gasp ripped out of her at his words. Words she hadn't heard in...

"Where'd you hear that name?" she whispered.

He took a deep breath. "Sophie."

She would *kill* her sister.

"Well, then she also probably told you about how I..."

"Yeah, yeah, how you were unpopular, and probably a little weird and you had bad skin, bad teeth, a limp, whatever."

A limp?

"But, Brynn...you've got to get over it."

Hot anger rushed over it. "Don't you dare. Don't you dare tell me how I'm supposed to feel. You don't know what it was like."

His face softened slightly. "You're right, I don't. And I hate that kids were mean to you. Hate that *I* was mean to you, even though all I ever wanted was for you to *look* at me. Bullying is real, and it's vicious, and I wish like hell that I could go back and beat up anyone who ever made you cry, my past self included. But it was what, fifteen years ago? You've *got* to stop letting it ruin your adult life."

It was as though his words ripped through her very soul, reaching for its most damaged nerve and searing it.

And in that moment, she really, truly hated him.

Hated even more that there was truth in his statement. Truth she wasn't ready to deal with.

"Get out," she said, after several tense moments passed between them.

He closed his eyes briefly. "If I walk out that door, I won't be coming back, Brynn. Ever."

Her stomach lurched. *Ever?* "But..."

He met her eyes. "I can't do this anymore. You're killing me from the inside out. You'll be able to walk away with a tiny little battle wound. But me? I'll be..."

Will didn't finish the sentence, but her heart began to pound anyway. "What are you talking about? You can't do *what* anymore?"

His face crumpled slightly as he reached out a finger toward her cheek. "Brynny. Do you have any idea what I felt when you showed up on my front porch that night three years ago?"

She tried for a smile to lighten the mood. "Horny?"

He didn't smile back. "I felt like my entire life was finally about to start."

Brynn literally felt her heart skip a beat.

"But it was just sex," she whispered.

He didn't respond.

"Wasn't it?" she asked, her voice cracking.

He continued as though he hadn't heard her. "I waited *so long* for you to come to me. I was on top of the world. And not even a week later, I find you on a date with some other guy."

Her mind reeled, remembering. "You came over to return something my mom asked you to drop off, not to see me. And if I remember correctly, you were a total dick. Two days later, you were gone."

His jaw tightened. "Did you care that I moved?"

No.

Yes.

Yes, I cared.

"I just thought you might have mentioned something that big, even to me," she said softly.

"I didn't mention it because I didn't know I wasn't going to move until I got on the plane."

Brynn shook her head. "What do you mean you didn't know? You moved across the country; you must have had *some* idea."

"Nope."

"That's ridiculous. Who changes three time zones without a plan?"

He gave the smallest of smiles. "You and your plans."

She took a deep breath. "So you moved because we slept together?"

Will went very still, his eyes dark and pleading. "I moved because I couldn't stand the thought of watching you with other guys. Not after we'd been together. I moved because I didn't want to be your dirty little secret, Brynn. I still don't."

Brynn froze. "You mean...you want..."

"Yeah," he said with a harsh laugh. "I *want*. I want to hold your hand, and take you to the movies, and be *with* you when we go to your parents for dinner, and I want you to call me when you have a flat tire."

"I did call you when I had a flat tire." It felt like the safest thing to say at the moment.

"You think that wasn't planned?"

She snorted. "How could you plan a flat tire?"

He just looked at her and her jaw dropped.

"You gave me a flat tire?"

Will didn't bother looking the slightest bit guilty. "I would have done anything to get you to notice me."

Her world tilted slightly at the implications of that. "Notice you how?"

"You know."

She did know. But still her brain rejected it. "You... That's why you moved next door? That's the game you were playing?"

"It was never a game, Princess. Not to me."

"So you...you've wanted us...me...you...to be like, a thing?"

He gave a curt nod.

Brynn's fingers dropped again to the mark on her hip. "One step closer to what, Will? What does it mean?"

His hands were on her shoulders again, only this time he pressed her into the wall, his breath coming harsh and fast as he lifted her to her toes, shaking her. "Not one step closer to *what*, Brynn. One step closer to *who*. One step closer to *me*. After all these years, you finally came to me. Finally took a step in the right direction. And I didn't want you to forget it."

Brynn's vision went fuzzy and her mouth went dry. *"All these years . . . ?"*

He closed his eyes briefly, and when he opened them again, the emotion was so raw that she almost gasped.

No.

She put a hand up to stop him. "Will."

He grasped her fingers, refusing to be silenced. "I've loved you every day. Every single Goddamn day since you first flicked your hair at me on the football field in that tiny cheerleading skirt."

Brynn's entire body trembled even as her brain shied away from his words.

Will Thatcher loved her.

And she . . .

She had never felt so lost. She had no idea what to say. Had no idea how to make this go away, or how to fix it.

She opened her mouth to say something. Anything. But her brain couldn't put the pieces together. Couldn't reconcile that the Will who'd always hated her had never hated her at all.

And that the Will she hated could be . . .

No. They'd spent their entire lives making each other miserable, and he wanted to push that all aside for something that could never work?

She was ice and order and calm. He was fire and instinct and chaos.

He would hurt her. And she'd already hurt him.

There was nothing for her to say.

Brynn forced herself to watch his eyes. Forced herself to recognize the exact second that he gave up.

The moment he realized that she wasn't going to be saying it back.

All the fire and heat dropped from his gaze as he gently let her drop down to her feet. His hands fell away from her, arms falling loosely to his sides.

Brynn felt the loss of contact acutely. She wanted it back.

"Will, can't we just...I need time."

He gave a quick shake of his head, before planting a tender kiss on her forehead. "You've had plenty of time, Brynn."

A sob hiccuped in her throat as she felt the meaning behind that kiss. She knew what that kiss meant. Knew Will well enough to understand what he wasn't telling her.

He wanted all or nothing, and he was done waiting.

That kiss had been a good-bye.

CHAPTER TWENTY-TWO

Routine is the path to your future.

—Brynn Dalton's Rules for an
Exemplary Life, #37

I look like a freak."

Brynn sat back in her chair and set her distal end cutters on the tray before peeling back off her latex gloves. She tried for her most reassuring smile, but the truth was, she was bone tired. Tired of painstakingly attaching metal to misshapen teeth only to get petulant complaints in return.

"You don't look like a freak."

Abby Cornwell's fourteen-year-old face scowled up at her, and Brynn felt a pull of sympathy. Between the thick glasses, the frizzy hair, the acne-ridden skin, and now the mouthful of metal, Abby hadn't exactly hit the adolescent jackpot.

It will get better, sweetie.

Except sometimes it didn't. Even when you did everything right, there were no guarantees. Because having straight teeth didn't bring happiness. Apparently, neither did creating them.

"You look great," Brynn said, leaning forward and giving Abby's arm a quick squeeze.

Abby gave her an *oh, please* look that was apparently written into the female DNA to develop around the age of eleven.

"Well, yeah, okay, braces suck," Brynn heard herself say. "But I promise that one day you'll realize there are a lot more important things in life."

"Yeah, yeah, I know. My mom tells me all the time. Looks are passing, but brains and kindness are forever...all that crap."

Good mom.

"Your mom's right," Brynn said.

"Easy for you to say. You're perfect."

Brynn leaned forward and gave her a little wink. "I work hard to make people think so."

She escorted Abby to the reception desk to wait for her mom, knowing that nothing else she could say would make Abby hate her reflection any less, but silently sending up a prayer that life would be kind to the girl. That she would be *happy* instead of perfect.

Brynn swung by the staff fridge to grab her yogurt before heading to her office for a quick break. She glanced at her watch and winced. She felt like she'd been here for hours, but it wasn't even half past ten.

"That's probably the tenth time I've seen you check your watch today,"

Brynn gave Susan a wan smile as she peeled off the yogurt top and dropped it in the trash before sitting on the corner of her desk.

But Susan didn't let up. "Never known you to be a clock-watcher, everything okay?

No. No, everything's not okay.

Brynn shrugged. "Having a little trouble settling back into the daily grind."

Susan folded her arms and tapped plain fingernails against her forearm. "Interesting choice of words. Watching the clock, taking long lunches, leaving the office as soon as possible in the afternoon...referring to your job as a grind?"

Brynn raised her eyebrows at Susan's detailed assessment. "If you're concerned I'm not pulling my weight, just say so."

"Oh gosh, it's not that," Susan said with an exasperated wave of her hand. "I know you'd never give less than your best to your patients, and to the practice. But ever since you got back from vacation..."

At the concerned look on her partner's face, Brynn's yogurt started to taste sour. "I thought the break would help, ya know?"

Susan nodded slowly. "It should have. I know I felt better after getting away for a few days, even though it was for unhappy circumstances."

Brynn gave a sympathetic smile. "I'm sorry about your mom. But she's doing better?"

Susan shrugged. "As well as can be expected, I guess. But yeah, she'll make it. We're grateful."

Immediately Brynn felt awful that she was moping around for no good reason while Susan actually had a reason to be down, and instead she was going about her business happily and professionally.

"Well, I just wanted to see if everything was okay," Susan said. "I know you just came through a rough breakup and all, so if you need to talk..."

"It wasn't really a breakup since we were never together," Brynn muttered.

Susan tilted her head. "What do you mean? Weren't you guys together for like two years?"

Ohhhhhh. She was talking about James.

"I was kind of...seeing someone over the past few weeks. Casually," she rushed to add.

"A rebound!" Susan said with a grin. "Sexy!"

"It was sexy," Brynn admitted. "And then it blew up in my face."

"Aha, I *knew* it was guy issues that were getting you down."

Yeah, if by "guy issues" you mean your worst enemy telling you he's been in love with you since forever and then promptly disappearing and not returning any of your phone calls. Yeah, that had gotten her down all right.

Even worse was that nothing else in her life seemed to get back to normal either. She was barely doing her job, all of her old friends were boring, and worst of all... despite the fact that her life list had returned to its status on her nightstand, she hadn't once opened it.

Didn't *want* to open it.

"I'm a mess, Sue."

"It'll get better, I promise. Guys have a way of making us...crazy. But it'll fade and you'll feel right again."

She smiled at her friend's well-meaning advice. Even though she knew she was dead wrong.

Brynn didn't want to go back. But she didn't know how to go forward either.

* * *

It wasn't that Brynn had never been on a bad date before. She'd had her fair share. But she'd never been on a bad date that *should* have been great.

Like many little girls with romantic inclinations, Brynn had spent a fair amount of her younger years daydreaming about her future husband. He'd be tall, naturally. Dark, personal preference. Handsome, that was a given.

He'd also be smart, successful, and kind, but never boring.

James had almost made it. Minus the boring part. And considerate and kind weren't quite the same thing, but he had been a good guy.

But Michael Alden?

Oh baby—he was literally the stuff of fantasies. *Her* fantasies.

She even prided herself a little in branching out from her doctor/lawyer dating pool. Granted, he was CIO of a pharmaceutical company, which meant he mostly worked with doctors. But still.

Take that, Will Thatcher. I'm not such a creature of habit.

She could change it up.

She could be different.

She could be open-minded.

Case in point, Michael had a dog. Brynn was not a dog person. At all. But was she writing Michael off just because of that? No, no, she was not.

And yet she wanted to go home. Badly.

"Is everything okay? You seem a bit quiet," Michael said as he topped off her wineglass with a delicious Pinot Noir.

"Sorry," Brynn said sheepishly. "Long day."

They were all long lately. Ever since that awful showdown with Will, her days had somehow become an endless string of the same old coffee, the same old commute, the same old workday. Same salad for lunch, same problems, same triumphs...

She half listened to Michael as he told a story about how his nephew's space shuttle drawing looked disturbingly like male genitalia. And even though she laughed in all the right spots...even though the anecdote was genuinely entertaining, it was all...wrong.

He was wrong.

The hair was too dark. The eyes weren't the right color. His shoulders weren't quite as broad as she might like.

And he didn't excite her.

Her heart starting to pound, she quickly put him through her Future Filter. That mental game she played with every potential partner where she fast-forwarded five years to the point where they had wedding bands and family trips to Disneyland and a homemade-ice-cream maker for special treat days. She could see it all.

And she didn't want any of it. Not with him.

Oh my God, oh my God.

"Are you all right?" he asked, looking alarmed as she put a hand over her suddenly tight chest.

Maybe. Probably not. Could be a heart attack.

Or perhaps, more appropriately...an attack of the heart.

Oh my God, oh my God.

"Would you...excuse me, just for a sec—"

She was moving away from the table before she'd even finished the sentence, weaving around the white table-cloths on her way to the ladies' room.

She burst into the first empty stall and braced her hands on the wall, not once stopping to consider that her palms were resting on germ central. Her face was hot and it was getting increasingly hard to breathe.

Brynn slowly turned and lowered herself to the toilet seat before pressing her hands to her flushed cheeks.

Very slowly, very carefully, Brynn let herself go into her Future Filter again. Let her picture herself in five years as the new Brynn.

No goals. No bullshit. No rules. Well...*fewer* rules.

There were still wedding bands and children. But the husband wasn't a brunet, and the kids weren't the tidy, well-behaved, matchy-matchy-clothes type of children.

They were blond, and wild and mischievous.

Just like their dad.

And they would still do Disneyland, but they would do other crazy stuff too. Unexpected stuff like running through the mud on a random Tuesday morning, and having food fights. With nonstaining ingredients, of course.

But there would be no white couches, and probably too many age-inappropriate horror movies, and the kids would only have to have goal lists if they wanted to. If any of them took after her, they probably would.

And they would be happy.

She would be happy.

With the wrong man, who was so damn *right* it made her literally ache inside.

The man she'd thrown away because she was still trying so hard not to be Dumpy Dalton that she'd become a complete shell of a person instead.

A rough choking noise escaped her throat, and she heard two friends at the mirror falter in their conversation, but she didn't care.

She'd pushed him away. Thrown Will aside like he wasn't fit to take out her trash, when really he'd done nothing but love her the way she needed to be loved.

She gave a watery snuffle as she realized that her little epiphany was starting very much the way this crazy journey had begun—with her crying in a bathroom stall feeling sorry for herself.

Which was pathetic, because the only one who had made a victim out of Brynn was herself.

Starting with that stupid list and a lifetime of pointless, self-inflicted expectations.

Brynn glanced down at her feet. She was wearing the same boring nude pumps as before, and this time she knew they were all wrong.

The black leather clothes had been all wrong too, but that was okay.

It was time to discover the real Brynn Dalton.

The version of herself that Will deserved.

CHAPTER TWENTY-THREE

~~Spontaneity is overrated.~~

—Brynn Dalton's Rules for an
Exemplary Life, #7

Where's Will?" Marnie asked, setting a platter of avocado crostini in front of them. "These are his favorite. He's usually here by now."

Brynn nearly opened her mouth to answer her mother's question. To tell Marnie that she didn't give a flying bat where Will Thatcher was because the guy was an irrational jackass who seemed to think that just because she slept with him, she was supposed to be fawning over him.

But then she realized that her mother hadn't been asking her—nobody ever thought to ask Brynn about where Will might be. Because nobody knew that Brynn had seen parts of Will that Sophie never had. Intimately.

Stop. Thinking. About. It.

Sophie snagged a piece of avocado off the plate and slurped it off her thumb noisily. "Will moved to Boston."

Dimly Brynn heard the sound of shattered wineglass, absently noting that shards of wineglass would be hell for someone to pick up.

It took several seconds to realize that it was her *wineglass that had shattered.*

Marnie came bustling over to fuss over the broken glass, but Brynn's eyes never left Sophie's face.

"What do you mean he's moved to Boston?" Chris asked, looking nearly as stunned as Brynn felt. "We just saw him last Sunday and he didn't say a word about it."

Sophie shrugged and explained that he'd simply had a new work opportunity come up, and made a last-minute decision to move to Boston.

Brynn wanted to shake her sister. Why was there not more detail? Like when would he back? What was he doing there?

And why?

"He's sorry he didn't say good-bye," Sophie was saying.

Brynn had thought she'd known just what a selfish, thoughtless prick Will was, but looking at her parents' wounded faces, and the unmistakable sting of hurt on Sophie's, made her livid.

The Daltons had always treated him like family.

Apparently he didn't think of them as the same.

"Well, that's just...just....I don't know what to say," her mother sputtered, speechless for once.

Me neither, Brynn thought.

"He said he'll be back someday, Mom," Sophie said gently. "And I'm sure he'll come visit."

Marnie gave a little head shake and went back to tossing the salad, her motions more violent than before. Brynn's dad had turned back to the baseball game, but he too looked crushed. Probably because nobody else in the family could talk Mariners stats the way Will could.

Brynn finished picking up the last of the big chunks of wineglass before absently getting the broom and sweeping up the worst of it.

Blindly, she turned to the sink, her eyes fixed unseeingly on her parents' backyard landscaping.

She didn't know how long she'd stood there with the water running before her sister came over and put a hand on her arm.

"You okay, Brynny?" Sophie asked.

No. Not even close. And I don't know why.

"What? Oh, sure," she heard herself say. "Did Will say why?"

Sophie shook her head. "Nope. Maybe he just wanted a fresh start."

But why the hurry?

"Brynn, the water?" her mother said.

"Oh, right," she muttered, returning to the task of washing her hands.

Out of the corner of her eye, she saw her mom and sister exchange a puzzled glance. She couldn't blame them. She should be thrilled to have Will out of her life. Or at least indifferent.

Instead she felt . . . confused.

And maybe a little bit broken.

* * *

Telling Michael Alden that she had feelings for someone else had been surprisingly easy. And freeing. And as she drove home—drove toward Will—she sang at the top of her lungs, feeling the best she had in weeks. Months. Forever.

She'd thought that she'd been seeking freedom after James had ditched her, but that had merely been fear causing her to move *away* from something.

It was nothing compared to the euphoria of moving toward something.

Moving toward some*one*.

Brynn slapped a hand over her mouth as a little giggle escaped.

I'm in love with Will Thatcher.

The thought felt...right. No, it felt *wonderful*.

"I'm in love with Will Thatcher." Felt even better to say it out loud.

She rolled down the window, and yelled it again just because she could, not caring that nobody else on the freeway could hear her. She only needed Will to hear her.

As she exited the freeway, she let her mind flit back through the years in a sappy, heart-thumping montage of the two of them. Will punching her prom date right before pictures, and her throwing a punch in his face in retaliation. And then he'd asked her to dance that one last dance, and she'd been so *mad*, and yet that too had been right.

Will letting the air out of her tires. Just so he could help her afterward.

Her sneaking into the boys' locker room and cutting out the crotch of his favorite jeans.

Her knocking on his door that night three years ago.

That moment when she'd found out that he'd moved to Boston.

The moment that she'd learned he was back.

The moment she'd learned that he'd come back for *her*.

Brynn mentally cursed the slowpoke speed limit on her street, but just because she was done following *all* the rules didn't mean she wasn't going to follow *some*.

As she crawled closer to her house, it took her brain several seconds to register what she was seeing.

"No," she whispered. "Oh God, no, please. Not again."

Brynn careened into Will's driveway before spilling out of her car, not noticing that she lost a shoe as she burst through the open front door.

"Hello?" she yelled. "Will, what the *hell*!"

A male face appeared at the top of the stairs. Not Will's. "Who the hell are you, lady? I don't think you're supposed to be here."

She turned wild eyes on the burly stranger. "There's a moving truck out front. Why is there a moving truck?"

The guy rubbed his greasy hair as he moved aside as two other men scooted behind him carrying a mattress.

"Put that down!" she shrieked. "Where's Will?"

"The guy who owns the place? Never met him. Hired us over the phone and told us to pack it all and move it."

This couldn't be happening again. Not when she'd finally figured things out. Not when she'd finally *gotten* it.

"Moved where?"

The guy rolled his shoulders and stared down at her, taking in the missing shoe and the fact that she was now literally tugging on her hair.

"Don't know that I should tell you that. Who'd you say you were again?"

"I'm his friend. Neighbor. I'm his girlfriend," she said, everything running together in one big burst of panic.

"Riiiight," he said, leaning down to pick up two enormous boxes like they were Kleenex. "Well, we respect our clients' privacy, and if your 'boyfriend' didn't tell you where he was movin' to, I don't think that I should either."

"No, look, you have to," she said desperately, kicking off her other shoe and climbing the stairs even as he came down them. She scooted along the walls, careful not to bump him while he was carrying stuff but also really wanting him to just stop and listen to her.

"See, we had this fight, you know?" she said, trotting after him toward the truck. "And I thought he wasn't the one. Because he's so...unpredictable, and kind of mean, and, well...he's been with lots of other women, although now I don't know if that's even true, and..."

"Lady," the guy said, setting the boxes on the back of the truck. "You've gotta go. And move your car, or I'm calling the cops."

She clasped her hands together and tried to do that sweet, desperate-female thing that Sophie had perfected at the age of seven, but Brynn could never bring herself to try. "*Please*," she said. "It's really important that I find him."

The guy looked at her for several seconds before jerking his thumb over his finger. "Don't forget your shoes when you go."

Brynn's hands fell to her side as he hoisted himself into the truck and began scooting boxes toward the back.

Watery eyes fell on the shoe lying discarded on the lawn. She didn't even know where the other one was.

The stupid boring pump represented everything she hated about herself.

Everything that had driven Will away.

"Keep the shoes!" she hollered as she opened her car door. "I've got a boyfriend to win back."

* * *

"What do you mean you shouldn't say?" Brynn said, clutching her cell phone and pacing her living room. "I'm your sister. You can't even tell me where he is?"

"He's my best friend," Sophie said softly. "You hurt him."

Brynn knew that. Had known from the look on his face when she hadn't said she'd loved him back that it had cut him deeply. But hearing it out loud felt like someone was squeezing her heart.

"I know," Brynn said quietly. "It's why I want to make it right."

Her sister was silent for several seconds on the other line. "I don't know, Brynny. He seemed really...done, you know?"

Brynn swallowed painfully, her gaze locked on Will's deserted house. "Done, how?"

Done with me?

Sophie's continued silence confirmed her worst fears, and Brynn felt the urge to throw up. How could he be done? He'd said he'd loved her forever. He'd waited so long. That kind of love didn't fade in one evening, did it?

Except... she'd behaved horribly.

Really, truly, *awfully* horribly.

Maybe he'd realized what Brynn had been realizing all day. That she didn't deserve him.

But she had to try. "Soph, please. *Please.* If he's completely done with me, I'll walk away and leave him alone. I just need him to know how I feel."

"And you're really sure about how you feel? You're sure this isn't just wanting what you can't have?"

"That's not it. I've never even thought about him as someone I could or couldn't have. I *really didn't know.*"

"And now that you do know that you can have it, you've all of a sudden decided you want it."

"Stop saying it like that!" Brynn yelled into the phone.

She pinched the bridge of her nose. She'd done more yelling in the past week than she had in a lifetime. She'd yelled at Will, yelled at the movers, yelled at Sophie. Yelled at herself.

She'd done a few things quietly too. She'd quit her job. Or at least she was in the process of it. The legalities of turning over an orthodontist practice would take some time, but when she'd let Susan know that she was looking to sell, her partner could not have been more supportive. Probably because she was tired of Brynn's dead weight around the office.

She'd also talked to her parents. Explained to them that although they would never see her tattoo, the tattoo did in fact exist. She'd confirmed that Will had seen it. Up close. *Really close.* She hadn't added that last part, but she was pretty sure they knew it anyway.

They hadn't seemed all that surprised about her and Will. Neither had any of her friends when she'd told them. Brynn was definitely getting the feeling that everyone else had known what she hadn't.

That she and Will belonged together—had *always* belonged together.

Now she just had to convince him.

"You really care about him, Brynn? Really?" her sister asked.

Brynn's fingers subconsciously moved to the written words on her hip. "I love him."

She could hear her sister thinking things through.

"Okay, then," Sophie said finally. "Here's what we're gonna do..."

CHAPTER TWENTY-FOUR

Brynn, that guy is totally looking at you."

Brynn didn't pause in the dance steps she was trying to master. She'd always thought cheerleading was a lot of waving pom-poms in the air, but this was hard work.

"Ohmigod, that's Will Thatcher."

Still, Brynn didn't look up. If she'd learned anything in her first four months of high school, it was that most girls thought most guys were uhhh-mazing. But most of the ones she'd seen so far had been overhyped.

"Whoa, Brynn, do you know him or something? He's eating you up with his eyes."

Brynn finally registered that the rest of the freshman cheer squad was gawking at someone over her shoulder and curiosity finally won out.

Her eyes collided with a tall, blond-haired boy and her stomach did a full flip. The girls had gotten it right this time. This one was hot. Seriously hot. He was taller than most of the other guys, but not in a gangly way. He had dark blond hair that flopped perfectly over his fore-head.

She was too far away to see the color of his eyes, but she could feel his gaze. It was piercing.

Who was he? Her eyes never broke contact with his. It didn't matter that he was standing on a crowded football field with the rest of his team or that she was standing with the rest of her squad on the sideline.

It was as though they only had eyes for each other.

She mentally scolded herself for the ridiculousness of her thoughts. She didn't even know the guy.

But it felt like she did. Or felt like she was supposed to.

Stop being an idiot.

"Who is he?" she asked out loud.

"Will Thatcher," Amy repeated. "Pretty much the hottest guy in the junior class. He was already starting quarterback last year even though he was only a sopho-more."

Brynn couldn't care less about what he was on the football team. She wanted to know who he was.

Dimly, Will became aware of a man yelling, "Thatcher! Thatcher!" and his eyes reluctantly tore away from hers, looking back once over his shoulder before he jogged to his coach.

Brynn watched his back for several more seconds, ignoring the jealous giggling of the other girls.

"Will Thatcher," she said softly, out loud. It felt right.

And even though she was only fifteen . . . even though

her brain insisted that nobody fell in love at fifteen, her heart said something different.

Her heart said, This one.

* * *

Brynn loved her sister. She really did. But she should have known better than to think that Sophie would have a plan other than *show up and wear your most low-cut shirt*.

Especially when "show up" meant flying across the country.

Because when Will ran, Will ran *far*. The thought made her smile as she impatiently waited for everyone to file off the cramped airplane. It was just like him to do things drastically. When he'd wanted to win her, he didn't just move back to the same city. He'd moved next door.

And when he'd wanted to flee her, he'd jumped time zones.

She was already a sweaty mess by the time she wheeled her suitcase to her rental car thirty minutes later.

Chicago in the summer, Will? Really?

But she would have flown to Madagascar if she'd had to.

Trouble was, she wasn't *exactly* sure what came next. Sophie had given her the name of the hotel where he was staying until he figured out his more permanent housing. The house hunt Brynn planned to put a stop to immediately, because the only permanent housing he was going to need was with her.

But right now, her strategy looked a little something

like: show up in the hotel lobby and camp out there 24/7 until she saw him. And then beg.

Not her best plan.

But he wouldn't respond to her calls, texts, e-mails, or any other form of communication she could think of.

He'd told Sophie the name of the hotel only for emergencies, and then had gone off the grid. Sophie had called him a dozen times, but he wasn't even picking up for his best friend.

Perhaps because his best friend was related to the woman who'd treated him like shit.

"Checking in?" the valet guy asked.

Brynn nodded stupidly and gave a too-bright smile, her hands suddenly clammy.

Really didn't think this one through, Brynn.

Which was kind of the point. No more psychotic planning as life passed her by.

But this *might* have been one time where a little bit of forethought beyond *go there* would have been useful.

Taking a deep breath, she headed toward the reception desk, already scanning the lobby for any sign of him.

There was nobody but an old couple, a family with two tiny kids, and a pair of twentysomethings who apparently hadn't been able to wait to get to their room before making out.

"Checking in?"

Brynn felt a little seed of an idea sprout when she saw the hotel employee was an attractive guy about her age. Her eyes skimmed his left hand. No ring. And he was straight, if she had to bet on it. Perfect.

She let her hand go in for a casual hair twirl, only she hadn't gotten used to her shorter haircut, and instead ended up swirling a big circle in the air in the vicinity of her boob. *Shit.* When had all her flirting skills gone out the window?

"Checking in?" he asked again, placid expression never changing.

"Right. Yes. Yes, I am." Brynn leaned in closer, letting him get a glance of the boob shot Sophie had made her practice. She peered at his name tag. "So, Tyler...the thing is, my boyfriend's here on business, and he doesn't know I'm here to surprise him for our anniversary. Is there *any* way..."

Tyler expression didn't change. Nor did he stop typing on his computer. Or even sneak a peek at her boobs. "I'm sorry, I can't help you, it's against our privacy policy to give any guest information."

Normally Brynn would be quite approving of such rules, and even more approving of those who followed them. No exceptions.

But...

"Not even for..." She fished a couple twenties out of her wallet. Sophie's idea.

"Ma'am, I can't do that, but if you'd like to leave a message for your boyfriend, or we could have a note delivered to his room..."

"And the number of that room would be...?"

This time Tyler's expression *did* slip, but luckily it was into an indulgent smile instead of an *I'm gonna call the cops* look.

He leaned a little closer, and Brynn's stomach leaped in relief. He was going to help her.

"I'll tell you what I'm gonna do," Tyler said softly, looking from side to side.

"Yeah?" she said eagerly.

"Well, how about you tell me the name of your boyfriend. I'll look him up in our system, and *if* he's staying here..."

"Right, good..."

Tyler continued whispering. "And if he is staying here, I'm going to suggest he give his girlfriend a call."

Brynn's face fell. "You're not going to help me."

Tyler straightened. "Not in the way you want. But look on the bright side, I also wouldn't give anyone *your* room number either, so you don't have to worry about strange men knowing where you sleep."

Brynn scowled. "But I'm not a strange man."

"You're not a man, no, but strange...?" Tyler said with a wink, as he slid the envelope with her room key across the counter. "I'll be here until eight tonight if you want to give me his name. Maybe I can stick a note into his locker."

Brynn made a *ha-ha* face and resigned herself to camping out in the lobby.

Except she wouldn't have to. Because there he was, as though she'd summoned him out of sheer love and desperation.

Tall, golden, and wearing a suit, of all things. She hadn't even known he owned a suit.

And he had his arm around a very, *very* attractive redhead.

"Will!"

His name burst out of her mouth before she could think it through. Before she could think *anything* through. But in all her mental scenarios about this moment, another woman had not been involved. She also hadn't pictured verbally accosting him from across the lobby with a dozen spectators watching.

"Oh dear," she heard Tyler mutter.

Will slowly straightened as he looked in the direction of her voice. He was too far away from her to read his eyes, but the tension in his shoulders and his unsmiling mouth told her most of what she needed to know.

He wasn't happy to see her. At all.

Brynn mentally crossed off the run-into-each-other's-arms scenario as she slowly, purposefully made her way toward him. She felt the redhead's curious gaze on her profile as she approached. Hell, she felt the entire lobby's eyes on her. But her eyes never wavered from the one person who mattered.

She stopped a foot away from him, not caring that they were blocking the path to the elevators behind Will. She didn't care about anything but getting him back.

"So, you moved to Chicago," she said with a little smile.

"What the hell are you doing here, Brynn?"

Her smile wanted to slip, but she kept it pasted there as she turned to the other woman. Unlike Lily, who she'd subconsciously known along was part of the game, this woman was a threat. Tall, thin, and composed, she looked like the premium version of the woman Brynn used to try to be. Perfect hair, perfect clothes, perfect posture...

What if he's already trying to replace me?

"I'm Brynn," she said, extending a damp hand.

"Dana."

Brynn watched the other woman carefully for the classic female signs. The narrowing of eyes, the proprietary shift toward Will, the *Who are you?* gaze. There was nothing.

And yet this woman had walked out of the elevator with Will. Had they come from the same room?

The thought of Will with his hands on another woman made her want to puke, but she forced herself to see this through. She owed it to herself. Owed it to them.

"Can we talk in private?" she asked, turning her attention back to Will.

"I'll have the rental pulled around," Dana said quickly, starting to move away.

Will grabbed her arm. "You can stay. Brynn and I don't have anything to talk about."

"That's bullshit," Brynn said primly, refusing to be pushed aside.

His eyebrow arched up at Brynn's assertive tone and public swearing, and he released Dana, who made a fast getaway.

"Can we sit?" Brynn asked, gesturing at a cluster of chairs that were at least slightly more private than the main corridor.

He didn't move.

"You have two minutes," he said, checking his watch.

"So, out in the open, then, huh?" she said with a deep breath.

He glanced at his watch again.

"Are you sleeping with her?" Brynn asked, jerking her head in the direction Dana had gone.

"You're hardly in a position to be possessive."

"Are you sleeping with her?" she asked again. She had to know.

He ignored the question again. "How about you start

by explaining how you happen to be at the same hotel where I've quite intentionally come to be as far away as possible from you."

It stung. She'd known she was the reason he'd left Seattle, but it stung to hear it out loud.

"Are you sleeping with Dana, or not?"

He narrowed his eyes. "Not currently, no."

"Do you plan to?"

He crossed his arms over his chest. "Can't say that I'd thought much about it. Thought I'd give myself a break from women for a while."

Her shoulders slumped in relief. "Then what's she doing here?"

"She flew in from Austin to discuss an investment opportunity."

Brynn's eyes narrowed. "Your hand was on her waist. And she's pretty."

"My hand was on her waist because she almost tripped in her ridiculously high heels. And you have one minute."

She licked her lips and gave him a pleading smile. "Can we please just go up to your room for a second?"

"Brynn, if the low-cut shirt didn't soften me up, that pleading smile's sure as hell not going to work either. Spit it out. What do you want? Another fuck?"

She heard someone behind them gasp.

"No, I just want..."

"You've got another itch you want me to scratch? You wanna go bungee jumping, or swim with sharks, and you need a partner who won't tattle on you after?"

"I quit my job."

His head snapped back slightly. *Aha. That got him.* "Quit, like another month of playtime, or quit for good?"

"For good," she said, feeling oddly proud of something so wildly irresponsible.

"Why?"

"It wasn't making me happy."

He faked an appalled expression. "What about your list? However will you be mentioned in ten premiere medical journals before the age of thirty-five if you quit now?"

Brynn's eyes narrowed. "You've been reading my list."

"*Lists.* Plural. I've been reading those notebooks since you started stashing them under your mattress. Makes for great shitter read."

She didn't let herself get riled. "You know, it really wasn't fair to give me a time limit if you were going to hog all of the talking time."

For a second she thought he might smile. Or at least relax. Instead his jaw tensed. "Fine, twenty-second extension. Go."

Twenty seconds. It was enough.

Brynn took a deep breath. "I want to do this. For real."

"What's *this*?"

"Us. You and me. Out in public."

He started to move past her. "Pass."

She grabbed his sleeve, panic clutching at her throat at his quick dismissal. "You can't pass! I came all the way to Chicago to tell you that!"

"So it was a couple hundred bucks out of your savings account. Maybe you can go shopping while you're here or something so it's not a total waste. Find something classy and boring for your next hotshot job and statue boyfriend."

"Please," she said hoarsely. "Don't tell me I'm too late.

You didn't give me any time to think before you told me ... you know."

"That I'd loved you? Please. You had plenty of time. You had more than fifteen Goddamn years to figure it out."

"You're talking in past tense." Her voice broke.

"Well, what did you expect, Brynn? That I could keep it up indefinitely? That I'd keep loving someone who saw me as a boy toy she couldn't stand outside of the bedroom?"

"You're being unfair—you never once even hinted that it was anything else. I thought we were on the same page."

He pulled his sleeve away from her grasping fingers. "You're right, it's not fair, Brynn. It's not fair that I had to watch you throw your heart at countless other men while I had to make do with a string of vapid women who would never be you. And now that I'm finally ready to move on ... finally ready to get on with my life, you want to drag me back in?"

"Yes," she whispered.

"For what?"

She was crying for real now, and she folded her hands loosely in front of her before shrugging and saying the only thing there was left to say.

"I love you, Will."

She saw that it rocked through him. He shuddered and closed his eyes briefly, and her heart nearly broke at the searing emotion on his strong, familiar features.

He turned on his heel and walked away from her.

"Wait!"

He didn't.

"William Thatcher, you can't walk away from this! You didn't stick this out for half of your life to chicken out now."

He kept walking.

"Shit," she muttered. "Shit!"

Tyler gave her a reproving look from the front desk, but she barely noticed as she went tearing back out into the humid Chicago air.

She saw him start to get into the driver's seat of a car and sprinted full speed toward him, not stopping until she slammed into his side.

He glanced down. "You're embarrassing yourself."

"I don't care," she said, wiping at her cheeks as she dug through her purse. "I came prepared for you to be a stubborn ass, so I brought something."

"I can hardly wait to see."

She shoved a large cylindrical Tupperware at his chest. "Here."

He stared down at the container in confusion. "You brought a plastic tub full of shredded paper to prove your love."

Brynn nodded in earnest, shoving it closer to him so he couldn't give it back. "Not just any paper. My lists."

His lips parted for a second as his grip tightened on the container. "Your book? It's all in here?"

"Well, not the cover...it was too thick to shred. But the contents. The thirty before thirty, forty before forty, the ten characteristics of a respectable husband, the ninety-nine rules of leading an exemplary life...all in there."

"Why?"

"I don't need them anymore," she said simply. "I

thought they were helping me live my life, but they were actually keeping me from it. I thought that by planning everything, that by doing everything just right, that I could stop being Dumpy Dalton. And I guess I succeeded, but I also turned into..."

"A bitch?" he supplied.

She swallowed and pressed on. "*You're* my life, Will."

Brynn heard an awkward clearing of a throat, and belatedly realized that Dana was in the passenger seat. She didn't care. She only cared that Will would hear her. Want her. Love her.

Will slowly, deliberately unscrewed the plastic top from the container and turned it upside down. Tiny shreds of paper fell to the ground, not even bothering to flutter in the breezeless air.

Brynn closed her eyes and let the tears fall.

He didn't want her. She'd offered him everything. Been as bare as she'd ever been before, but it had been too little too late.

Incoherent with pain, she started to drop to her knees to pick up the paper. Needing something, anything to ground herself.

She'd lost him.

Rough hands gripped her shoulders and yanked her forward. Will's hands slid up to cup her cheeks as he rested his forehead on hers. "Goddamn you, Brynn Dalton."

She choked out a laugh, hardly daring to hope as her fingers clenched his shirt. "Give me a chance, Will. Let me try to be the woman for you."

"You idiot." His fingers clenched in her hair. "You've always been the only woman for me."

"I love you," she said. "I love you so much. I think somehow I always have."

"Do you have any idea how long I've waited to hear you say that?" His voice sounded suspiciously choked up, and she wiggled closer to him.

"You might have heard it a lot sooner if you hadn't tried to woo me by running my bra up the flagpole my freshman year."

"Foreplay, baby. Fifteen really long years of foreplay."

And then he kissed her, long and hard. It was the first kiss they'd shared in front of other people, and it was all the sweeter because of it.

And when a sudden gust of hot summer air dragged up the scraps of paper at their feet before scattering them in a mess of confetti, that was okay too.

The new Brynn—the *real* Brynn—had all she needed.

EPILOGUE

"It's a lovely housewarming party, Brynn, honey."

Brynn smiled in satisfaction. It really was a perfect party. The night was unseasonably warm for fall in Seattle, but there were a couple of those fancy heat lamps scattered around for when the sun went down. She'd even put out a couple of warm blankets for anyone who wanted to stay late and cuddle up under the stars.

Emphasis on the cuddle.

On second thought, she hoped nobody else would stay around for that part.

Brynn set out the last of the condiments on the table. "I've lived here a year and a half, Mom. I don't think you can call it a 'housewarming' anymore."

Marnie Dalton linked arms with her eldest daughter

and gave her a secret smile. "Yes, but I suspect it's just now starting to feel like a home, yes?"

Brynn's eyes involuntarily went across the deck to where Will was manning the grill and drinking a beer with her dad. It was a scene she'd envisioned a dozen times before—outdoor barbecues, friends and family, and a partner that helped her do it all.

Oddly, she'd also been seeing this scene for years—Will talking to her dad, Will as part of the family. She just hadn't been able to reconcile her dream vision with the reality.

She had now. And it was wonderful.

"It's not like we're living together, Mom. He has his own apartment in Seattle."

Marnie sniffed. "I still don't understand why he sold his house. A perfectly good piece of real estate..."

Brynn only gave her mom half an ear. Will hadn't bothered to try and buy back his house when he'd returned to Seattle. It seemed silly for both of them to have big houses right next door to each other when they were spending their nights in the same bed.

Will *had*, however, insisted on getting his own apartment so as not to rush her. But she suspected there was another reason...Despite all his live-on-the-wild-side lectures, Will Thatcher had a streak of old-fashioned in him, and didn't want to shack up with a girl who wasn't his wife.

But she was wearing him down.

"Brynny, do you have a Taser? Trish's kids are awful," Sophie said, appearing at her side, slightly out of breath.

"No, but you can bribe them with marshmallows," Brynn said, gesturing at the s'mores table for later.

"Yeah, because that's what they need. More sugar," Sophie said, her own cheeks now full of said marshmallow.

"I think they're cute," Brynn said, looking over to where her cousin's twin daughters ran frantic circles on the lawn.

"The chubby one bit me."

"You're an elementary schoolteacher, you're supposed to love kids."

Sophie stuffed another marshmallow in her mouth. "I like them between the hours of seven and three p.m. Not so much on weekends when I want my wine."

Brynn gestured toward the large silver bucket where several bottles of white wine were nestled amid the ice, but Gray was already on it, pouring a hefty glass for his wife.

"Can I help you with anything, Brynn?" Gray said, neatly popping the cap off a beer bottle and walking it over to the trash can.

The tidy action made Brynn smile. It was exactly what she would have done, whereas Sophie and Will would have flopped the cap on the table to be picked up later. By somebody else.

She met her brother-in-law's eyes and they seemed to smile back at her, as though to say *opposites attract*, and all that.

"How's Jenna?" Brynn asked Gray, after moving the flower arrangement just a few inches to the left and deciding that it was good enough. And that was another thing Will had taught her in the past few months since she'd coaxed him back from Chicago. When it came to the little stuff, sometimes, *good enough* was just right.

"Jenna's on an absolute tear," Gray said.

"Yeah, she mentioned that the guy she's moving in with is trying to break up with her."

Sophie snorted. " 'Trying' is the operative word there. Nobody's going to break up with that girl unless she wants it."

"Seriously," Brynn muttered. "I hope that guy's ready to part with his testicles."

After she and Will became official, Jenna had sent a succinct e-mail that read "Finally." The two women had become pen pals of sorts since then. The most recent e-mail had been a scathing note about how the love of her life was having an existential crisis and could no longer handle Jenna's fabulousness.

Jenna had mentioned a plan, and Brynn had silently said a prayer for the sake of the poor guy. She knew exactly how plans could blow up in your face.

"Grill's preheated," Will said, coming up behind her and tugging on her ponytail. She was growing her hair back out to its original length, and the blonde was here to stay. But no longer was she painstakingly straightening it with a flat-iron every day.

It was a little bit looser nowadays.

Just like her.

"I'll get the plates," she said, turning to head toward the kitchen after sneaking a quick kiss.

He snagged her elbow before she could go back inside. "I want to say something first."

Brynn sent him an alarmed look. "If you tell anyone that we have matching tattoos," she hissed.

"Not that," he said, kissing her temple. "That's just for us."

"Well, and my parents, seeing as you told them—"

Will ignored her. "Hey, can I get everyone's attention for a few minutes?"

The chatter abruptly stopped, and friends and neighbors who'd been standing in various clusters around the backyard turned to face them.

"What are you doing?" she hissed. "I'm not singing another duet with you; that was a one-time drunken thing..."

Will continued to ignore her as he addressed the group. "As you all know, my Brynny here has made some recent changes in the past couple months."

"Cheers to *that*," Sophie added.

"...she no longer has to consult a chart to decide what to wear each Monday, she's no longer collecting brochures for her post-sixty Alaskan retirement cruise..."

"Only 'cause you made me," Brynn hissed. "That cruise is supposed to be a spectacular treat for the elderly..."

Will put a hand over her face, playfully stifling her. "Anyway, point being, our little planner has taken great strides in embracing spontaneity."

Brynn rolled her eyes, even as she flushed with pleasure at the pride in Will's voice.

"But..." Will said, holding up a finger.

Brynn's smile slipped.

"...our girl's been hiding a dirty little secret under the mattress in the guest bedroom."

Her face went hot as she grabbed his arm. "Wait, I can explain..."

"No need, honey, I think most of the women here will be able to relate..."

He moved toward one of the side tables, pulled a thick notebook out from under a bowl of chips, and held it up for everyone to see.

Sophie cried out in glee. "Oh, Brynny, it's your wedding notebook."

Marnie turned to her husband. "I have about *six* of those for each girl...of course, Sophie had to go and elope..."

Brynn's dad and Gray each put a hand on Marnie's shoulder and pressed. Hard.

"I thought we said no planning," Will said with a teasing smile as he dangled the book in front of Brynn's face. "But flipping through this, it looks like you've got quite a few things figured out."

Only since I was six, she thought.

"Oh, that thing's still around?" Brynn asked, her voice too high. "It must have escaped the shredder. Here, give it to me, and I'll get rid—"

Will lifted the book higher and out of her reach before handing it to Sophie for safekeeping.

"I think maybe this is one of your planning notebooks that we'll keep," Will said, hooking a hand behind her neck and tilting her face up to him.

A few months ago, Brynn would have been mortified at such a blatant show of affection in front of so many people.

But now? Now she couldn't care less who saw them together.

"I'll get rid of it, really. It's silly, and I don't care about any of that—"

He stamped a hard kiss on her lips. "Yes, you do. And so do I. I may not have a wedding notebook, but I've been carrying something around with me since I was old enough to afford it."

"So he was like twelve," she heard Gray mutter.

All of the chattering around her turned to a dull hum as she watched Will drop to his knee.

"Will..." she said in a warning voice.

He shook his head. "We're doing this the old-fashioned way. You're not the only one who's had a few dreams tucked away for future use. This is mine."

Her eyes watered when he pulled out a perfect small, unmistakably sized jewelry box.

She opened it with shaking hands, her hand covering her wobbling lips at the perfect ring.

Her ring.

"See, Princess, this isn't the first time I've seen your wedding notebook. That night after prom when I drove you home after your date ditched you...it was lying on your desk. You'd circled a picture of a ring, with a sticky note saying *the one*."

She couldn't speak. Couldn't breathe.

His eyes clouded slightly as he clenched her fingers a little harder. "It is still the one, right? Your taste hasn't changed?"

"It hasn't changed," she whispered, sliding the ring onto her finger. "It's still the one." *Just like you are.*

He chin dipped slightly in relief. "So that's a yes?"

"That's a hell yes."

Brynn heard her sister give a little yelp of excitement, and her mom gave a definite sniffle as Will climbed to his feet and looked down at her newly adorned left hand.

"It doesn't stop here, you know," he said, rubbing a thumb along her fourth finger. "I want babies. Lots of them. And I want them to grow into precocious little monsters that have their entire lives planned by the age of seven."

Brynn laid her palms on his cheeks, her fingers tracing his familiar features. "I want that too. But you know what? I'm more excited for the day when our kids see the light and get *rid* of the lists."

Will smiled into her eyes. "Yeah?"

"Of course," she said, pulling his head down for a kiss. "Because that's when life really begins."

Party girl Sophie is enjoying her Las Vegas trip—
until an uptight businessman mistakes her
for a prostitute.

But when that gorgeous man turns
out to be her new boss, they soon realize
their Vegas misunderstanding might lead
to the real thing...

Please see the next page for an excerpt from

ONLY WITH YOU.

CHAPTER ONE

If only the boots had come with some sort of warning label.

Perhaps a succinct sticker reading, HOOKER.

Or even a tasteful note card indicating, "These shoes will change your life."

But the knee-high, rhinestone-covered boots said neither of these things, and so Sophie Claire Dalton made the most crucial decision of her life without having all the information.

Not that Sophie *realized* the magnitude of the choice she was about to make. If someone were to ask her about the most important decision of her life, the feminine dilemma of shoe choice probably wouldn't have been on her radar.

She might have thought it was the tearful junior prom date decision between Adam and Gary.

(Adam. Way cuter. Less acne.)

Or perhaps the melodramatic soul-searching about whether to pursue soccer or cheerleading.

(Cheerleading, totally. Boxy athletic shorts hadn't stood a pubescent chance against a flippy little skirt.)

It could have been her long-deliberated college destination.

(Stanford. Yep, Sophie was one of *those* girls.)

Then there was the choice that had nearly ripped her heart out. Jon McHale had dropped to his knee their senior year of college with a diamond ring the size of her face and the promise of yuppie housewife security.

(Answer: No. Although *that* decision had been particularly rough. The ring had been Tiffany and the man had been sweet.)

Or perhaps most likely, Sophie might have guessed the proverbial fork was the debate over whether to finish her stint at Harvard Law or drop out and pursue a life of, well...aimlessness.

(Current occupation: cocktail waitress.)

And yet, none of these decisions would be as life-altering as the choice she was about to make.

Classic strappy black sandals, or...The Boots.

Clueless to the magnitude of what she was about to decide, Sophie teetered over to the full-length mirror of her Las Vegas hotel room, tugging at the hem of her black miniskirt. She extended the black sandal on her left foot for inspection and winced. Surely that white, flabby, and unshaven stump wasn't *her* leg.

Damn. The testicle-shaped birthmark above her left

knee said the limb was definitely hers. And the pasty complexion looked just about right for a lazy Seattle native in the middle of January.

As for the shoes, the delicate high-heeled sandals had potential. Sexy but understated. Very Audrey Hepburn. Very Jackie Onassis.

But on the other hand...

Sophie pivoted awkwardly to extend her other leg and inspected the boot option. They'd been an impulse buy (okay, fine, a slightly *tipsy* impulse buy) from the Lover's Package sex shop for last year's Halloween costume of Sexy Space Girl.

Alas, due to some unflattering Halloween-day bloating, the Sexy Space Girl had never made an appearance, and Sophie had tackled Halloween as the green M&M for the third year in a row.

The boots had sat abandoned and unworn in her closet, awaiting their destiny.

Sophie chewed on her lip and considered. The boots were certainly tacky, but wasn't that kind of the point of a bachelorette party in Vegas? Particularly a bachelorette party for which the slightly unhinged bride had declared a theme of Totally Trashy? These boots were practically the poster children for trashy.

Not to mention they'd cover the glow-in-the-dark-white shade of her calves.

Decision made, Sophie flipped off her old standby black sandal. There'd be plenty of time to channel first ladies and iconic movie stars at job interviews and bridal showers.

The bride's pouty voice echoed in Sophie's ear. *I want my bachelorette party to be hella skanky and memorable. If you're going to be on your period that weekend, fix it.*

Which was totally reasonable, since all women could *totally* just up and regulate their uteruses with a firm talking-to.

Sophie was a sucker for traditional wedding hoopla, bachelorette parties included. But she wasn't looking forward to this one. Had the bride not been her cousin, and the maid of honor not been Sophie's sister, she would have bailed. But family was family, so here she was in a hotel room she couldn't afford, dressed like some sort of space-station call girl.

Grabbing her cosmetic bag, Sophie teetered into the bathroom and eyed the multiple mirrors. She pulled the magnifying mirror away from the wall and stared at herself in rapt horror. No pasty American female in her late twenties would have thought it a good idea to zoom in on skin that had been maybe just a *tiny* bit free with the gin and lax on the sunscreen.

Sophie pushed the judgmental mirror away and gave it the bird. She didn't need a crappy little mirror calling attention to her flaws. She had a mother and a sister for that.

Turning toward the normal, less judgmental mirror, she began applying her makeup with a heavier hand than usual. And the last step in the transformation to tart?

Fake eyelashes.

They'd been deemed mandatory for all bridesmaids. A Totally Trashy uniform of sorts. Sophie squinted at the elaborate packaging. Not only were these things like an inch long, but they had little fake gemstones on them. She shrugged. At least they'd match her boots.

After twenty minutes and a good deal of cursing

(Jackie O was long gone by this point), Sophie managed to attach something that looked akin to bedazzled pube clumps onto her normally pale, stubby lashes.

Lovely, she thought. *Really lovely and classy.*

Last, she wound her blonde hair around a curling iron to create a mass of showgirl curls. Stepping back, she surveyed the overall results in the mirror. Not bad, considering.

This was not the Sophie Dalton who'd been dumped over the phone yesterday afternoon while standing in the airport security line as the TSA agents were disassembling her carefully packed bag.

A bag that contained The Boots. And a purple vibrator. Which the judgmental little security man had *sooooo* not believed was a gag gift for Trish.

But *that* loser version of herself wasn't here tonight.

No, the Sophie in the mirror had her shit together. Granted, it was trampy shit. And she would have to blame the slightly red, puffy eyes on the dry Las Vegas air. Still, she thought she was hiding the pathetic pretty damn well. At least she wasn't wallowing at home with a pint of Ben & Jerry's.

Sophie yanked the curling iron plug from the wall and blinked back the tears that would probably send her fake eyelashes sliding down her cheeks. She wasn't even sure why she was crying. It wasn't as though Brian had been The One. He was the fun guy, not the husband potential you brought home to Mom. They'd only been dating for eight months and Brian had switched jobs no fewer than three times.

For once, *Sophie* had been the stable one in the relationship.

Which was why it stung when he'd told her yesterday that she simply didn't have enough *drive*. That he needed a woman who knew what she wanted, whereas Sophie was just floating.

Floating, he'd said. Right before the Sea-Tac Airport TSA agents had loudly commanded her to hang up the phone and repack her "pleasure toys."

Whatever. His loss.

Slopping on a glittery lip gloss that claimed to "plump" lips into a sexy pout with God only knew what kind of chemicals, Sophie took one final glance in the mirror.

Skirt the size of a Band-Aid? Check.

Scrappy halter top barely covering her nipples? Got it.

Pole dancer makeup? Definitely.

And the final touch: boots that belonged in a brothel.

Perfect. She looked like a girl looking for no-strings-attached sex.

Exactly what she needed.

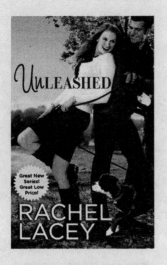

Fall in Love with Forever Romance

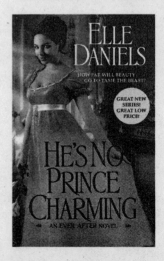

Fall in Love with Forever Romance

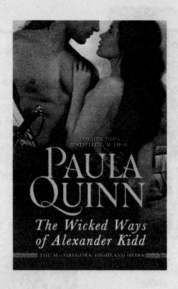

THE WICKED WAYS OF ALEXANDER KIDD
by Paula Quinn

The newest sinfully sexy Scottish romance in *New York Times* bestselling author Paula Quinn's Highland Heirs series, about the niece of a Highland chief who stows away on a pirate ship, desperate for adventure, and the pirate captain whose wicked ways inflame an irresistible desire...

Find out more about Forever Romance!

Visit us at
www.hachettebookgroup.com/publishing_forever.aspx

Find us on Facebook
http://www.facebook.com/ForeverRomance

Follow us on Twitter
http://twitter.com/ForeverRomance

NEW AND UPCOMING TITLES

Each month we feature our new titles
and reader favorites.

CONTESTS AND GIVEAWAYS

We give away galleys, autographed copies,
and all kinds of exclusive items.

AUTHOR INFO

You'll find bios, articles, and links to personal websites
for all your favorite authors—and so much more.

GET SOCIAL

Connect with your favorite authors, editors, and
other Forever fans, and share what's important to you.

THE BUZZ

Sign up for our monthly romance newsletter,
and be the first to read all about it.

VISIT US ONLINE AT

WWW.HACHETTEBOOKGROUP.COM

FEATURES:

OPENBOOK BROWSE AND SEARCH EXCERPTS

•

AUDIOBOOK EXCERPTS AND PODCASTS

•

AUTHOR ARTICLES AND INTERVIEWS

•

BESTSELLER AND PUBLISHING GROUP NEWS

•

SIGN UP FOR E-NEWSLETTERS

•

AUTHOR APPEARANCES AND TOUR INFORMATION

•

SOCIAL MEDIA FEEDS AND WIDGETS

•

DOWNLOAD FREE APPS